I0713626

WENDY B. TRUSCOTT

DEAD SERIOUS

by Wendy B. Truscott

Copyright © 2023 by Wendy B. Truscott
Published by Gordian Books, an imprint of Winged
Publications

Editor: Cynthia Hickey
Book Design by Winged Publications

All rights reserved. No part of this publication may
be reproduced, stored in a retrieval system, or
transmitted in any form or by any means —electronic,
mechanical, photocopying, recording, or
otherwise —without the prior written permission of
the publisher. The only exception is brief quotations
in printed reviews. Piracy is illegal. Thank you for
respecting the hard work of this author.

This book is a work of fiction. Names, characters,
Places, incidents, and dialogues are either products
of the author's imagination or used fictitiously.
Any resemblance to actual persons, living or dead,
or events is coincidental.
Fiction and Literature: Inspirational
Christian Romantic Suspense

ISBN-13: 978-1-959788-76-8

Dedication

As always, to my greatest cheerleaders, my family,
for their constant encouragement,
especially to my husband, Paul, who has always
believed in me and given me the confidence to believe
in myself.

Author's Notes

Some years ago, I failed a brief course on mystery/romance writing. "Failed" might be too strong a word. More accurately, I failed to complete it. I did not want to write romance. I was there to learn the mystery part. However, the instructor was adamant: I must write both. Forced to comply, this usually cooperative student, became unusually uncooperative, and in a small act of rebellion, scribbled a chapter or two based on the most outrageous idea that came to mind. Because I missed the last class, I don't believe I ever received an evaluation (or perhaps my merciful memory simply refuses to recall it). Those chapters were then shelved for at least ten years, while I completed and published two historical novels, *Haunted Journey* (2016) and *MacGregor's Curse* (2020)

Finding a renewed interest in that earlier attempt, I discovered the previously outrageous idea actually made a fairly good premise for something a bit different and decided to expand on it. When I later asked that same instructor, romance-mystery author, Dee Lloyd, to critique several chapters, one of her important suggestions was that I add more tension by giving my characters an actual crime to work with— perhaps my villain could kill someone! (There was more, but I won't spoil the mystery for you.) Strangely, for a fan of murder mysteries, the idea of inserting a murder into my own novel had never occurred to me. I then had the somewhat macabre pleasure of deciding which unfortunate character would die and why. A writer can begin to feel like a master of a universe, building a world, populating it, then deciding who survives and who doesn't. Thanks for your guidance, Dee!

While *Dead Serious* is a work of fiction, the Toronto neighbourhood known as The Beach, where it's set, was home during my formative years and has played a significant role ever since, especially its boardwalk and the unnamed church in this story. As an adult, I enjoyed participating in many amateur productions in its auditorium where, as far as I know, no murder ever took place! However, despite my deep skepticism about the supernatural, on a day when I was utterly alone in that vast building, with the doors locked, the slow and heavy footsteps I heard did convince me it might be haunted!

Thank you for taking the time to read this book. I hope you'll enjoy it and consider leaving a review on www.goodreads.com. Reviews are important to authors.
Also by Wendy B. Truscott

Haunted Journey and *MacGregor's Curse* available through Amazon, Barnes & Noble, Chapters/Indigo and other distributors or at www.wendytruscott.com .
Follow me on Facebook at Wendytruscottnovels and on Twitter: LoonEcho@TruscottWendy

Acknowledgments

Although I've always had an interest in writing, I know, without a doubt, I would not have progressed to actually putting words on paper without the initiative and encouragement of my local libraries, which established the Baysville and Bracebridge Libraries Writers' Circle. This group began with memoir writing but evolved into fiction and brought together a marvelous group of people who offer constructive critiques and constant cheerleading. I owe them all many thanks.

The Muskoka Authors' Association, of which I am an original member, continues to be a source of inspiration offering speakers, workshops, authors' nights, and more friendships.

Thank you also to these good friends and invaluable Beta readers, who read all or parts of this novel: Ethna Barlow; Yvonne and Don Gray; Jane Low; Janet Prueter; Amy Truscott; Heather Truscott. A special tribute goes to my late friends, Jean and Don Murray, Beta readers par excellence!

To those who offered advice on covers, contracts, and a myriad of other items: Nancy Beal; Beverly Brewer; Wendie Donabie; Kim Fahner, V.P. Writers' Union of Canada; Brian Henry at Quick Brown Fox; Ann Malley, author; Grant Millard, Plant 48.com; Neil Petrunia, Publisher, Frontenac House; Sheridan Rondeau, author, *Dear Tony, A Caregiver's Loving Journey Through Alzheimer's Dementia;* Shelley

Truscott; Tara Truscott; Judy Vanclieaf; Eric Williams, 5310 Publishing; and to those I'm sure I've missed listing, please know how much I appreciate all your contributions.

I am grateful to Kaitlyn Sutey, member of The Muskoka Authors' Association, who edited my manuscript before I began submitting. I have the honour of being Kaitlyn's first official client, as she embarks on what I hope will be a successful editing career, and I am pleased to highly recommend both her work and her delightful manner. kaitlynjnsutey@gmail.com

Sincere thanks to realtor Trevor Fontaine of Sotheby's for his photo of the famous Beach Boardwalk, Toronto, Ontario, Canada.

Contents

Chapter One

The first thing Dana Williams saw that morning was a dead rat sharing her pillow, its teeth bared in a sick half-smile. A black lace bow encircled its thin, stiff throat.

She leaped out of bed, screaming. Unable to take her eyes off the obscene thing, she raced, crab-like, to the furthest corner of her bedroom. Managing to tuck her long limbs close to her chest, she squeezed herself into the awkward space between dresser and wall, where she sat, curled in a fetal position. Little mewing sounds escaped her mouth, but Dana felt separate from them, as if they were coming from a stranger.

Oh, God! Please help me! How did that thing get in here? Someone must have been in the apartment. Then, a more terrifying thought: *They could still be here.*

She strained to listen for signs of an intruder in her apartment, but her heart thudded so loudly she wouldn't have heard a nuclear explosion.

What kind of sicko would do something like that? And why? Why?

She shrank even further into the corner, willing herself to be invisible as she tried to calm her body and mind with deep, yogic breaths. From this vantage point, she could no longer see the hideous thing.

An urgent knock on her apartment door broke through her thoughts. Reacting automatically, Dana unfolded from her cramped position and stumbled into the living room. As she scurried across the carpet to open the door, she realized she had no idea who might be out there and came to a sudden halt. Her body tensed as she listened, terrified, and afraid to breathe.

"Dana? Dana, it's Mrs. MacGyver. Are you all right, dear?"

Mrs. MacGyver! Dana was so grateful to hear her landlady's voice that when she opened the door, she almost threw herself into the sweet woman's arms. Except, Mrs. MacGyver wasn't alone. A tall man stood behind her, his dark scowl and stiff stance exuding an almost palpable tension.

"Dana! What's wrong? I heard screaming! You're shaking, my dear. What is it?" Mrs. MacGyver's usually calm eyes were filled with worry.

The man stared at Dana, appraising both her and the situation, as he glanced over her shoulder and into the room behind her. If he came to any conclusions, his face did not reveal them. She couldn't speak.

Oddly, she did note Mrs. MacGyver's smart pantsuit and the stylish new cut of her blonde, bobbed hair. For a brief moment, she wondered if her widowed landlady had acquired a new male friend, before dismissing the idea as both none of her business and highly unlikely – the guy was way too young —early to mid-thirties, she guessed, maybe just a couple of years older than herself. Still, to see a strange man in the house at this hour of the morning, and in the company of Mrs. MacGyver, was most unusual.

Crazy thoughts flew around her brain. Suddenly and absurdly afraid of looking foolish, she considered not explaining what happened. She could make up a plausible explanation, a particularly vivid nightmare, perhaps. At the same time, she simply could not go back into the bedroom and face that *thing* alone. After all, she admonished herself, there was nothing for her to feel foolish about. There was a dead rat in her bed, and someone had deliberately placed it there.

Maybe it was meant to be a joke, she thought, desperate for any reasonable explanation and recalling the black lace bow tied like a macabre necklace around its neck.

That's it! It was just a horrible prank someone tried to pull off. This possibility brought no comfort, however, only more disturbing questions: *But who would do that? And why? And what was "reasonable" about that explanation anyway?*

Fighting off a rising hysteria, she found refuge in her sense of dark humour.

"I just found a present, Mrs. MacGyver."

"A present? A present made you scream like that?"

The poor woman looked confused, *And no wonder*, Dana thought. *I'm confused myself.* She gave her head a shake as if to clear it.

"Yes," she continued, still shaking, "It's a big, fat rat. I didn't think there were any in this house, but I certainly found one."

Her landlady recoiled at the idea, bristling at the implied insult. "No, dear. We've never had rats in this house. Never! Could it be a big mouse?"

Not waiting for a reply, she added, "Let's have a look then, shall we? Where did you see it? Maybe it found a way in from outside. It only takes the tiniest opening for them to squeeze through, you know."

She started to enter the apartment. The stranger remained standing in the hallway but reached out as if to put a restraining hand on her arm.

"Oh, no. It's a rat, all right. And it even came gift-wrapped, tied with a bow." Shivering, Dana wrapped her arms around herself. She was becoming giddy and fought an urge to giggle. *Was she going into shock?*

"Gift-wrapped?" Mrs. MacGyver gave her an odd, assessing look. She appeared to notice Dana's discomfort and put an arm around her. "You need a sweater or a throw to wrap around yourself."

Realizing she was wearing her briefest pajamas, Dana grabbed a knitted afghan off her sofa and wrapped it tightly around herself, and not only because she was shivering. She couldn't take her eyes off the tall man. *Why is he standing there like that? Now,* he's *starting to freak me out, too.*

Following her gaze, Mrs. MacGyver seemed to remember she hadn't arrived alone and spoke to the stranger. "Philip, do you think you could give us a hand with this mouse?"

To Dana, she explained, "This is my nephew, Philip Marshall. We were just getting ready to go out for breakfast when you screamed. I'm sure he'll be able to take care of this for us, dear. Now, where do you think you saw this mouse? I suppose it could be anywhere by now. We'll likely need to set a trap."

Dana gave the nephew a wary look and silent appraisal. His deeply tanned and slightly lined face still bore an angry expression, accented by the jut of a strong chin. Yet in his tired-looking eyes, she noted concern for his aunt. His lean frame was casually dressed in what she thought must be travel clothes— one of those vests full of handy pockets, and light cotton slacks full of creases. She was aware of being assessed in return and could read the obvious conclusion in his intense gaze. She was not to be trusted.

"Dana?" Mrs. MacGyver interrupted her thoughts. "Where was the mouse, dear?"

Without another word of explanation, she led the two

to her bedroom. Standing aside at the doorway, she ushered them in ahead of her. Not wanting to advance any further, she mutely pointed at the bed and closed her eyes.

Chapter Two

Dana heard a sharp intake of breath and then Mrs. MacGyver's strained, "Mother of God!" followed by a deep, guttural curse in a male voice. When she opened her eyes, she saw them standing stock-still. Her landlady looked a little ill, her face drained of colour.

"What kind of crazy person wraps a bow around a dead rat?" her nephew demanded, turning to give Dana an odd look.

Oh, good heavens! He thinks I did this!

"I beg your pardon? Are you implying that *I* did this? I've been scared half to death by this … this disgusting thing, and you think I'm crazy enough to put something that gross in my own bed? Why on earth would I do that?" She was aware her voice was rising almost to a shriek but couldn't stop it. "It seems to me you're the one whose thinking is a little twisted here, mister!"

"Now, dear, calm down. Philip didn't mean to imply any such thing. It's just so...so awful...that it's taken us by surprise."

Philip didn't apologize, but when he spoke, his manner was a fraction milder. "How did it get here?"

"I don't know!"

"Well, it didn't just walk in. Who else has a key?"

"No one. Just me. And your aunt, of course."

"Did you have a friend over or let someone in?"

"No, no one."

"Is there any sign of a break-in?"

"I don't think so. I haven't had time to look around." Her eyes searched the room, looking for clues. Philip walked over to the window and peered out. The house backed onto a sloping ravine at the bottom of which was another street of homes. At this time of year, even though the trees were in full bud, the view remained clear.

Mrs. MacGyver shivered involuntarily and said, "Let's get the thing out of here first. Then we'll have a look 'round."

Her nephew turned from the window. "Have you got a shoebox or anything I can put it in? And work gloves? I don't want to handle it without them. The darn thing could have rabies."

Dana hadn't thought of that. "No work gloves, but I've got a shoebox."

"There's a pair of gardening gloves in a basket by the back door," his aunt said. "They'll be small for you, but they'll do in a pinch."

Dana opened her closet, tossed a new pair of strappy sandals out of their box, and without looking at Philip, handed it over.

He tossed it on the bed and left the room without another word. She and her landlady stood immobilized, listening to his pounding footsteps on the stairs as he went in search of the gloves.

Chapter Three

Mrs. MacGyver appeared frazzled, rubbing her arms as if for warmth and looking in need of comforting and a little lie-down herself. However, she bustled Dana into the living room, saying, "Come, dear. Would you like a glass of water or some tea? "

"Please don't fuss. I'll be fine, thank you. I just need a few minutes to gather myself together." She felt almost ill. *Well, who wouldn't, waking up to that?* The throw had slipped off her shoulders and she pulled it snugly back around her.

She ran a nervous hand through her hair. Twirling a finger through her long, thick strands had, since childhood, soothed her in moments of stress. What she found instead was her newly cropped cut, the result of a dramatic impulse she'd momentarily forgotten. Moving to a new part of the city in hopes of starting a new life had seemed to require a new look, too.

"Here's Philip again." Her landlady turned to her nephew who was standing in the doorway.

Philip looked at the two women and seemed to hesitate for a moment. In his right hand, a pair of bright yellow gardening gloves held at chest level reminded Dana of a spring bouquet, their sunny colour and floppy fingers mimicking flowers. *I'm going mad. A spring bouquet!*

"What do you plan to do with it? Put it in

the garbage?" Mrs. MacGyver asked.

"I don't know. Maybe we should see about getting it tested."

Looking at Dana again, he asked, "That's how you found it? Dead on your bed?"

"Of course," she snapped, "what did you think? I tied a bow around it and was trying to turn it into a pet?" *Get a grip! This isn't like you, losing it like this.*

"No need to get mad. I'm just trying to figure this out. Any idea how long it's been there?"

Dana paused before she could give him another angry retort. "Sorry, I'm not sure. I haven't had time to think. It couldn't have been there long. I'd have noticed."

"Are you sure? Maybe it was hidden under the sheets."

"Are you crazy? Do you think I could sleep all night without noticing a dead rat in my bed?"

"That depends."

"On what?" she snapped.

"Well, I guess it would depend on the state you were in when you went to bed...if you'd had a big night out...?"

"Philip, please, dear," his aunt interjected. "You don't know Dana. She's not that kind of girl. Now, let's try to calm down and sort this thing out."

"Sorry, Aunt Iva," he smiled at his aunt apologetically.

Smiling at least made him look less formidable but no less annoying, Dana thought.

While Philip went into the bedroom to box up the rat, Mrs. MacGyver put the kettle on, even though Dana had said she didn't want anything. She supposed for some people, tea is always the answer to life's stressful moments.

Maybe they're right. It's either the tea itself or the simple act of preparing it that brings some desired sense of normalcy and routine.

Philip emerged with the closed shoe box and headed

for the door. He paused and turned to Dana. Although his look had softened slightly, his eyes still assessed her, as if he couldn't decide whether she was sane and trustworthy.

"Do you want to get it tested?" he asked.

She tried to concentrate on the question, but her brain wouldn't cooperate. What did it matter whether it was tested or not?

"I don't know," she said, trying to pull herself together. "I suppose maybe it should. What do you think?" She couldn't believe she was asking for his opinion.

"I think for my aunt's peace of mind, and my own, it should."

"All right, then. Will you do it, or shall I?"

He seemed to examine her face even more deeply before replying, "I'll take care of it. No problem."

"Thank you."

"You're welcome. I also took a quick look around in there for signs of anything out of the ordinary. There's no broken window or anything obvious. There's no other entrance besides the door in the living room?"

"Right. Only that one." Thoughts of an intruder stirred her fears again.

His aunt came out of the kitchen, consternation on her face. "Oh, Dana! I suddenly remembered. This is your big day. What an awful start to it!"

"Big day?' inquired Philip. "Like a wedding? Are you getting married?"

"No, no," Mrs. MacGyver rushed to Dana's rescue. "Dana is an author. Her first play is going into rehearsals today, or rather tonight. It's very exciting." She looked proudly at her tenant.

"It went right out of my mind with all this…" Waving a hand in the air, Dana searched for a word to describe what had transpired. She gave up. "I think I will have a cup of tea, after all. You, too," she pleaded with the older woman. "Please stay and have some with me."

Mrs. MacGyver looked questioningly at Philip.

"You stay, Aunt Iva. I'll wrap this up and put it in your freezer 'til we can contact the authorities."

"My freezer?" The poor woman's horrified expression was almost comical.

"Don't worry. It won't be there long. Won't do any harm," he assured her, moving towards the door. "I think I'll go outside, too, and scout around the house and yard a bit."

Pausing, he turned to Dana. "Well, goodbye. It's been...*interesting* meeting you."

Was that a smirk on his face? Dana felt like throwing something at his smug back but lacked the energy. Instead, she collapsed onto the sofa cushions and closed her eyes.

The rehearsal! Tonight. Thinking of her play suddenly seemed like something from another life, another world. How odd, when for years it had consumed her almost every waking moment.

Chapter Four

Dana barely tasted the tea Mrs. MacGyver insisted on preparing, and after once more declining her invitation to join her and her nephew for breakfast, closed the door behind the kind woman, grateful to be alone again.

She collapsed on her couch, overwhelmed by the trauma of discovering the disgusting creature in her bed and then the difficult, yet understandable, questions from Mrs. MacGyver and her stern nephew, as everyone tried to imagine what possible reasons might lay behind such a grotesque event.

Dana was alarmed at how clumsy her legs felt, as though heavy weights were strapped to them. *Probably another symptom of shock.* At the door to her bedroom, she hesitated and took a deep breath before forcing herself to enter. A vision of the rat's body played across her mind, producing a shiver. She didn't even want to touch her pretty sheets, which now seemed defiled, but, with a grimace, she gathered them up to throw in the wash.

I'll never want to sleep on them again. Then she chided herself. *Don't be ridiculous. You paid good money for them, you love them, and they're going into the wash anyway.*

Tidying up, she did a careful inspection of the apartment, searching for any indication of how the abominable creature might have arrived. She found nothing.

The clear morning air carried the screech of streetcars braking on Queen St., even though the windows were shut. Dana thought of all the city's commuters en route to work or school, each absorbed in the minutiae of his or her own life, largely unaware of the drama in others'.

A glance at the clock reminded her to get on with her shower, and she brightened a bit in anticipation of soothing, warm water easing her tense muscles. But as she turned on the faucet and the showerhead gushed, a storm of intense panic seized her, and she couldn't bring herself to step in. Never before had she been so acutely aware of being alone and vulnerable in this apartment.

I can't let this thing make me paranoid. I'm always alone in here. Nothing's changed.

Her feeble attempt at rationalizing failed. At a fundamental level, Dana knew everything had changed.

Chapter Five

Dana ran down the stairs leading out of her apartment, anxious to not be late for her yoga class. Her thudding feet must've alerted the neighbours, because the door to Mrs. MacGyver's main-floor apartment opened, and Philip Marshall stepped into the spacious foyer. She assumed by the tilt of his head and raised eyebrows that he wished to speak to her. Despite a flicker of annoyance at being waylaid, she came to a stop at the bottom of the stairs and waited for him to speak.

He still wore that dark look, but it didn't stop her from noticing how the colour of his shirt matched the blue of his eyes. She noticed how intense those eyes were. Some might consider them intriguing, but Dana thought their expression was unnerving.

"My aunt and I were wondering if you intended to call the police about this incident?" he politely inquired.

"The police? It hadn't crossed my mind."

And why hadn't it? Someone had entered her apartment to put that awful thing in her bed. That certainly wasn't normal, but was it meant as a threat? She couldn't imagine it was, but was she thinking clearly? And was it anything to call the police about?

"Aren't you concerned that someone might be trying to threaten you?" he asked. "Maybe this *should* be a police matter. My aunt is convinced there's nothing they can do because there wasn't an actual crime, but—"

"I think she's right," Dana interrupted. "It was probably a bad joke. A disgusting one, for sure, but not an actual crime."

"I don't think you believe that. Even if you can't prove there was a crime…" Philip shook his head in disbelief. "Look, finding a dead rat is one thing, but to find one tied up with a black bow is something else entirely. The more I think about it, the less I like it. This is your apartment, but we don't know if you're being targeted. It could just as easily have been my aunt."

"I hadn't thought of that," Dana confessed. "Do you think so? I can't imagine why anyone would want to hurt her."

"Neither can I. But who knows? Maybe someone wants to drive out her last tenant for some crazy reason."

Dana pondered this new idea for a moment. "That does sound crazy." She moved toward the door, adding, "I'll think about calling the police. Right now, I need to get to my yoga class on time."

His eyes flashed in annoyance. When he spoke, his voice was tight with disapproval. "I'm sure the teacher will understand if you're a bit late once you explain the circumstances."

"I *am* the teacher," Dana informed him. "If you'll excuse me, I have students waiting."

He didn't reply but watched as she went out the door and headed down the street. Unable to resist, she looked back to see him on the verandah, his heated stare following her. She turned away but felt them boring into her back until she knew she was out of sight.

Chapter Six

Dana proceeded completely unaware of the delightful spring morning as she half-walked, half-jogged along Queen St. Was it only yesterday, she'd been thrilled by the signs of tiny buds on the trees and the promise they held? The weather had been warm enough to enjoy a drink at an outdoor table. Today, it was as if time had flipped to summer. For the blissful, upturned faces of those soaking in the sun's warmth, breathing in the earthy scent of freshly raked lawns could only add to their pleasure. For Dana, the beauty of this day appeared to be wasted.

Dog-walkers swerved as if to avoid a collision with the lovely young woman lost in her own world. A keen observer might have noticed the young man enjoying his coffee on a park bench, who watched her approach with an appreciative gaze. He looked as if he might have dared to say good morning, then turned away. Was it the haunted look on her face that deterred him?

A half-empty streetcar rattled past as she waited to cross at the corner. She barely registered its presence. She couldn't get the picture of that tiny, ribboned body out of her brain or her brief conversation with Philip.

Philip. "Does Philip live nearby?" she'd inquired earlier when Mrs. MacGyver had brought her tea.

"No. He's from Guelph, but he's been working in Africa for the last three years, so this is the first time I've seen him in all that time." She'd leaned forward as she spoke, eyes shining with evident pleasure at her nephew's return.

"That's nice." Dana's brief reply had been absent-minded.

"Yes, it is. He'll be here a few days, and he's offered to do some small repairs for me, so I might ask him to fix that sticky window you've been having problems with. It probably needs oil or a light sanding. Would you mind if I let him in to do that while you're at work? Shouldn't take him long."

"No, that's fine. I'd like to let some fresh air in, now that it's warming up."

She didn't like the idea of a stranger being alone in her apartment, but Philip Marshall wasn't really a stranger, was he? He was Mrs. MacGyver's nephew, and surely his aunt would be with him.

A new and unsettling thought brought her to a halt on the sidewalk, almost causing a collision with the dog-walker behind her— exactly when had Philip Marshall arrived? Was it that morning, or had he been there the night before? If he had been there overnight, would he have had access to his aunt's master key?

This was a very disturbing line of thinking, but then something very disturbing had happened that morning.

*****

Dana was still absorbed in her thoughts when she arrived at her destination. Most days, simply entering the yoga studio soothed her soul. The muted, earthy colours of the decor and the unobtrusive, soft lighting underscored by a relaxing melody floating over the sound system worked magic on those who passed through its doors. Today, however, was not most days.

The new receptionist, Nora, was a young woman of

about twenty. She sat behind her desk in the lobby with a fresh cup of coffee next to the keyboard. When Dana walked through the front doors, she chirped a cheerful greeting. "Hi, Dana. Your students are here and ready…." She stopped, concern on her overly made-up face. "Are you all right? You look —"

"I'm fine." Dana cut in, not wanting to discuss anything right now, especially with Nora. The girl had only been there for two weeks and, though she seemed to be a reliable worker, was a complete stranger.

"I'm running a bit late, but I'm ready to go. See you later!"

Moving down the hall, she found her locker and threw in her jacket and street shoes but carried her backpack into the studio. Eight friendly faces greeted her, and a few called out, "Morning, Dana." She was glad to see her friend Julie in the group; although, Julie was scrutinizing her in a way that made her feel overly exposed. *She doesn't miss much.*

Elaine, the perpetually sleepy night-shift nurse, had placed her mat beside Julie's. Behind the two of them sat Delores, a retired teacher, and Marcus, a community college student. Nancy and Jean were a few feet off to the right. The slightly older women were co-workers at a local bank.

There were two unfamiliar faces this morning: a man and a woman looked at her with expectant faces. The arrival of new students was usually a pleasant event, so she was taken aback by how unnerving it was today. Why hadn't Nora forewarned her? Well, in her rush, she'd hardly given the girl a chance to tell her anything, had she?

With some effort to hide her nerves, she managed to begin. "Morning, everyone. Sorry I'm a bit late. It's one of those days, you know?" *Could they see through her lie?*

As she unrolled her mat and plugged her iPod into the docking station, a few sympathetic murmurs reached her. The early spring light was intense, so Dana walked over to the high-set windows and pulled a few blinds.

"I'm happy to see some new faces," she said, smiling at the two. "Welcome. I'm Dana." It was an effort to be cheerful and act as if this were a normal morning, but she was determined to give it her best shot.

The woman, an exquisitely-groomed thirty-ish blonde offered a slight, shy smile. "Thank you. I'm Anna."

"Hi, Anna. Are you new to yoga?"

"No, I've done some in the past, but it's been a couple of years."

"Well, I hope you enjoy the class. Try to relax and don't push yourself."

Anna could be a mother with children in school, who was able to fit in an hour of physical activity. Then again, she could also be a local businesswoman who managed to fit an hour of yoga into her busy schedule. Despite not having done any yoga in a while, it was clear she managed to find other ways to keep in shape.

The man spoke up, "I'm Brad. It's the same with me. It's been a while since I've taken a class. Thought I'd give it another try."

Brad appeared to be about thirty and fit. Another actor or student, Dana thought. Or possibly a stay-at-home dad for a change. She noted his deep, early tan. *He's either been south on vacation or he works outdoors. Could also be an actor who likes tanning salons, of course.*

"Welcome, Brad. Glad to have you with us. Take it easy today and don't push yourself beyond your comfort level. I'll come around and help if you need me."

To the whole group, she said, "Let's begin, shall we? Stretch out on your mats, lie on your backs, and assume the corpse pose with your eyes closed."

As she turned on her iPod, soothing classical guitar music washed over her, and she allowed herself to relax in the comfort of a familiar routine. Lowering herself onto her mat, she closed her own eyes and breathed in deeply. This was the place where she felt safest.

Chapter Seven

"Shanti. Thank you," several students said to Dana as they quietly filed out of the class. It pleased Dana to see them relaxed and to know the hour had benefitted them. She noted Anna and Brad walking down the hall chatting and wondered if they had come together. She hadn't gotten that impression in class, but in her state of mind, she would have missed even a big *Just Married* sign hanging around their necks.

Now that class had ended and Dana was alone, Julie approached with concern. "You look like you need a coffee. How 'bout it? We can sit outside again today. It's gorgeous out there."

Dana suddenly felt distracted and uneasy. During the class, her mind had attempted to wander, but she had kept re-focusing on what needed to be done then and there. Now, the morning's events were resurfacing, and her mind filled with the horrible image of "that thing". Although she enjoyed Julie's company, the idea of pretending everything was fine was overwhelming.

"Oh … I'm not sure, Julie. There's a lot to do with rehearsals starting tonight..."

"I can tell something's happened, Dana. Have you had bad news? It's not your mom, is it?"

"No, it's not Mom. She's fine. I'm fine." Dana's mom had been going to the doctor with some as-of-yet-undiagnosed mystery ailment, which Dana suspected was psychosomatic. She certainly hoped that's what it was.

Taking in Julie's earnest face, she found it difficult to brush off her friend's obvious concern. *She has a good heart. Maybe it will help to talk to her about it. Maybe things won't seem so bizarre in the light of day.*

"Okay, let's get a coffee. But a quick one."

"Great! It's my treat today."

The cafe was just down the block on a sunny corner. Planters of welcoming pansies and hyacinths flanking the door greeted customers. Spring blooms always gave Dana a mood lift and the scent of the purple hyacinths was divine. She and Julie went in and ordered from the barista, chatting a bit about the class while waiting. Outside, they chose a table not too close to the late-morning coffee-and-newspaper crowd and sipped their herbal teas.

"Why do we still say, 'let's go for a coffee' when we both drink tea?" Dana pondered.

"Old habits die hard, I guess," Julie replied. "We're the only tea grannies in our crowd. So, everybody just says 'coffee'."

Our crowd. Interesting phrase. What is our crowd? *It's usually Julie and me or one or two others from yoga class.*

Since moving to this area, she had begun to lose touch with her downtown friends. She told herself this was due to how busy she'd been finishing her play, but who was she kidding? The real reason was more complicated.

She realized that aside from Julie, she hadn't given herself time to meet others in her new neighbourhood. And even with Julie, it was more that Julie had pursued the friendship than she had.

"Anyway, I don't miss the caffeine, do you?" Julie continued.

"No. I sleep better without it." *But I might never sleep again, after last night.* "Anyhow, how are you? What've you been up to lately?"

"Not much," Julie looked down to examine the white metal tabletop in detail, as if wanting to avoid Dana's eyes. "Actually," she resumed slowly, "I did have something to tell you, but now I don't know if this is a good time or not. I can tell something's bothering you." She finally looked up, "Do you want to talk about it?"

"I'm not quite ready to speak about my problems, but now that you've piqued my curiosity you have to tell me! You can't keep me in suspense."

"Okay." Julie took a deep breath and then let it out. She watched Dana's face, assessing her reaction as she spoke. "Remember you told me once about that guy you used to be with, Dave Mitchell?"

The question came out of the blue. Dave Mitchell: less than a year before, Dana had believed with every fiber of her being she would be with the man forever. While he had never spoken the actual words, Dave had nevertheless made it clear he wasn't ready for a permanent commitment, but she'd been so blinded by love to begin with, that she'd half-accepted, half-ignored that particular fact.

Over time though, she'd come to acknowledge other, deeper flaws in their relationship. Dave never understood her need to write or her desire to make a career of it. To him, she was a precocious child with a passing interest in something she'd drop when the next thing came along. What was worse, she'd almost started to believe it.

For Dave, everything revolved around law school. Her needs took second place. At last, she knew she needed to pick up the pieces of her broken heart and leave, not only Dave, but their west-end Toronto neighbourhood as well. Otherwise, she'd not only risk running into him but the pitying glances of their mutual friends.

And that was how she'd landed where she was now, in The Beach, at the opposite end of the city. End of story. Well, maybe not quite the end— Julie seemed to have some kind of news, which judging by the way she was chewing her lips, was causing her some anxiety.

Dana took a careful sip of her tea and with some trepidation, said, "Yeah. What about him?"

Her friend's words came in a rush. "Well, you know how small the world is. I met a girl at work who knows him, and … maybe this isn't the best time to tell you, but —" Julie paused, examining Dana's face before continuing, "Anyway, according to her, he's getting married."

"Married? Dave?" Flabbergasted, Dana sat back in her chair. "Wow!" After a moment, she asked, "You're sure?"

Julie simply nodded, allowing her friend time to absorb the unexpected news.

"Coming from the guy who wasn't ready for a permanent relationship," Dana said with a disgusted sigh. "He said it would be years before he would consider settling down! Not that I was in any hurry, but still…"

"I hope you're not upset that I told you, but you were bound to hear sooner or later."

"No, no. Don't worry. I'm not upset, just blown away. Dave and I probably weren't meant to be, but I was in love with him for a long while. I thought things might change— hoped they would, actually. So, who's he marrying?"—

"I forget her name, but she's from Calgary. You probably don't know her. You're sure you're not upset?"

"No, not at all," Dana assured her, but she remained stunned as memories flooded back. She had to acknowledge that time and distance had wrought a change in her. Moving away had allowed her to move on as well, to heal from her heartbreak, and to write. A year ago, she wouldn't have believed that was possible. This profound realization brought a sense of clarity and, oddly, freedom.

Observing the obvious concern on her friend's face— the turned down brows and doubtful eyes, Dana added, "Actually, I'm glad you told me. It's made me realize I've moved on. It doesn't hurt as it might have a few months ago."

Julie's face cleared as if sunshine had blown away the clouds. "I'm glad. I was worried about telling you." They were quiet for a few moments, sipping their tea and contemplating Julie's news. "Now, what's up with you?" Julie asked. "And don't say 'nothing'."

Despite her best effort, Dana couldn't quite keep a slight note of despair from her reply. "I don't know what's up, Julie. And you're not going to believe it, anyway. "

Julie leaned in closer. "Try me."

Chapter Eight

The naturally inquisitive Julie would normally pepper Dana with questions as she related the morning's events. The fact that she sat through the narrative in stunned silence was an affirmation of how totally bizarre and ghoulish the incident was.

"You called the police, right?" Julie demanded. "Because this isn't funny, Dana. It's darned scary."

"No, I haven't called them."

"But you're going to, right? Some weirdo is out there, and who knows what a sick mind like that might try next."

"If you're trying to frighten me, Julie, you're doing a good job."

"If *I'm* trying to frighten you? Look, Dana. I'm trying to talk *sense* into you. You have to take this seriously. None of our friends would play a practical joke like that. It's sick."

"I know, but do you honestly think the police are going to take a dead rat seriously? They have more important things to deal with."

"Let them decide, okay? Promise me you'll call them." Dana didn't reply.

Julie became more exasperated. "What about tonight? You shouldn't be alone. I think I should camp out on your couch for a couple of nights. I'll bring my sleeping bag."

"Thanks, but tonight's the first rehearsal for my play,

remember? I'll be late getting in. You don't have to come over. I'll be fine. After all, Mrs. MacGyver's there, too."

"Mrs. MacGyver was there last night, too. A lot of good that did. And have you forgotten that I'm now part of your stage crew? We can leave together."

After a thoughtful moment during which Dana did not reply, Julie asked, "What about this nephew? What's he like?"

"Hard to say. He comes across as kind of angry and arrogant. I don't know..."

"How old is he? What does he do? What does he look like?"

Dana almost laughed at the rapid-fire questions. "Slow down, okay? I guess he's about our age. Maybe a bit older. Thirty-five, maybe? I don't know what he does. His aunt said he's been in Africa for three years. He just got back."

Aware of Julie's growing impatience, Dana added, "Okay. He's tall, slim, kind of intense, not bad looking if he'd learn to smile. Could be a nice guy or another Ted Bundy. How do I know?"

"Exactly! I'm not feeling good about this, Dana. I insist on staying over at least for tonight and maybe the rest of the weekend. I'll come home from the rehearsal with you."

Dana was deeply touched by her friend's kindness. "Thanks, Julie. Maybe it's not a bad idea after all. And thanks for this," she said, raising her now empty cup. "Next time, it's on me."

They parted with a promise to keep in touch by phone that afternoon and meet for dinner before the rehearsal.

Chapter Nine

Philip Marshall was not fooled. He was quite aware his aunt was attempting to hide her distress by putting on a cheerful front. In that way, she was like his mother. In other ways, they were quite different. Growing up, he'd always felt more at ease talking to his aunt rather than his mother who had folded in on herself after his older brother died. While his father had remained strong, he was never a man open to talking about feelings. Aunt Iva had been available and willing to listen to a boy's dreams and fears.

He sat at the familiar mottled grey stainless steel kitchen table with its arborite top and four matching chairs. Years ago, his mother had owned an identical set. They were once at the height of style, then trashed as outdated. According to the nabobs of fashion and décor in a magazine he'd recently read, they were now fashionably "retro." As he fondly observed his aunt, he smiled, thinking that she was likely unaware of her kitchen dining set's transition from in fashion, to out, and back in again; not that she would care. While he simply sat and enjoyed the heavenly aroma of bacon crisply frying and something deliciously sweet in the toaster oven, his aunt whisked some eggs and talked a mile a minute.

"No need to go out for breakfast, Philip. I've got a fridge full of bacon and eggs. I even bought some hot cross buns. I remember how you've always loved them. Even though Easter's over, they're still making some, and these are chock full of candied fruit. They look delicious. You wouldn't have had those in Africa, I imagine?"

"No, nor bacon and eggs often, either. The big hotels serve them, of course, for tourists. Once in a while, when I had a real yen for them, I'd go to a hotel for breakfast, if I was in a city."

"Were you ever homesick? I suppose that's a silly question to ask a grown man, but it's such a long way away."

"They kept me pretty busy. There wasn't time to get homesick," he told her. *Didn't want to think about home, anyway. Tried to put it right out of my mind.*

He needed to change the subject and found himself thinking of the young woman in the apartment above. "How long has Dana Williams been living here?" he asked.

"Oh, about six months, I suppose. She came last October after Mr. Syms moved out."

"Where'd she come from?"

"Downtown. Somewhere in the Annex neighbourhood near the university. She was taking some writing courses. Still does, at night school. Did I tell you she's written a play? I did, didn't I? There I go repeating myself. I'll have to watch that."

The ping of the toaster oven signaled the hot cross buns were ready. Philip got up to butter them while his aunt placed the eggs and bacon on plates and brought them to the table. They ate in companionable silence, and he savoured every mouthful. He'd almost forgotten the pleasure of sharing a home-cooked meal, no matter how simple. Sitting in his aunt's sunny kitchen was a treat.

He glanced around, taking in the familiar room, glad she hadn't gone on a decorating binge. It seemed his mother was constantly redoing rooms as if something in her was never satisfied. Aunt Iva's knick-knack shelf still held her collection of porcelain owls and the few familiar photos on one wall reminded him of his late uncle, whom he barely remembered. He thought about how long his aunt had been on her own, close to twenty years.

His mind returned to Dana and that gruesome rat. He didn't want to spoil breakfast by bringing it up again, but several questions remained. Trying to keep his tone light and casual, he asked, "Is Dana your only tenant right now? What about the third-floor apartment above hers? No one seemed to respond to her screams this morning."

"There's no one on the third floor right now. I'm not sure I'm going to rent it again. I thought you could stay there while you're here. I fixed up the bed, just in case." Her look was hopeful. "Of course, I know you're anxious to get back to Guelph, but anytime you're in Toronto, you'd be welcome to use it."

"Thanks. That's a nice offer. I'm not sure whether I'll be settling in Guelph again or not. I have a couple of meetings lined up with former colleagues, and I'll go from there. See what happens. But don't hold it just for me. If you need to rent it, go ahead."

"I don't need to rent it. For now, I'm happy only having Dana here. The last person I had on the third floor was a bit of a problem and not easy to get rid of. Dana's the perfect tenant, and she's become like a friend."

The perfect tenant, Philip mused. *I wonder.*

He thought about the young woman. She looked to be somewhere in her late twenties but could be thirty. It was hard to tell. He wasn't good at assessing women's ages —or assessing women, period. She was tall and lean and looked like she worked at keeping fit. *Nothing wrong with that,* he reminded himself. Despite the fact she'd just woken up and had a bad shock, she was not unattractive either: clear skin, deep blue eyes. Her short, light brown hair was boyish, not a look he usually appreciated, but not bad. All in all, nothing to make him think there was anything wrong with her, but who could tell these days? And what kind of an expert was he, anyway? None at all.

"What does she do for a living?"

"She works at the yoga studio along Queen St., part-time. Occasionally, one of her friends who owns a restaurant asks her to fill in as a waitress, but that's not too often. Her main focus is writing."

"Does she make anything at that? Enough to support herself?"

"She does movie reviews sometimes, too, for one of those magazines you get at the theatre. Once, she had an article in the food section of the newspaper. I have no idea how much she makes, but she's always on time with her rent."

Now that they'd finished their meal and moved on to coffee, Philip decided to bring up the one topic they'd avoided so far-what had happened in Dana's apartment that morning.. The best way to deal with it was head-on. His aunt was a sensible, capable woman; she didn't need protection from this kind of unpleasantness.

"What's your take on this morning's incident? How do you think that rat got there?"

His aunt looked off towards the window above the sink, as if searching for an answer. "I don't know, but I'm certain Dana had nothing to do with it, if that's what you're thinking."

She turned and looked at him directly, all pretense at cheerfulness vanished. "The obvious answer is that someone was in that apartment, in my house, without either of us knowing. I don't like to think that, but it's the only answer."

The distress in her eyes told him it was much more than just upsetting. She was badly frightened, and rightly so. After all, someone had invaded her home with malicious intent. He regretted his question, but he couldn't drop the subject. "Does Dana have many friends over? Couldn't one of them have a key?"

"I asked her that. She swore she hasn't given anyone a key. She doesn't have friends over as a rule. Occasionally, her friend Julie Chen comes over, but I think she tends to meet her other friends at a coffee shop or a restaurant."

"Do you want to call the police about this?" Her deep sigh indicated such a sense of helplessness, he was moved to reach out and take her hand. She gave him a grateful look in return. "I did think about that," she replied, "but what could they do? There wasn't any actual crime committed. I didn't suggest it to Dana, either, given the state she was in. I suppose it's her decision."

"There might have been a crime: breaking and entering."

"That's true, but I didn't see any sign of that. Did you?"

"No, but I'm no expert. The police might notice something we didn't."

"I'll talk to Dana when she gets home later. I don't know if she'll be back before her play rehearsal or not, though. What a terrible thing to happen, especially on her big day."

His aunt seemed lost in thought for a few minutes and Philip decided to let the matter drop for the time being. But he remained more than a little curious about this "perfect" tenant.

Chapter Ten

Dana passed the early part of the afternoon wandering in and out of the trendy little shops along Queen Street. The promising spring day and the main task at hand (scouting out a birthday present for her mother), served as a diversion from the traumatic manner in which her day had begun. Although it never completely dissipated, the horror receded sufficiently at times, enough that she could almost pretend nothing out of the ordinary had happened. *Almost.* She had to believe it was all a sick practical joke. Any other explanation was too much to consider. But who did she know that would consider something so sick? No one. She could not conceive of any of her old girlfriends coming up with such an idea, let alone handling a dead rat! Neither could Julie, she was quite sure, nor Mrs. MacGyver, even though she had the greatest opportunity. But what about her nephew? That was a disquieting thought, as he was obviously going to be in the house a few more days.

Seeking diversion, she turned her thoughts to Julie's news about Dave. She had surprised herself with her reaction to it, or rather, her lack of reaction. It hadn't hit her nearly as hard as she would have predicted. Dave had obviously moved on from any thoughts of reuniting with her. That was a good thing, wasn't it? Unless he still harboured a grudge against her? Would he go so far as to plant that horrible thing in her bed as revenge for the way things ended? No! She didn't believe Dave had that kind of vindictiveness in him. But what about some of his friends? She knew most of them well enough to dismiss this idea, too. And yet, could she afford to dismiss everyone so easily? There might have been one or two of Dave's friends who would think scaring the heck out of her on behalf of their pal would be a great idea.

She recalled two of his friends who had planned to play a prank during initiation week that had seriously backfired. Instead of being funny, their juvenile joke had been rather cruel, and they were lucky not to get kicked out of school. *But that was a couple of years ago. Now, they're both young lawyers, like Dave. Surely, they've outgrown that kind of immature behaviour?* At three o'clock, her cell phone sang its jaunty little tune in her pocket. "Hi, Julie."

"Did you have a nice morning, Dana?" The distorted, almost mechanical voice was most definitely not Julie. Confused, she checked the call display. It showed a private number.

"I'm sorry, who's this?"

"Did you like your present?"

Dana's throat closed. Her palms became slick with sweat. The phone slipped, but she gripped it tight before it could fall and hit the sidewalk. "What are you talking about?"

"I thought the black bow was a nice touch."

It was clear now who she was speaking to and that she was, indeed, the target of this morning's madness —*not* Mrs. MacGyver. Anger flooded her senses, enabling her to find her voice again. "Who are you?" she yelled into the phone. "What do you want with me? Are you sick or something, you freak?" Passers-by slowed down and stared, startled at the sudden outburst. Then, perhaps unnerved by the scene, they hurried on.

"Now, now, Dana. That's not nice. I thought you liked presents."

Horrified, Dana threw the phone as far as she could and watched it hit the sidewalk several meters away. The sound of plastic shattering shook her. She bent over, hands on her knees to keep from fainting ,and was appalled to find herself sobbing.

A concerned-looking, middle-aged woman who had observed the scene stooped to pick up the pieces of Dana's phone, all the while regarding Dana with uncertainty. The poor woman obviously wanted to be helpful but was wary of coming too close.

Who could blame her? I must look insane. Dana slumped against a nearby lamppost and tried to regain her composure.

"Are you all right?" The woman's sympathetic eyes probed Dana's as she placed the telephone pieces in her hands. Such concern from a total stranger prompted even more tears to flow.

Was she all right? How many people had asked her that already today? Too many. She had to stop losing it like this.

"I'm sorry," Dana told the kind woman. "I received some bad news, that's all. I'll be fine. Thank you for asking."

The woman seemed relieved by her answer, enough to say a quick "take care," before moving on.

Dana stared at the fractured phone before she slipped the pieces into her pocket and headed home.

She was relieved not to be greeted by Mrs. MacGyver and ran up the stairs, wanting nothing more than to sink into her easy chair and close her eyes. She didn't want to think about anything for a little while. She wanted to be alone.

At the top of the stairs with her key in the lock, she froze. The same sense of panic that had seized her when she tried to shower that morning gripped her again. *Take a deep breath. That's it. Breathe!* She repeated those words several times until they had some effect. After a few moments, only slightly calmer, she turned the key and opened the door.

Everything looked as it had when she left. The tightness in her neck and shoulders eased slightly. Dropping her backpack on the floor, she tossed her jacket onto the couch before heading straight to the worn, comfy armchair across the room. Before she could sit down, a shadow moved across the sunny patch on her carpet. Her breath caught in her throat. Someone was in her bedroom!

Chapter Eleven

Dana moved as quickly and silently as she could towards the door, only for Philip to emerge from the bedroom. "I'm sorry if I startled you. Aunt Iva wanted me to look at that window you're having trouble with and I..." He stopped abruptly, frowning. "You look ill!" Crossing the space between them in two big strides, he took her arm. "You'd better sit down."

"That was my plan!" she almost shouted. "Before you scared the living daylights out of me!" Shaking off his hand, she retreated to the door and opened it, motioning with her free hand for him to leave.

"I said I was sorry. I'm only here because of that stuck window. Did you forget I was coming?"

She had forgotten and immediately regretted her sharp tone; he hadn't done anything to deserve it. Closing her eyes, she took a deep, calming breath. "I'm sorry, too. I guess my nerves are a little on edge."

"No need for you to apologize. I'd worry if you weren't a bit edgy after what happened this morning. By the way, you didn't lock the door behind you. Do you usually leave it unlocked?"

Dana dropped into the big chair, suddenly too tired to stand. "Sometimes. If it's just your aunt and me in the house, I don't always feel I need to lock it. "

"Maybe that's not such a good idea now." He

examined her face. "Look, can I get you a glass of water or something? I can boil water. Tea's not beyond my capabilities. You look like you could use some. Or maybe you'd prefer coffee?"

His concern seemed genuine, and she almost felt sorry for him, but she was still wary. She realized her emotions were all over the place. Even his simple question about locking the door had put her on the defensive. Still, she found the idea of someone fussing over her surprisingly appealing at that moment. Forgetting her previous desire to be alone, she said, "I think I can manage that. Will you have a cup, too?"

"If you're sure you want company."

"I didn't, but I do now." She managed a smile. "You can tell me about the window."

As they stood in the tiny kitchen waiting for the kettle to boil and discussed the needed repairs, they found their tension easing.

Returning to the living room with their drinks, Dana sank into the easy chair while Philip took a seat on the couch, carefully moving her jacket aside. As he lifted it, the broken pieces of her phone slid out of the pocket.

"I dropped it," she said, unsure why she felt the need to lie.

"Looks more like it was run over."

"Well, it landed on the sidewalk."

"Still, it takes a lot to break up a phone that badly."

Her old anger rose again. "You don't believe me?" she challenged him.

"Take it easy. I didn't say I didn't believe you. I just said it takes a lot to break one, even on pavement. You'd almost have to hurl it to do that."

She was so startled by that remark that the truth must have shown on her face.

"*Did* you throw it? Come on, Dana. What happened?"

A tear slid down her cheek, and her horrified look told

the story.

"Tell me!" Philip urged. "For heaven's sake, you can't keep it all to yourself. Other people are involved here."

Could she trust him? She was struck by how much she wanted to be sure of him. Deep down, she needed to believe in him.

"Dana, did you get a call from someone? A threatening call? If you did, we need to let the police know. You see how serious this is, don't you?"

She looked at her hands wrapped around her hot mug. They should feel warm, but they didn't. Her whole body felt chilled to the bone, and she noticed she was shaking.

Putting his cup down, Philip rose and crossed to her chair. He stood looking down at her for a moment, then dropped to one knee, so he could look her in the face. "Tell me."

She refused to look at him, choosing instead to fix her eyes on the patterned rug. "He asked if I liked my 'present' this morning. That's what he called it, a present."

"Bastard! Who was it? Did you recognize his voice?"

"No. It sounded funny. Kind of tinny and distorted. At first, I thought it might have been a woman, but I'm sure it was a man."

"Is that all he said? 'Did you like your present?'" "He said…he said he thought the black bow was a nice touch."

Philip swore under his breath. "Anything else?"

"No. I got so freaked out I tossed the phone away, and it smashed to pieces on the sidewalk."

She was startled as he bolted upright. "We have to call the police," he insisted.

"But there's nothing to go on."

"Doesn't matter. We can't take any chances. I've got a sick feeling he won't stop at this. Maybe they can trace his call."

"Look at my phone! Do you think that's likely?"

"We won't know if we don't try. Do you want me to

make the call?"

"No. I will." Part of her remained reluctant and he must have sensed that.

Reaching into his hip pocket, he pulled out his phone and handed it to her. "Do it now, Dana. Don't wait."

Chapter Twelve

The young officer perched on the edge of Dana's couch looked dubious. She knew if she was hearing this tale of a dead rat tied with a black blow for the first time, she'd have looked the same way. It still sounded outrageous to her, and she had lived through it. However, when Philip removed the shoebox he retrieved from his aunt's freezer and displayed the now frozen rodent, Officer Green had turned the colour resembling his name.

Dana almost felt sorry for him. He looked so shiny and polished and earnest in his uniform. One might almost think it was his first day out of the police academy. As he listened to her account and questioned Mrs. MacGyver and Philip, he took copious notes, and his colour slowly returned to a healthier shade.

"And you're positive no one else has a key to your apartment, ma'am?" he asked once again.

"No," Dana repeated once again for the record. "I have never given a key to anyone." *Ma'am? Did he just call me ma'am?* She wasn't that much older than this officer, but the day was taking its toll. Maybe she looked as tired and ancient as she felt.

He nodded and turned his attention to Mrs. MacGyver. Stiff-backed with tension on the edge of a hard chair, her earlier bright and polished look vanished. The cheerful lipstick had been chewed off. and the blush on her cheeks had faded. "Is there a master key, ma'am?"

Startled by the question, she looked to Philip, then at Dana before replying, "Well, yes, officer. There's a master key that fits each of my apartments. It's for emergencies. I don't believe I've ever used it."

"And how many apartments are there?

"Just the three: my own, Dana's, and one on the third floor. It's unoccupied at the moment." Again, she glanced at Philip for reassurance.

"Right," the Officer said, scribbling a brief note in a room so quiet the scratch of pen on paper was audible. "And where is the master key kept, ma'am?"

"On a hook inside the broom closet in my kitchen. It's where I keep my car keys, too. But surely, you don't think…" Mrs. MacGyver's eyes widened in fear as she considered the implications.

Officer Green spelled it out for her, "So, anyone could have access to it if they knew where to look?"

"Well, I suppose so," she hesitated to admit. "But few people would know that, and they'd have to get into my apartment first." Shaking her head, she rejected the idea. "I don't see how that could happen. I'm there almost all the time, and when I'm not, I always lock up."

"Have you ever had a copy made for anyone? Perhaps a former tenant or a repairman?"

"Never!" she declared. Her indignation was so strong it brought a blush of colour back to her cheeks.

With a nod, Officer Green turned to Philip, who was standing protectively behind his aunt's chair. "And you, sir. You said you just arrived this morning, shortly before the incident happened. What time was that?"

"About 7:30," Philip replied, adding, "I had planned to take my aunt out for breakfast."

"So, you definitely weren't here last night or earlier this morning?"

"No. My plane got in last night at eleven, and I

checked into the airport Hilton. I picked up my rental truck at 6:30 this morning and got here at 7:30."

"Where did you fly in from?"

"From Kenya via London. British Airways," he replied. "That should be easy enough to check out." Dana noted an edge to Philip's voice with this last part.

"Yes, sir. Now, ma'am," he said turning back to her landlady. "Can you show me that broom closet, please?"

"Yes, of course." She rose somewhat stiffly with Philip taking her arm to help.

"I'll come with you," he stated.

"I'll wait here," Dana said, anxious to be alone, however briefly.

After the three filed out she closed the door behind them, then sank with a deep sigh into her most comfortable armchair. Aware of a dull pain forming behind her eyes, she massaged her forehead in gentle circles to ward off a full-blown headache, at the same time trying to imagine what lay behind such a macabre situation.

After a few minutes, she rose and wandered into her lemon-yellow kitchen, a room that always brightened her mood.

The clock on her microwave read 5:13 p.m. She'd better text Julie and tell her she couldn't make it to dinner. The cast was to gather at 7 o'clock. Surely, she wouldn't be delayed that long.

She reached for her jacket where she had stashed her cell phone that morning, only to come up empty. *Shoot! It's in pieces.* She'd have to add replacing that to her list of things to do. *If I can remember. My mind is turning to mush. I'm exhausted. If only I could stay home tonight.*

Was it only last night that she went to bed brimming with the excitement of starting rehearsals this evening? The nervous energy had been enough to keep her awake longer than usual. *How life can change in a blink of an eye.* Trite but true. Now, the play was taking a back seat to the horrible episodes of finding the rat and then receiving that creepy phone call.

Dana left the sunny kitchen that failed to brighten her mood and slumped into her chair again, leaning her head back. She allowed her gaze to drift around the living room. Its soft green hue usually soothed her soul, but even her few favourite pieces of memorabilia left her unmoved today. Was she ever going to feel safe in her own home again? She wasn't a timid person and life in the big city had never unnerved her. Ever since she'd arrived five years ago, she'd been reasonably street smart and moved about with ease, not continually looking over her shoulder like some, but now she felt she might have to start.

Closing her eyes again, she tried to take advantage of these few precious minutes to calm her mind with a short meditation. It wasn't long before she realized it wouldn't help. Was she losing her mind?

Hearing footsteps and voices heading upstairs, she went to open the door. An enticing aroma followed her landlady and the two men up the staircase, wafting into her apartment ahead of them. *Pot roast!* It reminded Dana that she hadn't eaten all day. She'd only had that cup of tea with Julie.

"Well, the key is still there," the young officer announced, seeming pleased. "That doesn't rule out the possibility that it might have been taken at an earlier date and then replaced. Anyone could have made a copy."

"As I said, I looked around outside earlier," Philip said, "but I'm no expert. You'll probably want to look around, too."

"I intend to," the officer affirmed. Looking thoughtful, he added, "This house has an odd configuration: that extra set of stairs from behind the kitchen to the second and third floors."

"The old servants' stairs," Mrs. MacGyver explained. "Some of these older houses have them. The main staircase was for family and friends, but the servants were to keep out of sight by using the rear stairs. There was usually only one servant or maid in a house this size. and they would have slept on the third floor if they were live-in help. Many of those staircases have been removed as people remodel."

"So, theoretically, if someone got in through your back door and knew where the master key was kept, they could have used that staircase," Philip conjectured.

"Exactly my thoughts," Officer Green commented. "And with that ravine out there, he might not have been seen coming or going."

"But there didn't appear to be any sign of forced entry," Dana pointed out.

"A good set of lock picks is all anyone would need," the young officer said. "Even if the deadbolt was on. You'd be surprised how easily most of them can be picked." Turning to Mrs. MacGyver, who was becoming agitated as she considered this possibility, he added, "You might want to consider an alarm system, ma'am." To Dana, he said, "Now, Miss, I'll just have another look at your bedroom window before I head outside. Then I'll write up a report. Since nothing has been stolen, it's an odd situation. It would appear, at the moment, that someone wanted to throw a scare into you." He gave her a considering look. "You're sure you didn't recognize anything about the voice when you got that phone call?" When Dana shook her head in frustration, he continued. "We could try to get a look at your phone records, but I doubt whoever called you has left a trail–probably used a burner phone or a stolen one. Let's hope it was a one-off, and that's the end of it. If anything else happens, call me." He handed her a card with his division number on it.

"Of course. Thank you." As she watched the officer depart, she thought, After that creepy call, there's no doubt I'm the target. But why? What have I done?

Chapter Thirteen

It was now too late to meet Julie for dinner, so she used Mrs. MacGyver's landline to call and cancel, suggesting they meet at the rehearsal instead. Grabbing some granola bars from her cupboard, she shoved them into her coat's pocket and headed for the streetcar stop.

The ride to the old church where the cast was meeting was short and uneventful. Since she was travelling west against rush hour traffic, the car was only partly filled. Dana was relieved to find no one on board suspiciously talking to themselves and no overly ripe street person attempting to share her seat. Usually, she was as sanguine as the next urban dweller about these realities, and certainly not without a great deal of compassion, but on this particular evening, she didn't think she could have coped. The only other passengers appeared to be average, "normal" citizens like herself. However, she was beginning to doubt her ability to judge "normal." It was a disquieting feeling.

With the car stop right at the corner of the street where the church was situated, it wasn't far to walk alone. Besides, it was still daylight and a lovely spring evening. Although it was difficult to leave the day's events behind, especially after calling in the police, she tried to put her mind resolutely to the excitement of seeing her play performed in rehearsals.

As Dana reached the top of the uneven stone steps, the building's dark-oak double doors opened before her. With a huge grin, Bud Watson (the show's producer) folded his tall frame into a mock bow and proclaimed, "Here she comes! The playwright herself! Welcome, madam, to our humble theatre."

Bud's infectious good humour proved to be the tonic she needed. They embraced as friends do, and then theatrically, with an air kiss on each cheek. She leaned back and smiled at his open, good-natured face. Such a handsome combination of expressive eyebrows, warm brown eyes, and a straight, Roman nose did not go unnoticed by most women. Much of Bud's charm lay in his apparent lack of awareness of how attractive he was.

Lacing an arm around Dana's waist, he ushered her into the large auditorium where several people waited. Some paced deep in thought while others perched on hard metal chairs studying copies of the script. All appeared to be rehearsing lines. *Her lines!* Exhilaration rushed through her. She couldn't help beaming. *Finally! Her lines! Her play!*

"Dana!" Julie called, waving madly as if Dana were a passenger on an ocean liner pulling into port after an extended absence. Dana returned the wave, but Julie had already disappeared through double doors near the stage.

"A little over the top, your new friend," commented Bud. "Is she always this manic?"

"Manic? Not Julie. She's pretty steady as a rule. She's just excited about being a part of the crew."

"Her role is pulling curtains. That's important, but nothing to get so hyper about."

"I'm sorry, Bud. I'm sure she'll be fine."

"No need for you to apologize, Dana. I guess she's just a little caught up in the excitement, as you said. Now, have a seat, milady."

He led her to a wobbly card table stacked with copies

of the script and random sheets of scribbled memos with yellow sticky notes slapped all over them.

"My humble office," he smiled and shrugged. "A place for everything and everything in its place!" With a flourish, he pulled out a chair for her to sit.

Dana laughed, her mood lightening. Bud had that effect on her.

Chapter Fourteen

Assembling the cast and crew, Bud proceeded with a brief rundown of how the evening should proceed. The two of them had selected the cast from auditions the previous month, an exciting experience for Dana, but one which had also opened her eyes to the competitive nature of many actors. She also became aware of how fragile some egos could be when several actors were rejected. Obviously, thick skin was required to survive in this business. *And this is only community theatre. I can't imagine what the egos must be like on Broadway.*

As Bud spoke, a young woman across the room wouldn't stop staring at her in a manner Dana found unnerving. The face was familiar from auditions, the first name Linda sticking out like a sore thumb in her mind. The only reason Dana could remember her name was because Linda had hoped to snag the lead but instead been cast in a secondary role. The woman's continued stare made Dana increasingly uncomfortable.

I'm probably being paranoid. Guess I'm going to need thicker skin, too!

All technical support had been rounded up by Bud. Dana knew none of them. She trusted Bud's judgement and experience to choose those who were qualified for the job.

"How are you doing with Small Props?" Bud asked a short, slender young man named Elvis. Instead of thick, glossy dark hair, he sported a sparse comb-over. On top of it, he appeared sallow-complexioned and shy. Perhaps his enthusiastic parents had hoped for an electrifying entertainer in the family. If so, the closest they'd get to that dream was Small Props in an amateur production.

Elvis reported, "I'm still looking for a Murphy-bed and a decent looking loveseat. If anybody has any leads, let me know."

"Wardrobe," Bud went down his list. "Do you have enough help, Audrey?"

A tall, bespectacled young woman with a lapel full of straight pins and a measuring tape looped around her neck replied, "I'll need a volunteer to iron a few costumes next week, and I need to take some inseam measurements tonight. I'll be coming around to get those during our break, so be ready." She raised her eyebrows a couple of times, Groucho Marx style, looking slightly lascivious. Everyone laughed.

Looking up to a booth high at the back of the auditorium, Bud asked, "Lights?"

It was impossible to make out faces, but someone flashed a spotlight and gave a thumbs up. From backstage the sound man stepped out in front of the curtains and gave Bud the high sign.

"Right. We'll do a full technical rehearsal at a later date. If there's nothing else right now, I'd like to walk through Act I Scene I so everyone can find their marks. If you're not in this scene, take a seat. No chatting, please. Pay close attention to what the other actors are doing." With a smile and a nod, he concluded. "Places everyone."

*****

And so, it began.

The idea for the plot had taken form during the first

heady days of her romance with Dave Mitchell. A breezy, funny love story set in the heart of a big city in which the star-crossed lovers encounter obstacles (mostly misunderstandings) with a love-conquers-all ending. Her own love story hadn't ended so happily. When Julie had broken the news that morning, her only reaction had been surprise. Six months ago, the thought of Dave marrying someone else would have been devastating, but, in a way, forcing herself to finish writing this play after their breakup had given her perspective. *And probably saved my sanity, too.*

Writing a love story the way she hoped her own would've played out not only gave her clarity on her relationship but proved that writing was not a passing fancy like Dave believed: it was her passion.

There were times she wanted to abandon the project altogether, because of the failure of her own love story. Any sane person would have! Instead, in a contrary move, she had made an intense effort to distance herself emotionally to complete it without constantly thinking of Dave.

Not only had that effort proved unexpectedly therapeutic, but she had left Dave far behind and also proved she could be content on her own. Someday, another relationship might be nice, but if it never happened, she was strong enough now to know she'd be fine.

And now, here she was, about to see her play performed. For the next hour, she could push aside all other thoughts and lose herself in the rehearsal. Perched on the edge of her seat, Dana leaned forward with anticipation as the leading man entered stage left.

Chapter Fifteen

A blood-curdling shriek cut off the lead actor's dialogue mid-sentence. It clearly emanated from the kitchen off the auditorium.

"What the…! Who…?" Then, in answer to his question, Bud said, "Shirley went in there to make coffee!"

Elvis, looking even paler than usual, was already dashing through the swinging kitchen doors. "I'll check on her! Maybe she's burned herself," he called over his shoulder.

"Great," Bud commented rather ungraciously. "Does anyone know first-aid? Is there a first-aid kit around here?"

"In the pantry off the kitchen," a young woman offered. "I noticed it earlier."

"Maybe I can help," an older man spoke up. "I took a Red Cross course."

As he stood and headed for the kitchen, Elvis emerged with a middle-aged woman that had to be Shirley. She was leaning heavily on him and verging on hysteria. Although her robust appearance gave the impression of hardiness, she looked ready to faint at any second. Elvis gently lowered her onto a nearby chair and knelt at her side, rubbing her hands as if they'd been frostbitten. Shirley leaned forward, attempting to put her head between her knees. It was clear something had happened other than being burned.

Cast and crew huddled around Elvis and Shirley, expressing equal parts sincere concern and puzzled apprehension.

Shirley's chest heaved as she released a deep, shuddering sob. Elvis looked like he might join her at any moment. "The coffee pot," he mumbled.

"What?" Bud asked. "The coffee pot? Did she burn herself?"

"No," Elvis said with more force. "It's *in* the coffee pot! Go and look for yourself. I can't go back there." Shuddering, he resumed his attempt to comfort Shirley.

Bud moved past them and through the swinging doors. Silence hung heavily in the auditorium as the puzzled group awaited further explanation. When Bud returned, his pallor matched Elvis's. Holding the coffee pot at arm's length, he looked as if he didn't know what his next move should be. Finally, he placed it on the table already set with refreshments and stepped back. One or two curious souls moved forward to peek into the pot and see what the fuss was about. "Oh, my —!" shrieked the leading lady before she ran off with her hand covering her mouth, looking as though she might vomit.

"Don't keep us in suspense," a young man demanded. "Is it old, mouldy coffee or something? What's all the drama?" Looking sheepish, he added, "Pardon the pun."

Dana's stomach knotted. She had an unpleasant flashback to waking up this morning. *It couldn't be! That's ridiculous. Why would it be here? It simply couldn't be.* But her intuition said differently.

As she inched toward the coffee pot, her feet felt like they were encased in cement boots. Taking a deep breath, she peeked into the pot and then spun around, seeking a place to sit down. Her legs gave out before she found one. Bud caught her and someone else neatly slipped a chair under her.

"Put your head between your knees," Bud urged. "I'm

sorry. I should have warned you. What the heck is going on here?" He scanned the room, searching for a guilty face. "Is this someone's stupid idea of a joke? It isn't the least bit funny, and when I find out who's responsible, it's not going to be pretty. This is sick!"

Several people shook their heads. A hum of low, anxious chattering vibrated through the cast, passing the news from ear to ear. No one claimed any knowledge of how or why a dead rodent had come to rest in the coffee pot.

Dana couldn't speak. She also didn't want to. She didn't think it would be wise to mention the rat she'd found at home that morning. The appearance of a second one in this coffee pot, complete with a lacey black bow, erased any doubt that she was indeed being threatened.

She jumped when Julie took her hand. She hadn't noticed her approach. "Is there anything I can do? Would you like a drink? The kettle has boiled. Shirley got that far before...oh, darn! I can't seem to stop putting my foot in my mouth."

Dana almost smiled. Poor Julie looked so upset with herself. "I'll be fine, Julie, but I simply couldn't face anything from the kitchen right now."

"Of course not. I'm so stupid." Julie flushed and her head dropped in embarrassment.

"Don't be silly. You were trying to be helpful."

"Right. Only I'm doing a lousy job of it. But one thing I can do is sleep on your couch tonight. I won't take no for an answer."

Before Dana could argue the point, Bud broke off a whispered conversation with a man she didn't recognize and hurried back to her. At his approach, Julie's expression became inscrutable, but it was clear she wasn't pleased. The conversation was dropped when she turned around and slipped away with no further comment.

Chapter Sixteen

Bud brought the rehearsal to an abrupt end. No one could concentrate. Most assumed that whoever had pulled this prank must've been part of the rehearsal crew. If a stranger had left it behind, surely those using the church beforehand would've noticed? Puzzled and disheartened, the cast and crew gathered their belongings, packed up props and lights, and left the building.

Bud locked up the church and insisted on driving Dana home in his small SUV. She gratefully accepted. Julie took some dissuading but couldn't insist on going home with her without disclosing to others the frightening fact that this was the second beribboned rodent of the day. To Dana's relief, her friend seemed to sense that she didn't want that fact mentioned.

Bud was quiet on the short drive to Dana's apartment, for which she was grateful. When they arrived, he walked her onto the verandah and waited until she dug her key out and had it in the lock before speaking.

"It's been an upsetting evening, Dana, but try not to let it get to you too much. I know that's easier said than done." He passed a hand over his forehead in a gesture of frustration and shook his head. "Someone is playing a prank even though it isn't remotely funny. We'll start fresh next week. Speaking of which, don't forget rehearsal will be Thursday instead of Friday because of the holiday weekend. Too many people are going away."

Dana simply nodded, unwilling to continue any speculation at the moment. "Thanks for the ride, Bud. I'll see you next week." As she turned to enter the house, Bud wrapped his arms around her and drew her to him, surprising her with a gentle, tentative kiss on the lips. She lingered a moment, savouring the strength and reassurance in his embrace but not unaware that the kiss was but a prelude.

"Dana...." The sound of her name emerged as a soft, guttural cry that was full of longing.

Drawing back, she bestowed a small, wistful smile on him. "I'm sorry, Bud, but this has been one heck of a day all 'round, and I'm a little tired. I need some time alone."

His arms dropped to his sides as his handsome head dropped to his chest in defeat. It was clear he was hoping for reciprocation, but she didn't have any energy left within her after the day's events. "Of course. I understand," he whispered.

As she somewhat regretfully moved inside, still lost in the lingering pleasure of Bud's embrace, she didn't notice Philip until she'd almost collided with him. He reached out to steady her as she stumbled forward. When she could stand on her own, he quickly removed his hands.

"Oh, sorry! I didn't see you lurking there."

"I wasn't 'lurking'!"

Her eyes narrowed. "Were you spying on me?"

"Of course not," he huffed. "I don't lurk *or* spy. We heard the car, so I came out to tell you your mother called."

"My mother? Oh, shoot! Did she call your aunt's number?"

He nodded. "She's beside herself because she couldn't reach you on your cell. I wasn't aware you don't have a landline. My aunt says you can use her phone until yours is replaced."

"Oh," Dana felt chagrined. She'd been meaning to call

home for over a week but, as usual, it had been easy to find reasons to postpone doing it. She should know better by now that conversations never went well when it was her mother who had to chase after her to see how she was doing. Dana wondered whether all mothers possessed a guilt-inducing gene or only hers.

"I guess I should come in and call her now, then, if it's not too late."

Philip wore a rather stiff and strained expression, obviously holding back something he wanted to say.

I think I've hurt his feelings! she realized with surprise and some dismay. Hastening to apologize, she said, "I'm sorry. This hasn't been the best day of my life, but that doesn't excuse rudeness. I know you weren't spying."

"Forget it. You had a nasty shock this morning. Anyone would be on edge."

"Thank you." Dana wondered if she could trust him with the news of what happened at rehearsal. She had no idea who she could trust, and that was unnerving.

Chapter Seventeen

Ever thoughtful, Mrs. MacGyver suggested Dana use the phone in her kitchen for privacy. She and Philip were in the living room enjoying a ball game on an old, boxy television, the kind people rarely saw anymore. Dana passed through glass-paneled doors into a dining room, skirting a heavy table and set of chairs to reach the kitchen.

She'd never been in her landlady's apartment before and was struck by the "hominess" of a collection of owls in the kitchen and the delicate, crocheted cloth on the dining room table with its side chairs covered in intricate needlepoint. Framed family pictures (some quite old and sepia-toned), covered the top of a side buffet. Near the phone hung a larger photo of a pleasant-looking, middle-aged man with an engaging smile whom she presumed must have been Mr. MacGyver.

She hesitated a moment as she mentally prepared herself for her mother's usual over-the-top anxieties. With a deep breath, she punched in the numbers.

"Hi, Mom. How are you? I'm fine. Nothing's wrong. I dropped my phone this afternoon, and it fell apart, that's all. ...Yes. I'll get another one tomorrow. Don't worry... I know, I didn't think they broke that easily either...I'm sure they'll replace it."

Dana crossed her fingers for that little white lie.

Talking to her mother often made her feel ten years old again. Thankfully, her mother changed the subject, only now she was on to the minefield of Dana's younger sister and her confused life.

"Caroline? No, I haven't talked to her in a couple of weeks. Why? Okay, I'll call to see how she is, but I'd rather not get into anything else, Mom. If she's seeing somebody new and she wants to keep it to herself, that's her business, not mine. I know you're her mother, but she's an adult now. If it's that important, why can't you ask her yourself?"

With a sigh, Dana realized yet again that her mother was never going to change in this one regard. When she needed to vent about her problems and issues, Dana was her sounding board. She hated that role and constantly resisted. It was emotionally exhausting, and it didn't help her fragile relationship with the ever-changeable Caroline, either. "Okay. I'll call you back in a day or two but don't count on anything. How's Dad? Oh. Well, I'll talk to him next time. I have to go, Mom. I promise. Yes. In a couple of days, okay? Yes, Mom. Bye."

She hung up but stood for a moment holding the phone, her head spinning. She didn't need any additional family drama, but as always, she'd do what her mother asked and call Caroline. It was easier than the fallout that would ensue. She wasn't going to call tonight and maybe not tomorrow, either. Her nerves were too taut to deal with Caroline yet.

Dana lay the phone down and returned to the living room to say goodnight.

Philip stood as she entered the room, an old-fashioned gentlemanly gesture of respect that, like the boxy television, was uncommon. She found it oddly endearing. Such manners reminded her of happier times spent in the company of her father and grandfather. Not that there was anything remotely fatherly or old-fashioned about Philip

Marshall. She wondered about his upbringing and his family. By all appearances, he was certainly fond of his aunt. *Goodness, was she staring? How embarrassing!* His gaze had locked with hers, and she had the uncomfortable impression he was reading her mind. Feeling a flush creep into her cheeks, she was the first to look away.

"How did your rehearsal go?" his aunt asked, full of genuine interest. She struggled to get out of her deep, comfy chintz-covered chair.

"Please don't get up!" Dana protested. "Everything's fine."

"I was just going to turn the sound down. The remote's over there, beside the TV."

"I'll get that," Philip said. As he moved across the room, his aunt settled back into her chair and glanced at her watch. "You seem to be back earlier than I'd have thought."

"Um, yes, a little. There were one or two little glitches, so we wrapped up early. It'll all be sorted out by next week."

"That must have been disappointing. However, you've had quite a day, so an early evening will likely do you good. Would you like company? I'd be happy to sleep on your couch if you'd like."

"Oh, my goodness! Thank you for offering, but I couldn't ask you to do that. I'll be fine. I'm so tired, I'll probably be out the moment I fall into bed," Dana lied.

"You're pretty cut off without a phone," Philip reminded her as he pulled his own from a pocket. "Take mine." Seeing Dana open her mouth to refuse, he insisted. "Just for tonight. I don't expect you'll need it, but it might give you some peace of mind. Keep it until you get a replacement. I won't miss it for a few days."

Dana had been about to refuse but then had second thoughts. Being independent was important to her, but maybe there were times when common sense trumped independence. As she accepted the proffered phone, Philip said, "The code's easy. It's 1984, like Orwell's *1984*."

She smiled. "I think I can remember that. Thank you. That's very thoughtful. I'll have to buy a new one tomorrow. I doubt they'll replace it. I can't lie and say I dropped it."

She realized by Mrs. MacGyver's puzzled look that Philip mustn't have told her about the sick phone call that afternoon. She wouldn't know that Dana had flung her phone to the pavement in a panic.

Glancing at Philip, she added for his aunt's benefit, "I was a bit too rough with it, so I guess I'm responsible for replacing it." Bidding them both goodnight, she tried to ignore their worried looks. Philip followed her out and stood at the foot of the stairs as she climbed up to her apartment and unlocked her door. Willing herself not to look back, she took a deep breath before going inside.

Chapter Eighteen

Well, that was fun! *All that reaction was certainly exhilarating. Not only stupid Shirley but greasy Elvis and Bud-the wanna-be. Wanna-be director, wanna-be lover of Dana. Wanna-be lots of impossible things. Then that other girl who nearly puked and ran away! Dana didn't do much better even though it was her second "present" of the day.*

It sure put the "break" in coffee break. Hey, that's a good one: 'the break in coffee break"! I should try writing plays. Could probably do better than that snotty Dana any day of the week. Will anyone show up next Thursday night? I can't wait to see.

The black bow around the neck was a nice touch. And I thought of that myself. An original. No copy-cat. That's not my style. I'm an original. Always have been. No one ever gave me credit for it, though. They gave me lots of other names, but they missed 'original." Oh, well, give them all a bit more time and they'll see how original I can be. Knock, knock! Who's there? Unique. Unique who? Unique up on me, and I'll neek up on you! Ha! Ha! Funny, too! I kill myself laughing at my own jokes.

That phone call was cool, too. Caught her on the street and freaked her right out! Nice work from the voice-disguiser, too. Have to try that again. Maybe tonight. Or is it too soon?

Should I let them all simmer for a few days? Keep them at a boil so to speak, wondering when the next shoe's going to drop? Bit of mixed metaphor there. Things happen in threes, they say. Maybe she'll be thinking that's it; the third thing already happened.

Wonder if she told the old lady about tonight? If they call the cops again, they won't be able to prove anything. No crime was committed. There's no evidence. Careful is my middle name!

Sleep well, Dana. We'll be in touch!

Chapter Nineteen

Dana had thought she'd be relieved to shut her door on all of them, well-meaning as they were. Now, having dropped her backpack on the floor, she leaned her back against the door, almost afraid to advance one step further into her living room.

Her total exhaustion was no surprise, but the unaccustomed feeling of fragility certainly was. She craved sleep above all else at this moment but somehow doubted she'd find it. The bold, square numerals of the clock on her iPod dock read 10:45 p.m. She couldn't wait to see the end of this day. Moving to the couch, she slipped off her jacket and shoes and laid down, wiggling her toes and stretching. *Ah-h-h, heaven! I'll get up in a minute and put the kettle on, then...*

Dana sat upright on the couch, her heart thudding. Something awful was happening! What was it? Her fuzzy head led to a sense of disorientation. Terror and dread rose together in her throat. It took a moment to realize she'd been caught in a nightmare of giant, hissing cats and enormous mice with razor-sharp teeth.

The image brought on a wave of nausea. She squeezed her eyes shut and concentrated on not throwing up, but the grotesque thoughts wouldn't leave her. Bile filled her mouth and she raced to the bathroom. Kneeling before the toilet, she waited for her stomach to purge itself but there was nothing to bring up. She'd hardly eaten the whole day. The retching and dry heaving, however, produced a sweat.

Eventually, she rose from the floor and turned on the tap to splash her face with cold water. Now thoroughly awake, she had no desire to fall back to sleep for fear of revisiting her horrible dreams.

Wobbling back into the living room, she took her spot on the couch once more. She was certainly not going to climb into her bed tonight. Deciding that reading might make her drowsy, she picked up an art magazine from the end table and flipped through it as her thoughts wandered.

She tried to think of anyone she might have offended enough that would make them do something so horrible. Someone who'd be crazy enough to enter her apartment while she was sleeping and leave a dead rat in her bed. She didn't think she knew anyone sufficiently disturbed, and yet...someone had to be.

Even more disquieting was the realization she couldn't afford to discount anyone.

Unable to sit still a second longer, she paced the room, hugging herself tightly. She was wound up like a child's top, ready to spin out of control at any moment. Chilly and shaky, she thought she might have a fever, but she knew better. *Face it, this is nerves.*

Officer Green's earnest face popped into her head. *I'll have to tell him about what happened at rehearsal. I'll call first thing in the morning.* She wasn't looking forward to more questions and mystifying conjectures.

Another twenty minutes of straining for some morsel of memory or clue proved fruitless. Frustrated, Dana fell into her easy chair and pulled the afghan over her shoulders, feeling wide awake for the day. However, she soon submitted to her fatigue and fell into a deep and surprisingly restorative sleep that was mercifully uninterrupted.

Until Philip's cell phone rang.

Chapter Twenty

It took Dana a moment to identify the sound and another to remember where she'd put the borrowed phone. Her groggy "Hello," sounded hoarse as well. *What time is it? Nine o'clock! Wow, I really slept.*

A lengthy silence ensued. "Hello?" she repeated.

"I've obviously got the wrong number," a hasty female voice said, as if ready to hang up.

"Wait! Who were you calling?"

There was a moment's hesitation, then, "I'm looking for a Philip Marshall, but I must have made a mistake."

"Hold on! This is Philip's number. You didn't make a mistake."

"Oh," the woman sounded nonplussed. "Who am I speaking to then?"

"I'm Dana Williams. Philip loaned me his phone because mine's broken. If you'll wait a moment, I'll get him for you."

"He's there?"

"Yes, he's right downstairs. It won't take me a minute to get him."

The woman's tone changed from suspicious to annoyed. "Don't bother! I don't think I want to talk to him after all."

"Are you sure? Could I take a message for him or let him know who's calling? It would only take a minute to get him for you."

"No, just forget it!" The line went dead.

Well, that was strange, Dana thought. *If I take the phone to Philip he could dial *69 and call them back, unless it's a private number.*

Halfway to the door, the phone rang again, and she made a natural assumption.

"Did you change your mind? Do you want Philip after all?"

"Who's Philip," a male voice replied. "Dana, is that you?"

"Bud? How did you get this number?" Her mind was still fuzzy from having been woken from a deep sleep by the first call of the morning.

"I couldn't get an answer on your cell, and I was worried, so I checked with Julie. She found your landlady's number, and then I got this one. What's going on, Dana? Who's Philip, and why aren't you answering your cell? I needed to make sure you were all right after last night."

"I'm all right, Bud, thanks. I broke my phone yesterday and Philip, Mrs. MacGyver's nephew, loaned me his until I get a new one."

"Oh. Her nephew? Does he live there, too?"

"No, he's just visiting." Did Bud sound jealous?

"Well, okay then. I thought maybe you had a new guy in your life I didn't know about." His soft chuckle was intended to be a slight attempt at humour. But, yes, he certainly did sound jealous.

It was kind of sweet that he was worried about her, but she didn't want to have to deal with anyone's romantic intentions. She thought back to the previous night's kiss. It had been nice and tempting, too, but she couldn't cope with someone else's feelings. She had to deal with this rat issue, and she *still* had to call the police.

"Um, Bud? There's something I have to tell you," Dana paused. "That rat last night wasn't the first one."

At the end of her explanation, Bud was quiet. Like Julie, he hadn't interrupted her with questions as she recounted the previous morning's horrible discovery. He seemed as stunned as everyone else by the bizarre story.

"You're right, you have to call the police. A very sick mind is behind this, and I have to tell you, it frightens me. Are you certain you're safe there? Maybe you should move out."

"And where would I go on such short notice, Bud?" She hated sounding so short-tempered, but she was overtired and disliked reminding everyone she was capable of looking after herself. "Besides, I'm happy here. If we can just find out what's going on, I know I'll feel much better. In the meantime, Mrs. MacGyver and Philip are here. Maybe having a man in the house will make this nut think twice about trying anything else."

"But you can't count on that, Dana. Look, you know there are three of us sharing this house. There's room for four. Why not think about moving in here and sharing expenses? You know Jane and Bruce. They're nice people and I'm not so hard to get along with, either."

The complete unexpectedness of the suggestion stunned Dana. She thought fast. "That's a nice offer, Bud, but I want to stay here. It's convenient to the yoga studio and the streetcar. Plus, I like the neighbourhood and Mrs. MacGyver, too. She's a great landlady. I'd hate to leave."

"And Philip? Does he have anything to do with your wanting to stay?"

"Of course not! Don't be ridiculous. I only met him twenty-four hours ago!"

"I'm sorry. I just want to be sure you're safe. I'm concerned about you."

"Thanks for the concern, but I'm fine. I'm going to call the police again shortly. They might want to talk to you about last night and maybe the others, too."

"You're probably right. I don't have a problem talking

to them, but I don't want the cast to get spooked about this." He sighed and she could hear his frustration. "I suppose they'll have to question them, though. It probably can't be helped. Okay, go ahead and call them. Let's hope they can figure this whole thing out fast."

They said their goodbyes, and Dana stood there for a moment to gather her thoughts. Then she headed downstairs and knocked on Mrs. MacGyver's door.

Chapter Twenty-One

Uncertain of how to begin, Dana postponed the topic of rats and attempted to return Philip's phone, which he refused to accept. She explained, "There was a call for you this morning, but they hung up before I could get a name or number. I thought maybe you could try Star 69."

"They?"

"A woman. She thought she'd called the wrong number. Then I explained you'd loaned me your phone. When I offered to get you for her, she said she didn't want to speak to you after all and hung up."

"Oh." His face darkened, and she thought he might've been angry but the red colouring in his cheeks made him seem embarrassed more than anything. "It's all right. Thank you. I think I know who it might have been."

"Well, that's good, because I forgot I had another call after that which means Star 69 wouldn't have worked. She addressed Mrs. MacGyver and said, "Bud mentioned he got my number from you. I'm sorry he bothered you."

"No problem, dear. He sounded rather frantic about reaching you."

"He was." Dana took a deep breath. "I'm afraid something else has happened. Maybe you'd like to sit down for this." Watching their puzzled faces as they took their seats, she felt wracked with guilt about what she was going to tell them. Nevertheless, she launched right into the story of the rat in the coffee pot.

As she described poor Shirley's and Elvis's reactions to it, as well as Bud's stricken look, Dana tried to inject some humour in hopes of lessening the horror for her listeners. The attempt failed; she sounded shallow even to herself.

"I'm going to call Officer Green as I promised, even though nothing happened here, thank goodness. I can't deny the two incidents are related and that I'm the one they're meant to upset."

"Oh, dear," his aunt added. "This is terrible. To think anyone could do something like this! And to you, Dana, of all people! You must call the police right away."

"I will. I imagine they'll want to check out the rehearsal hall and talk to the cast and crew. What a mess. I hope it doesn't cast a pall over the play. It means a lot to Bud and everyone, not just me."

"If you have to go down there, I'll drive you," Philip said. This wasn't put forth as an offer for her to accept or reject, it was stated as a fact: he would drive her there.

"Thanks, but that's not necessary. It's a short streetcar ride or a good walk."

"I know that, but I think you should be careful until you know what this is all about. I don't mind driving. I think the two of us would feel better." He looked at his aunt who was nodding her head in vigorous agreement.

"I'm sorry to worry you with all of this, but I can't have someone with me every minute. I want to carry on as normal."

"But nothing is normal right now, dear. Let him drive you. I know you can't have someone with you every minute, but once in a while might be a good idea."

"I don't want to seem ungrateful, but let me think about it and let you know after I talk to the police. Okay?"

Dana could tell neither one was happy with her answer, but she felt she couldn't give in to being watched and guarded. No matter how well-intentioned they were, she'd feel like a prisoner.

As she climbed the stairs, the phone rang yet again. She stopped on the landing to answer it.

"Dana! Thank goodness! Are you all right? Has anything else happened? Why aren't you answering your phone? Bud told me you're borrowing someone else's."

"Julie, take a deep breath. I'm fine. My phone's broken, that's all. I dropped it on the street yesterday. I'm going out to get a new one shortly. Philip didn't think I should be without one in the meantime."

"So Philip … is he being nice or something? He seems protective of you like a knight in shining armor coming to the rescue." She giggled.

Dana entered her apartment and closed the door before answering Julie's question. She felt annoyed by the silliness of it, not to mention the giggling. *Giggling!*

"He's just being careful, Julie. That's all. I think it's to make Mrs. MacGyver feel better. This has thrown her for a loop."

"Well, it's thrown all of us for a loop. Although, the guys at rehearsal don't know about the thing you found yesterday morning. Holy smokes, Dana! Who's doing these freaky things? Have you got any idea?"

"No, not a clue. I'm going to call the police again. I don't think last night was any coincidence. I think someone planned both...incidents. I've got to get to the bottom of this, before..."

"Before what?"

"I don't know. Before it gets even weirder, I guess. I don't understand it, Julie."

"Do you think you should stay there, Dana? Don't you think you should maybe consider moving out? I mean, maybe nothing else will happen, but we don't know for sure. Maybe it's not safe for you there." Julie sounded more and more shrill. She wasn't a calming influence in a crisis.

Bud had been right last night; Julie could be a little manic.

"I already had this conversation with Bud this morning. I don't know where I'd go, and besides, I like it here. I'm going to call the police now, Julie, so I have to go." Dana was beginning to realize that the longer she talked to her friend, the more uneasy she felt. *I don't need this right now. I have to stay calm and focused. Calm and focused.* She repeated the three words like a mantra as she entered her apartment and closed the door behind her. Pulling Officer Green's card out of her bag, she punched in the numbers. *Calm and focused.*

Chapter Twenty-Two

Although he maintained a professional telephone manner, Dana clearly deciphered Officer Green's uncertainty and hesitancy in the pauses between his questions. She couldn't blame him for being incredulous.

"It's an unusual situation, that's for sure. However, no actual crime has been committed, and you haven't been threatened…"

"For heaven's sake!" Dana's voice rose in a shrill panic. "What about the phone call? Whoever it was tried to disguise his voice. I'm sure of it. It sounded tinny and strange."

"But he didn't specifically threaten you with harm, did he?" The officer's voice was irritatingly calm and logical.

Her voice shook with anger and frustration. She astonished herself by yelling into the phone. "What else could it mean when some freak is leaving dead rats for me to find and making creepy phone calls? I don't understand why you're not taking this seriously!"

"Oh, I'm taking it seriously, believe me."

He sounded offended. What did he have to be ticked off about? She was the one being harassed!

"I'm sorry I yelled at you, but something needs to be done." Now her voice sounded pleading.

"I'm making note of all this, but again," he repeated with great patience, "our hands are tied unless whoever this is makes a direct threat or breaks the law. But I want you to keep in touch if anything else does happen. And try to think of anyone who might have a reason to scare you."

"Great!" If only she had a landline, she'd have taken great pleasure in slamming the receiver down, an entirely satisfying gesture. Instead, she calmed down enough to say, "Well, thank you anyway."

"On the other hand," Dana had been about to click *end call* and put the phone away when Officer Green spoke again.

"Yes?" she said, hope rising in her chest.

"Maybe I can find a moment to meet you at the scene of the crime, so to speak." His rather weak attempt at humour failed, but she was grateful for this change of direction.

"Being a Saturday, it may take a while to find someone who can give us access," he continued.

"My director has a key. Bud Watson. He locked up last night. I have his number right here." Rummaging in her bag she came up with a notepad and read off Bud's number.

She promised to keep her phone on and remain available. She had a class scheduled for 4:00 p.m; it was now 10:25 a.m. With luck, she'd be able to make that class. Finding a replacement in such a short time and on such a gorgeous spring weekend would be impossible.

If Officer Green hadn't called by then, she would leave Philip's phone at the front desk with Nora. The young woman could take a message or interrupt her class. Dana concluded this was the best she could do under the circumstances.

She set about gathering laundry and tidying up her small space. *There's always laundry,* she noted. And as odd as it might seem, she found comfort in the most mundane tasks.

When the call came in at noon, she was so absorbed in the mindlessness of cleaning that the phone's abrupt ringtone startled her. As she picked it up, she surveyed the results of her efforts. She now had an apartment that shone and sparkled as never before. At any other time, she'd have felt elated. Today, she simply felt flat.

"Ms. Williams? I called Bud Watson. He can meet us there in an hour. It shouldn't take long. I don't imagine we'll find anything useful, but we'll have a look 'round anyway. By now, someone's probably gotten rid of the evidence."

"With any luck, it might still be there. there's a good chance the janitors haven't been in yet today, being a Saturday. They might come in at some point this afternoon or evening to clean up before church tomorrow."

"You seem familiar with their cleaning schedule."

Was there an element of suspicion in this remark?

"I know nothing about it," she retorted, allowing her irritation to show. "I'm simply drawing on experience. I grew up going to church."

"Where was that?"

"Up north in Bracebridge, but I've lived here five years now." Why did she feel obliged to add that particular fact?

"Okay, so we'll meet at the church in one hour. It shouldn't take long as I said."

"Right." Her reply was terse. "Thanks," she remembered to add before ending the call. His last questions had rattled her. Had she imagined a suspicious tone? *Am I getting paranoid? Or does he suspect me of something? Is that why he agreed to meet me?*

She hadn't expected to feel grilled about the events. *He's only doing his job,* she tried to reason with herself, but the uneasy feeling remained.

A sharp pain in her right temple foretold a blazing headache. *Shoot! not now! I need to think clearly.*

Next step: Do I go alone or do I accept Philip's offer to drive me? Remembering his words hadn't come across as an offer or suggestion but a definite statement, both her mind and independent streak rebelled. *I don't need a chaperone. I'm going by myself!*

My byself! My byself! her mind shrieked at her, a mocking parody of her childhood self. Whenever her stubborn or independent traits came to the fore, her parents were inclined to remind her that, 'Me do my byself!' was one of the first phrases she had ever spoken. Well, so far it had done well for her. She had learned to stand on her own two feet.

She needed to shower and organize her gear for her four o'clock class. As much as she recoiled at the idea, she had to face that new fear sooner or later. *Might as well be now.*

As she was stepping into the shower stall, the phone rang again, and she hesitated briefly before deciding to answer. She wasn't sure how to retrieve messages on Philip's phone and didn't want to have to ask him to do it for her, especially if the message was from Officer Green. A part of her didn't want to have to explain about meeting the policeman at the church.

Wrapped in a towel, she stepped back into the living room and picked up the still-ringing instrument. "Hello?"

Bud apologized for not being able to pick her up as he would have preferred. "I thought I'd have time to swing by and get you, but I'm in the west end and now traffic's all backed up for some reason. I'll probably be late getting to the church, too. Will you be all right going over on your own?"

Dana felt the need to count to three, otherwise, she'd erupt. *What is it with these men? It's broad daylight and I'm a grown woman. I can make it a few blocks on my own!*

"Don't worry, Bud. I'll be fine. Thanks for offering. I'll see you when you get there. Take care."

As warm water from the showerhead slid over her body and steam rose in the stall, Dana closed her eyes and lathered a lavender-scented shampoo into her hair. The scent, promoted as possessing soothing qualities worked its magic. It was a much-needed feeling. Deep, yogic breaths also helped. By the time she stepped out of the shower to dry off, she was halfway to the more relaxed state she sought. She prayed it would last.

Chapter Twenty-Three

The plan was to slip down the stairs and out the door unnoticed. Dana decided if she did run into Mrs. MacGyver or Philip she wouldn't lie, but she was under no obligation to advise them of her whereabouts. It would be easy to say she was off to meet a friend. Besides, Bud was a friend, so that would be telling the truth. She needn't feel guilty.

She almost made it to the front door when Mrs. MacGyver called to her. She prepared to fib her way through whatever questions came at her, but when she turned around, the shocking change in her landlady's appearance stunned her. The older woman had aged in the space of a few hours. Deep worry lines creased her forehead and her colour was almost blue. A china doll couldn't have looked more fragile.

"Are you feeling all right?" Dana asked, moving instinctively to the older woman's side. "You look like you should be in bed."

"I do feel a little under the weather. I intend to have a little nap shortly. I was wondering if you'd spoken to the police?" With shaky fingers, the woman worried a linen handkerchief, folding and refolding it into neat squares.

"Yes, I called Officer Green last night."

"Do you think he might want to come here again to talk to us about yesterday morning?"

Was she worried about such a visit or would she be relieved by one, believing it a sign the police were taking things seriously? It was difficult to read her at this moment. Dana was anxious to extricate herself from this conversation.

"I don't know. He might at some point. I'm sorry, but I have to rush. Please don't worry too much about all of this and make sure you have a nap. I hope you feel better soon."

"Thank you, Dana. Before you go, I do have another question if you can spare the moment. When you spoke to the officer about the events from yesterday, did he mention if he will be taking a look around the church, too?"

Before she could answer, the apartment door behind Mrs. MacGyver opened and Philip joined them in the foyer. It was clear he'd heard his aunt pose the question Dana had hoped to avoid.

Philip gave her an inquisitive look when she hesitated to reply. *Oh, those eyes! They seem to see right into my soul. I could never look into them and lie.* She lowered her own gaze and avoided looking at either of the two eager faces directly.

"Yes, he said he would."

"Is that where you're going now?" Philip's question was direct. "I did say I'd take you if that happened."

Darn! I almost made it. She wouldn't have minded trying to out-maneuver Philip, but she didn't have the heart to add to his aunt's obvious distress.

*****

In the truck, Dana rode in silence. She observed the usual Saturday parade on Queen St.: dog-walkers, bike riders, rollerbladers, coffee-sippers, window-shoppers, and one nervy skateboarder weaving in and out among them. Life-affirming, normal activities, and normally, she was part of all that normalcy. How could her life have taken such an abnormal turn?

Spotting two women sharing a patio table and chatting over coffee, she felt a stab of longing for a relaxed friendship. How long had it been since she'd truly caught up with an old friend? Too long. There were e-mails and quick chats with her Annex friends, but they weren't the same as an hour or two with no interruptions and no pressures.

In the six months since she'd moved to this part of town, she'd been so absorbed in fine-tuning her play that the only one person she'd spent much time with was Julie. While she was pleasant enough company, they didn't have a shared history for reminiscing. In fact, what did she know about Julie's history? On the odd occasion when she'd attempted to learn about Julie's family, her questions had been brushed off with humour. Dana got the feeling that her family was a closed topic and that she shouldn't press the issue.

In her present state of mind, she re-examined that decision. What if Julie was hiding something? *Stop it! This is pure paranoia! Julie is a sweet person and a good friend. Hasn't she proven that, offering to sleep on my couch? Yes*, another part of her mind argued, *but what better way to get into your apartment? No!* she protested. *I won't go there! Not Julie.* Except, the seed of doubt had already been planted.

"You're very quiet," Philip commented as he stopped for a red light. He turned to look at her.

She kept her gaze on the passers-by. "Sorry. I've got a lot on my mind."

"I guess so. A lot's been happening."

She turned to examine his profile as the light changed while he remained focused on the traffic.

"I haven't driven on such busy city streets for a long time," he continued. "I don't remember quite this much traffic around here before. We're barely moving."

"Well, it's Saturday. People come from all over the city to stroll along Queen and the Boardwalk, especially when the weather's nice like today. You get used to it."

"I don't know if I ever could —if I moved here, I mean."

"Are you thinking of moving here? Won't you be going back to Guelph?"

"For the short term. The jury's still out for the long term."

The light changed, and he concentrated on his driving again. She was surprised to discover she wanted to know more about his plans. "How long are you planning to stay now?" *Real subtle, Dana!*

"Not sure. I have an appointment with a friend from the university on Tuesday morning. I was planning to drive home after that, but I might stay on a couple of more days."

"I guess your family will be excited. You probably have lots of catching up to do." *Great! Now she was pumping him for information.*

"Hm-m-m." Vague. Non-committal. "Maybe. Right now, I'm more than a little concerned about Aunt Iva."

"She didn't look well today. It's probably all this stupid stuff with the rats. I feel awful about it."

"Well, it's certainly not your fault."

"She's a nice woman. I hate seeing her upset."

"Me, too."

"You seem close."

"Yeah, I guess we always have been. She and my uncle never had kids, so they spoiled us."

"How many of you are there? Brothers and sisters, I mean."

"There were two of us. My brother died a long time ago."

"Oh, I'm sorry."

"Here we are," Philip pointed out as he navigated a

right turn. The topic of family was dropped as they both concentrated on scanning the streets for a parking spot, a task that usually proved as fruitful as searching for a four-leaf clover. After turning a corner onto the next parallel street, Philip pulled into the only available spot in a small city parking lot.

After paying at the machine and leaving the ticket displayed on the dash, he locked the truck, and they crossed through a wide alley that came out directly across the road from the church.

Neither of them had spoken for several minutes. Dana didn't wish to return to the topic of family, and Philip seemed preoccupied. She wondered whether his silence had been brought on by her questions or by the meeting they were about to have with Officer Green. She decided that, sometime, she'd like the opportunity to learn a little more about the mysterious Philip Marshall.

Chapter Twenty-Four

On the sloping, off-kilter steps of the old brown brick church, the young police officer and Bud Watson waited. Their stiff postures broadcast an unease with each other. As Dana and Philip drew near, both men turned to observe them.

Dana introduced Philip to Bud and was taken aback by the sour look on Bud's face.

"Were you here last night, Mr. Marshall?" Officer Green asked.

Well, he's getting right to the point. No beating around the bush with him this morning.

"No. I just offered to drive Miss Williams over. Since this is the second dead rat in less than twenty-four hours, I'm more than a little concerned."

"You believe Miss Williams is in physical danger? Someone may just be trying to mess with her head."

Philip's eyes flashed with anger. Dana could see the effort it took to bite his tongue.

"Well," the policeman offered in a more conciliatory tone. "Let's get started here and see what's what."

He looked to Bud to unlock the door. For a moment, Bud stood rooted to the spot, glaring at Philip.

"Mr. Watson?"

As if returning from some other plane of existence, Bud looked up with surprise, then shook his head slightly.

He unlocked the oak double doors which bore scars and scuffs from generations of use and abuse. Entering the building, Dana thought of the lives that had passed through those doors for almost a century and a half.

Inside the brick-walled vestibule, a modest amount of sunlight penetrated the few clerestory windows above the doors, highlighting a host of dust mites dancing in the musty air. Bud sneezed. "Sorry, I'm allergic to dust."

While he fumbled with his flashlight to locate and flip on the light switches, Dana, Philip, and the police officer waited in silence. Bud then guided them into the deathly stillness of the cavernous auditorium.

Chapter Twenty-Five

A lingering and slightly sour smell hung over the space as if, over time, even the bricks and drywall had absorbed the residue from countless sweaty bodies in countless basketball games played here. Their echoing footsteps added to the strange feeling projected by the emptiness of the ancient building. Dana contrasted this scene to that of the previous evening when the enormous space had buzzed with the excitement of a first rehearsal.

Officer Green turned to Bud and Dana. "Where's the kitchen?"

Bud led the way through the kitchen doors and pointed out the coffee pots, no longer certain which one was *the* coffee pot. A cast member had tried to sterilize it after the rat had been removed. Dana could tell this bit of news disappointed Officer Green.

He lifted lids off two garbage bins. "Looks like you were right, Miss Williams. These haven't been emptied yet. Maybe we'll get lucky."

Reaching into an inner pocket, he pulled out a package of crime scene gloves like she'd seen television detectives do. As a writer, she knew this was an instance where she should pull out a notebook and make notes for future reference. Someday, there might be another play or story in all of this! She chided herself for such a self-serving thought. Except, now wasn't the time or place to let her inner writer roam free.

Bud moved over and watched as the policeman sorted through soggy packages. Boxes marked for recyclables sat along another wall. Dana observed Philip giving them a cursory glance, taking care not to touch anything. It was highly unlikely that what they were seeking was in those boxes, but he clearly wasn't going to take a chance on contaminating evidence.

A low, soft whistle caused their heads to swivel. "Gotcha! Funny place to leave it. Maybe someone wanted to give the church ladies a thrill tomorrow morning."

"I think the garbage would have been removed before then." Dana wanted to refute the idea that a cast member could have been so callous. However, it was likely that a member of the cast or crew had placed it in the coffee pot to begin with.

"Well, we'll get the janitor's schedule and check that out, too."

Once the rodent was bagged for evidence, Bud and Dana did their best to walk the officer through where the cast and crew had been before and during rehearsal, but there had been so much coming and going that it was almost a pointless exercise.

She was aware of Philip's silent presence. With great discretion, he managed to both stay out of the way of the investigation and remain close to her at all times. She found she didn't mind his obvious protectiveness. She appreciated it. Bud on the other hand was openly hostile, shooting dark glances Philip's way and placing himself between the two of them whenever possible. He was behaving in a manner some women might have found appealing or at least amusing, but Dana simply found it irksome.

"Might as well have a look at the other entrances and exits, and we can check windows for signs of a break-in while we're at it," Green said to Bud. "I assume you know your way around here?"

Bud nodded, and they proceeded with a thorough examination of all the nooks and crannies of the church. The original structure dated back to well over a hundred years, but subsequent generations had remodeled and constructed additions in such a manner that a labyrinth of low-ceilinged corridors and tiny rooms honey-combed the original basement. Above ground, additional corridors connected the more modern additions and a small, neglected inner courtyard seemed to exist solely to ensure that the light of day could showcase the sanctuary's southern wall of stained glass.

As they ascended from the basement, Bud said to Officer Green, "I don't know if you remember, but a few years ago a young woman was murdered a few blocks away. Her killer was never found. I wasn't living in the city at the time, but I heard that no woman would walk anywhere alone, even to put the garbage out in the evening. Even if this church was full, people would avoid going near all those old corridors and spaces. There are too many places for someone to hide, and if you were attacked down there, no one would ever hear your screams."

"I wasn't on the force then, so I don't know anything about that. But you certainly seem to know your way around this building."

Bud flushed. "I've done several plays here, and I came to Sunday School when I was a kid."

"It does look like anyone could get in and hide if they wanted to. Wouldn't be hard to stay behind after the place was locked up, either. A janitor couldn't possibly do a thorough check."

"You're right. On a couple of occasions, the minister or janitor has arrived in the morning to find someone sleeping in a pew."

"This is all very comforting information," Dana

commented with more than a hint of sarcasm. "But where does it get us with what happened last night?"

Bud scowled. "I guess that remains to be seen."

"And this woman who went into the kitchen and found the rat in the coffee pot," Officer Green interjected, "I'll need her name."

"Shirley Fox. There isn't anything more she can tell you that you don't already know. Besides, I don't want her to be bothered by the police. She's been through enough."

Green ignored Bud's tone. "Nevertheless, I'd like to get a statement from her."

"Elvis was there, too," Dana reminded Bud.

The incredulous look on Officer Green's face was almost comical. "Elvis?"

"Elvis Fox is Shirley's cousin," Bud explained. Then, almost as an aside, he muttered in a low voice, "Poor bastard."

Officer Green didn't miss it. "Why 'poor bastard'?"

"Well, as if walking around with that name isn't enough, he's been saddled with Shirley, too, since her parents died. He's all she's got."

"'Saddled' with her?"

Bud's face reddened. "I shouldn't have said anything." He was obviously annoyed with himself. "Not that it's at all relevant to what happened but, if you must know, Shirley has some problems. She manages fine most of the time, but sometimes she goes off her meds, and then there's trouble."

With stern glances at Dana and particularly at Philip, Bud added, "None of this goes beyond this room, you understand? As I said, it's not relevant. I shouldn't have brought it up. Shirley needs this group." Officer Green scribbled in his notebook as Bud glared at him, too. "I'm afraid it's not up to you to decide what is and what isn't relevant, Mr. Watson. Every piece of information has to be considered."

"If you question Shirley about her issues, you'll only set her back."

"It might turn out unnecessary to go there."

Bud's frown seemed to indicate he wasn't at all reassured by this comment.

"Since you seem to know her so well, what's the nature of her problems? Could she become violent?"

"Absolutely not! She hasn't got an ounce of violence in her." Fuming, Bud turned and stalked off. "Idiot!"

Dana could almost feel the heat of his anger as he brushed past her. With an abrupt about-face, he strode back and growled, "Shirley has no siblings, and last year she lost both parents within a short period. She hasn't coped well at all, and she's become … she's a hoarder, okay? That's her big problem."

Dana watched, impressed, as the officer stood his ground while Bud spluttered in his face. This calm manner had a bit of an effect as Bud stepped back and dropped his voice.

"She keeps all kinds of junk around. It's her way of coping, I guess. She's fragile emotionally but she's completely harmless." He jabbed an index finger in the policeman's direction. "I won't have her hounded by you or anyone else! Who knows what she might do to herself if she felt you suspected her of this sick stuff!"

The officer's scribbling stopped, and his notebook snapped shut. "Well, I think that's all for now." Ignoring Bud's outburst, he turned to Dana. "As I said before Miss Williams if anything else should happen, give us a call."

"There's nothing more you can do?" Dana asked, knowing the question was futile.

"I'm sorry, but as I said, no actual crime has been committed." With a curt nod in her direction, he headed for the exit.

"Except that someone broke into her apartment and left that rat!" Philip shouted in frustration, but he was talking to the officer's back. As the three of them also headed out, no one spoke, but Philip's protest seemed to echo through the vast and empty space.

Chapter Twenty-Six

Outside, the three of them stepped into a burst of spring sunshine that fell on Dana like a blessing, and she stepped forward, lifting her face to receive it. As they watched Officer Green place the bag containing the dead rat in his cruiser and pulled out into traffic, Bud turned to lock the heavy door behind them. "Heck of a lot of good that did."

Philip remained silent. Turning, Dana regarded the two men. They stood stiff on the steps leading down from the church, their expressions as dark and threatening as thunderclouds.

"Well," Dana said, feeling the awkwardness of the situation. Bud had clearly taken a dislike to Philip who was not unaware of it.

She searched for words but when they came, they sounded feeble at best. "I guess I'll see you next Thursday night, Bud. I'm sorry about all this."

"It's not your fault, Dana." His handsome face softened and as he stepped forward to put a possessive arm around her. Behind him, she caught a glimpse of Philip's darkening glare.

"Tell you what —let's have dinner before rehearsal. How about Trattoria? I'll make a reservation." His sudden light tone sounded forced.

"I'm not sure what my class schedule is next

Thursday," Dana stalled. She didn't want to hurt Bud, but she didn't want to encourage him too much right now, either. Was she beginning to distrust him? What a sad state of affairs that would be.

"I'll call in a day or so then," he persisted. "We'll set something up." He glanced in Philip's direction. Did she catch a hint of triumph in that look?

"Fine," she said. Surely, he couldn't miss her lack of enthusiasm.

*****

As she and Philip retraced their steps through the lane to the parking lot, Philip's expression remained almost as dark as the leather jacket he wore. Dana decided to leave him be with whatever grim thoughts were behind it. She had her own to contend with.

Thus absorbed, she didn't hear the teenager on a bicycle coming up from behind and jumped as he whipped past her, causing Philip to rouse out of his reverie, too.

Finally, he spoke, "Well, that was all quite interesting."

"What was?"

"Everything. It's all so bizarre. To begin with, there isn't a snowball's chance of learning who brought that rat into the kitchen. And what's with this Bud? He's got a chip on his shoulder as big as city hall."

Dana concentrated on the pavement as if needing to watch where she stepped. "I hadn't noticed."

She could feel the sharp look this brought. "Really?" The sarcasm hung heavy in the air. "You haven't noticed how he looks at you? It's obvious he doesn't want anyone else around you."

"Don't be ridiculous!" She did not want to discuss Bud's feelings for her with Philip.

"Okay. Pretend you don't know, but in your situation,

you can't afford to turn a blind eye to anyone or anything."

Dana started to wave her hand to cut him off, but he persisted. "I'm serious, Dana, and this is a serious situation."

"I know," she sighed, suddenly too tired to fight. Besides, she knew he was right.

They'd reached the car. Philip unlocked it and held the door for her. She put on her seat belt and leaned back while he came around and climbed behind the wheel without another word. She thought about his last comment. *This is a serious situation.* The fear and panic she had been trying to bury burst through her defenses, and she was suddenly horrified by unexpected tears streaming down her cheeks. Unable to stop them, she turned to look out the side window, making what she hoped was an unobtrusive gesture with her hand to wipe them away. Reaching into her backpack, she felt around for her sunglasses and put them on, all the while keeping her face turned towards the window and pretending to be engrossed by two little girls playing hopscotch on the sidewalk nearby.

She sensed Philip studying her as he turned on the ignition and pulled out of the parking space. Either her subterfuge had worked, or he was being discreet and not commenting on her emotional state. Either way, she was grateful.

"I guess we've both missed lunch. Maybe we should stop and get something. I don't want Aunt Iva to feel she has to keep feeding me. Especially when she isn't feeling well."

Dana was relieved by the change of subject. "Right. She did say she'd try to have a nap."

"Another good reason to eat out, then. But if you don't want to sit in a restaurant, we could get take-out to bring back to your apartment. Maybe you'd prefer to be alone."

Her first instinct was to confirm that she would prefer

to be alone. However, she realized that wasn't true. Being alone was the last thing she wanted at this point. She checked her watch. "I've got time for something quick. My next class isn't 'til four, but I'll need time to go home and change before that. Thank you."

"Great!" Philip beamed with pleasure and his surprisingly engaging smile elicited a definite skip in her heartbeat. She sank further back into her seat and for the first time in almost two days, despite her tears and skipping heart, she felt the flickering of something resembling a sense of normalcy. It would be nice to do such an ordinary thing as sharing a meal with another person.

Chapter Twenty-Seven

The limited availability of parking spaces would dictate their choice of restaurant, so when Dana finally pointed to a car pulling out of a spot, Philip claimed it. After, they looked around for the closest and most appealing place to eat, which was how they found themselves seated on the outdoor patio of a gourmet pizza parlour.

In Dana's mind, this was the perfect choice for a quick and casual lunch with no strings attached. It was unlikely anyone seeing them would receive the impression this was some kind of date. She didn't have the energy to deal with gossip or other complications.

Philip's face lit up, declaring it the perfect choice since he hadn't had pizza in all the time he'd been away. Inhaling the heady aroma of tomato sauce, cheese, garlic, and the endless variety of herbs and toppings baking in the brick ovens, he warned her he might begin to drool.

Food and people-watching provided fodder for easy conversation. They were careful to avoid the elephant in the room—the topic of greatest concern to each of them. They seemed to realize nothing more could be learned from rehashing the events of the past thirty-six hours; the only result would be more stress.

Turning away from the sidewalk parade, Philip leaned forward as if genuinely interested. "Tell me about being a writer."

Taken aback, she stumbled a bit. "Well, it's something I've always wanted to do. I love it, but it's not easy making a living at it, as you probably know. Right now, I'm getting some free-lance assignments, but I'd like to be able to do it full-time someday."

"Great. Meanwhile, you also teach yoga?"

"That's what pays the bills, but I think I'd do it regardless. I enjoy the people in my classes, and it's been good for me, physically and emotionally. I find it calming."

It was as if they both heard the unspoken words. *And that's what I need right now.* Philip smiled. "What's your play about?"

"Well, umm..." For some bizarre reason, shyness overtook her, making her reluctant to explain it to this man. He was still smiling, politely waiting for her reply. *Get a grip,* she

told herself, drawing a deep breath. "It's a bit of a romantic comedy."

"Oh? Comedy must be hard to write. Romance, too, I suppose. What inspired you to try it?"

"Well..."

"Sorry! I didn't mean to be rude. That was a dumb question." Despite his deep tan, his cheeks coloured with embarrassment. "I know nothing about writing, but I admire people who can do it."

"It's not a dumb question." Dana gave him a reassuring smile and tried to draw this line of conversation to a close. "I'm not sure why I chose this genre," she shrugged. "I guess an idea came to me, and I started putting thoughts on paper."

He seemed to accept that as a final answer, so Dana proceeded to inquire about his years in Africa. As he explained how most of his projects involved establishing wells for clean water in rural villages, he became more and more animated. His enthusiastic recounting of some of his adventures fascinated her.

When she asked why he'd decided to work overseas, his reply was sufficiently subdued and vague. This was a topic he didn't care to discuss. Had he been running away from something? Or someone? Remembering the woman on the phone, Dana wondered who she was and whether or not she'd call again. This reminded her that she needed to replace her phone and return Philip's to him.

"I intended to get a new phone today, but I don't think I'm going to manage that now. I wasn't expecting to spend this much time at the church, and I won't be able to fit it in before my class at four. I'm sorry." Rummaging through her bag, she continued, "But I want you to have yours. I'll be fine until the phone store opens Monday."

Philip started shaking his head the moment she began searching for his phone. "I don't need it, but you do. Keep it." He placed his hand on hers to stop her search.

She did stop momentarily, and as their eyes locked, Dana was completely thrown off guard by the intensity of her reaction to his touch. She turned her head away, hoping he hadn't picked up on it.

At that moment, their order arrived, and she had the impression Philip was as grateful for the distraction as she was. She made a conscious effort to push the moment away and tried to convince herself it meant nothing.

After all the tensions of the morning, she thought she'd lost her appetite but the aromas and the enticing toppings on the pizzas were so irresistible that the two of them simply dove in, agreeing to swap one slice, so that each had a taste of the other's choice. By the time they'd had their tea and coffee, she felt sufficiently relaxed in Philip's company that she decided it was a shame he was heading back to Guelph. If he were to stick around, they might become friends.

Chapter Twenty-Eight

Philip unlocked the door to his aunt's apartment and listened. In the dead quiet, the only sound was the ticking of the kitchen clock. Perhaps she had taken heed and went to lie down for a nap. He tiptoed through the living room and kitchen, placed his ear against her closed bedroom door, and listened until he identified the sound of light snoring. *Good!* He was glad for her sake that she could rest.

Spying a copy of the thin, local area newspaper on the kitchen table, he carried it into the living room where he settled down on the couch.

After a while, it dawned on him that he was reading the top story concerning a nearby home-invasion for the third time. The term "home invasion" was largely unknown when he'd left Canada, but he gathered this type of crime was becoming more common. Often, the invaders knew the occupants of the house, and either held a grudge against them or knew they had valuables worth stealing. Rarely were the victims randomly chosen.

In his opinion, there was a substantial difference between a burglary committed in an empty house and one where the burglar chose to enter a house knowing people were inside. The latter was much more appalling, leaving the victims terrorized. Would the police label what happened here yesterday morning a home invasion? He supposed, strictly speaking, it couldn't be termed a burglary as nothing had been stolen and there had been no evidence of a break-in. However, the house had been invaded, while two women were at home and asleep.

The police might assume the perpetrator knew their identities and that he had entered with the express intent of terrifying the women by placing a dead rat in Dana William's bed.

It wasn't only the rat that was terrifying, but the knowledge that someone had entered her bedroom to leave it there.

He was relieved that Dana had finally called the police. He hadn't thought she would.

That Officer Green was pretty, well...green when he heard the story and saw the rat for himself, but honestly, what can he do? There isn't any evidence that anyone entered the house. Other than the rat. That's evidence of a sort. Though they might conclude Dana is disturbed and put it there herself. Some kind of sick attention-seeking. He had considered this possibility himself at first, but now he wasn't convinced.

He thought back to the meeting at the church. *Bud Watson looks like he could be a problem. He's obviously in love with Dana and acting possessive. Exactly the kind that could turn into a stalker. How well does she know him?*

He was now reluctant to leave Toronto. *I need to keep an eye on things. Maybe I should move into the third-floor apartment after all. But how long can I afford to stay? At some point, I have to go back to Guelph to see Mom and Dad, and I have to talk to Guneet Sharma on Tuesday morning about a job. Much as I want to be here, I can't wait forever.*

Philip was fully aware that it wasn't only concern for his aunt that made him want to stay; Dana Williams had caused a tiny fissure to develop in the protective, turtle-like shell he'd drawn over himself three years ago. He'd grown comfortable inside that shell and wasn't certain he was ready to stick his head out and expose himself to the possibility of more hurt.

However, thinking about Dana and picturing her expressive eyes, as he was doing at this moment, made him wonder if it might be worth taking the chance. He smiled ruefully. *Less than forty-eight hours back in the country and already my carefully laid plans are being sidetracked by a woman.*

The smile disappeared when he remembered another woman, the one who'd caused him to form that protective shell, and the main reason he'd headed for Kenya in the first place. Could she possibly be the one who called that morning and asked for him? *It had to be her. But why would she call? What could she possibly want from me after all this time?*

A sense of dread crept over him as he pondered the distinct possibility that he'd been correct in his judgment of her three years ago. The woman was truly mad.

Chapter Twenty-Nine

A silent wraith staggered forward, gray and haggard. Philip sprang from the couch. "Good Lord!" He took his aunt's arm and led her to the couch. "Sit down. You don't look well at all. Are you sure you should be up?"

"I'm fine. Don't worry. I just haven't slept well with these strange things happening."

"Let me make you a good, strong coffee."

"Thank you, dear, but coffee would keep me awake even more." She waved a hand in front of her face. "I'll be fine. My head's just kind of foggy right now. I did doze off for a bit, but I had a nasty dream." She shook her head as if to clear it.

"Maybe we should go out for some fresh air. We could have dinner out," Philip suggested. "A change of scene would be good for you."

"Maybe." The reply was faint. His aunt looked down at her hands and then up at him again. Her distress seemed even deeper. "Philip, there's something I need to tell you. It's something…not very pleasant. It's dreadful, but I need to tell you." He dropped onto the couch beside her and held her hand, waiting for her to continue. *She's sick! She's going to say she's dying! Oh, please, God. No!* There was a buzzing in his ears. He felt faint with fear for her.

"A few years ago, a young woman I was quite fond of died."

"Oh," was all he could utter, so great was his relief she wasn't announcing a fatal illness. He hastened to add, "I'm sorry."

"She lived here for about six months. In Dana's apartment, actually. I guess the stress of all that's happened to Dana brought her to mind again."

"I guess that's natural. But try not to dwell on it. It isn't doing you any good."

"The thing is, you see, she didn't just die." A pause followed. Then a whispered, "She was murdered."

"Murdered?" The stark pronouncement caught him off guard. "Here? In this house?"

"No. The poor thing was attacked only a block away on her way home one evening. They never found who did it. There didn't seem to be a motive of any kind. It was declared to be a random attack."

Philip watched his aunt wipe away a tear. "Her name was Lynne Brown. She was such a sweet girl. Her family was devastated, of course, and so was I. I had a lot of guilt, too, because I believed I had failed her somehow. If she were in danger, was there something I'd missed?"

"You couldn't possibly have known. You said it was a random attack, no known motive."

"I know. I know. That's what I kept telling myself. The thing is, I was fond of her." She turned to him, "As I am of Dana. I'm so worried about her."

"But that all happened a few years ago, and there's no connection between her and Dana … is there?"

"Not that I know of, other than both of them living here. I'm a bit overwrought, I suppose, and I started thinking about poor Lynne."

"It's too bad what has happened to Dana brought this all back. I'm sure there's no connection."

Despite his attempt to reassure his aunt, a disturbing niggle of doubt stirred in Philip's mind. Could this be the same murdered woman Bud Watson had been talking about back at the church? If so, was it more than a coincidence that she had lived here— in Dana's apartment? Philip was not a believer in coincidences.

Chapter Thirty

At the yoga studio, Nora was nowhere in sight. Had she quit, or was she having a day off? The young woman replacing her didn't seem to know. Was it a case of poor management in this office that caused employees to leave or merely boredom? It couldn't be an exciting job for a young person, but they did get to meet lots of nice people.

She glanced into the classroom before going to her locker. The usual suspects had shown up for her Saturday afternoon class, which tended to be less well-attended than her weekday ones. She was glad to see Julie again, as well as Anna and Brad. It was a sign that they must have enjoyed their first session.

Oddly, the class was congregated around the coat racks at the back of the room and an animated conversation was in progress. Intrigued, Dana walked over to see what the fuss was all about. At her approach, everyone turned to greet her.

"Hi, Dana," Julie said. "We were just saying this would be a great night to go out for a drink after class. Brad suggested the Beach Arms. They've got a great pub menu if we wanted something to eat. What do you think? Are you in?"

Dana was touched by her friend's excitement of going out as a group, yet she vacillated. After the strain of the past twenty-four hours, she had planned to go home and cocoon. Retreating from the world held a great appeal, but she liked the idea of not going home and being faced with those horrible memories. Being around people would probably be better for her.

Brad spoke up, "Everyone thought it would be a nice way to start off a Saturday night. Most of us don't have other plans, and we're hoping you don't, either."

"We'd love it if you could come," added Anna. "It would be nice to get to know each other."

Her sincere expression and Brad's charming smile were difficult to resist. *Why not? I know I should be careful, but I can't retreat from the world. It's only a drink with my yoga class.*

"Sounds like fun," she said. "Thank you. Now, we should get started. Find a spot and roll out your mats." She tossed her coat and backpack in with the others and moved to the front of the room to plug in her music. This particular CD of relaxing music mixed with sounds of nature always moved her. Croaking frogs, softly hooting owls, and the soft tumbling of waterfalls slowed her heartbeat, and she felt rewarded when she observed its pleasing effect on some of the others, too.

The session finished well with her students sufficiently relaxed, and every muscle stretched to the best of its ability. As the group gathered their belongings, the eight who decided to have a drink together walked the three blocks east to the Beach Arms in a festive mood.

*****

Once they were settled in at the table made up of two pushed together to accommodate them, everyone examined the menu and considered their drink options. Dana thought back to her pizza lunch with Philip and wondered if this was the kind of impromptu time with friends and acquaintances he'd enjoy. She thought he would.

Why am I thinking of him and what he'd like? She couldn't come up with an answer, though it might have to do with the fact she didn't want to delve into the reasons of why she cared about Philip's interests.

A baseball game played silently on the enormous TV behind the bar. Closed-Captioning displayed the play-by-play across the bottom screen, complete with hilarious misspellings and misunderstandings. This early in the season, the hometown Jays were doing well, and hopes were high among their fans.

While Dana enjoyed watching a game, she didn't understand what the attraction was for the truly dedicated fans. It seemed to her that every spring their giddy hopes rose high, only to ride the highs and lows of summer, and finally be dashed in the fall. The following spring, the cycle would recommence. Watching Brad's face as he followed the on-screen action, she could tell he was a loyal Blue Jays' fans and smiled.

"You a Jays' fan, Dana?" he asked with hopeful enthusiasm.

"I enjoy a game now and then, but I don't follow the standings closely." His obvious disappointment made her laugh. "I bet you do, though. You can probably quote all kinds of esoteric stats and trivia. Am I right?" she teased.

"You bet. My dad took us to the opening game when the Jays first came to town. We're still big fans."

"Didn't it snow that day? I think I heard that."

"It did. That was part of the excitement. Great memories."

"My family was at that first game, too," Anna said. "What a super day."

Three of the other women added that they'd all been there as well. It was a pleasant, shared memory for all.

As they chatted, Dana thought it was interesting that Brad, being the only male, had felt comfortable enough to come along to the pub with seven women. When the waiter arrived to take their drink orders, Brad joked about having a night out with his harem. No one was offended by the comment as some might be in such politically correct times. Instead, the women seemed to get a kick out of it. Though Dana wondered if his interest in hanging out with a bunch of women had to do with one in particular. It didn't take her long to note that most of Brad's attention was focused on Anna. Whether or not Anna was aware of this was unclear; she was enjoying a conversation with Elaine about a cooking show they both followed.

"How long have you been teaching at the studio, Dana?" Brad asked.

"About six months. I'm one of the newer instructors."

"Do you teach anywhere else?"

"Not at the moment. I have taught at a few other places before, mostly for Parks and Rec, but also at a few private clubs."

"Is this your full-time job or do you have another life?"

Dana had the impression he was truly interested and not only making polite conversation. She rarely ventured into the area of her writing with casual acquaintances. Most weren't all that interested and she was shy speaking about it.

"I'm a writer," she stated. "Mostly freelance stuff but my first play is in rehearsals. We had our first one last night." There, she'd said it out loud, and it felt good! Though the feeling soon slipped away when she remembered how the rehearsal had ended.

Brad was observant enough to notice the change in her demeanor —even though it was slight —and she made an effort to cover it up.

"That sounds pretty exciting, seeing your work on stage. Were you pleased with it? You must have been nervous."

"It was fine. What do you do, Brad?"

"I'm a head-hunter." He smiled at her perplexed look. "Executive recruiting. I've recently gone out on my own and started a small company. I'm working from home, which is nice for a change. One of the perks is being able to come to your classes." He flashed a flirtatious smile.

"So, are you a househusband, too, taking care of the house and kids when you're not–hunting heads?" Dana wasn't actually curious about his marital status. She had asked the question for Anna's sake, who half-turned to hear the answer while Elaine continued describing a complicated-sounding recipe from the cooking show.

"I'm single, if that's what you're wondering," Brad smiled. "No wife and kiddies hidden away."

"There's an old feminist saying, 'Every woman needs a wife,'" Dana said. "Remember the old TV shows like *Leave it to Beaver*? Sometimes, I think it would be nice to come home and find dinner prepared and the laundry done, as old-fashioned as that sounds."

"Right on!" Julie chimed in. Brad laughed.

Amused by her friends' reactions, Dana glanced across the table to see Anna's. Nothing. There was no hint of a smile or frown of disapproval. As if unaware of their presence, Anna sat stiff-backed and trance-like, staring into space, her face an inscrutable mask.

With the arrival of drinks and much clinking of glasses all around, Anna snapped out of whatever spell she'd been under.

The others hadn't seemed to notice, but for Dana, the effect had been chilling.

Chapter Thirty-One

After a few amusing toasts and more laughter, in which Anna once again participated, Brad turned back to Dana. Abandoning his previous subject of baseball, he asked, "Who owns the studio? I don't think I've seen anyone around except the receptionists, and they seem too young to be the owners."

"The owners live in Markham. They're a couple, I think. I don't see them often myself. They hired me, of course, but other than that we rarely cross paths."

Nodding, he took an appreciative sip of his dark ale before asking, "Is it a chain? Do they have more than one place?"

Again, Anna seemed to lean her head in their direction as if curious about their conversation. Dana wasn't sure what to make of the woman after having witnessed her earlier trance-like state. On the other hand, she could be over-reacting because she was stressed.

"As far as I know, this is their only place, but I couldn't swear to that."

"Well, it appears to be a nice little business they've got going. Seems to be popular. Are they a young couple?"

"I'd say middle-aged. Their English isn't too good, so I think they're recent immigrants. Maybe they had a business wherever they came from and decided to start one up here." She shook her head. "This is all pure conjecture on my part. I don't know much about them."

Sipping her glass of Pinot Grigio, she enjoyed its silky softness sliding down her throat and the resulting tingle and warmth as it spread through her. She closed her eyes, losing herself in the moment. When she opened them again, Brad was absorbed in a replay being dissected on the Sports Network. She was about to speak to Julie when he turned to her again, but it wasn't to comment on baseball.

"It's interesting. A lot of immigrants from Hong Kong have money to invest in small businesses. I think I read somewhere that it's a condition of eligibility, but I'm not sure."

She had assumed the conversation about the studio was over, since it was obvious she didn't know much at all about it or her employers. However, for some reason, Brad remained intrigued.

"Oh, they're not Chinese!" she declared. "I have trouble figuring out accents, but if I had to guess I'd say maybe Russian, only because I once had Russian neighbours. But as I said, I'm not good at accents."

"No matter," he said, with his attractive smile. "I was just curious about the business. It seems like a nice little set-up, and I'm glad it's so convenient for me."

Maybe that's all it was: he was new to the neighbourhood and naturally interested in some of the local businesses. That was his area of expertise, after all.

Dana couldn't help a surreptitious glance in Anna's direction to see if she was still eavesdropping, but the woman had turned back to chatting with Julie. It didn't matter one whit to Dana if she was interested in Brad. She was more curious about Anna's episode earlier when she seemed to zone out. Dana continued to remain slightly unnerved by what she'd witnessed.

She told herself that under ordinary circumstances, she probably wouldn't have given Anna's behaviour a second thought, and she shouldn't now. Yet...how much did she know about Anna? Or Brad? Or anyone here with her now for that matter? How much did she even know about her so-called friend Julie?

Stop it! her mind screamed. *Just stop it!*

*****

Another hour or so passed pleasantly enough with no more questions about the yoga studio and no more strangeness from Anna. As everyone prepared to leave, Julie suggested a film, but Dana begged off, saying she needed an early night.

Her friend's expression displayed her concern, but Dana insisted, "I'm all right, Julie. This was good for me. Thanks for arranging it. I know it was your idea." Her little white lie seemed to have its desired effect as her friend appeared to take her at her word. When the bills arrived, Brad offered to treat her, but Dana politely refused. Some men would have pushed it, but he didn't, and she appreciated not having to go back and forth over it with him. As she unzipped the pocket of her backpack where she kept her wallet, something fell out and fluttered to the floor. Distracted by a comment from Elaine, Dana leaned over to pick it up and placed it on the table a second or two before her mind registered what it was.

Julie gasped and her hand flew to her mouth. Everyone turned to look while Dana sat immobilized. Against the white placemat, the lacy black bow stood out in sharp contrast. It seemed so innocent; a simple piece of black ribbon looped in a bow. Yet, to those who recognized its significance, it symbolized gruesome death and malevolence.

"What's wrong?" Elaine asked. "What's happened, Julie?"

"Dana, are you all right?" Anna hurried to her side and proceeded to take her pulse. Dana tried yanking her hand away, but Anna's grip was strong. "I don't like your colour," she said, her eyes examining Dana's face.

Brad cornered the waiter. "We need a glass of water. Fast!"

Dizzy and nauseous, Dana accepted the glass of water gratefully and took careful sips.

"Your pulse is quite fast," Anna stated. "Do you feel dizzy? Put your head between your knees for a few minutes."

Dana did so, recalling the same advice from the previous evening. *What the heck is going on? How did that get into my bag? Why is this happening? What did I do?*

Chapter Thirty-Two

As Dana's concerned friends gathered around and the nervous waiter hovered as well, all she could think was: *I've got to get out of here!* She couldn't tell them what had been going on. They'd think she was nuts. *And maybe I am!*

Raising her head slowly, she kept her eyes off the black bow. "I'm sorry. I'll be fine. I just got a little light-headed. Must have been the wine."

Dana scanned the entire room of faces for any sign of someone who might be targeting her. All she saw were the concerned faces from her yoga class, the pub's staff, and a nearly-full restaurant of strangers who weren't paying her any mind. No one looked the least bit suspicious, but what did she expect? To see a creepy person chortling at her reaction? As much as she wanted this harassment to end, she also hoped she wouldn't recognize anyone familiar, let alone someone she considered a friend.

"I'll call a taxi for you," Brad said.

"Please don't. Julie will walk home with me. The fresh air will help. I'll be fine. I promise."

"I go that way, too, so I'll keep you company," Anna said.

This was not a welcome offer, but again, she didn't want to refuse in front of the others. She noticed that Anna seemed to have caught Brad's attention when she spoke, and now he was the one wearing an inscrutable expression.

Julie and Anna insisted on holding her by an arm in case she passed out. The others, in a subdued mood, called for their bills. The party was definitely over. Dana faked a smile, said goodnight to her concerned friends, and left the bar. The black bow remained on the table.

*****

Dana couldn't have imagined a more mismatched threesome on the tense and awkward walk home: Anna, who was calm and collected; Julie, who was visibly emotional and trying not to panic; and herself, lost in a terrifying haze of crazy thoughts and images.

When they reached her corner, she drew herself up as tall as possible, attempting to project a strength and steadiness that wasn't there, and insisted she'd be fine walking the short distance up the street alone. They were having none of it, of course. Finally, to her relief, it was agreed there was no need for two escorts. Julie would go home with her, and Anna could go on her way.

She made a show of thanking Anna for her kindness, but Anna waved her off, saying, "You'd have done the same for me. Don't overdo things tonight. Try and take it easy, okay?" After promising to do so, she and Julie watched Anna depart before heading up the street.

Like a deflating balloon, Julie expelled a great gust of air. With it, her shoulders slumped, and her head dropped to her chest. "Holy smokes, Dana," she almost whispered. "I couldn't say anything before with everyone around, but I'm totally freaked out."

Putting a consoling arm around her friend's shoulders, Dana said, "I'm so sorry."

"You don't have anything to be sorry for!" Julie declared, stopping on the sidewalk. She tugged Dana's arm, forcing her to look her straight in the eye. "I don't mean to upset you more, but I hope you're taking this more seriously now."

"Believe me, I am. How could that possibly get into my bag? I always have it with me."

"Always?"

"Well, just about. It's always nearby, at least. Like today, it was at the back of the class with my jacket and everyone else's gear."

They resumed walking; their pace slowed as they considered the implications.

"Do you think that's when the ribbon got put in there?"

"I don't know," Dana anguished. The thought was thoroughly chilling. "When I think about it, I haven't been into my wallet since last night for the streetcar. No, wait, my streetcar tickets are in another part of my backpack, in a small pocket."

"Were you out anywhere this morning?"

The last thing Dana wanted to do was tell Julie about meeting Bud and the policeman at the church and her lunch with Philip.

Avoiding the specific question, she said, "I didn't have my wallet out again. Then I left my bag and jacket at the back of the class this afternoon. So, like I said, the last time I took my wallet out must have been sometime on Thursday or Friday, but you paid for our tea on Friday after class…"

They had reached the house but, almost by unspoken agreement, continued the conversation on the sidewalk.

"Okay, so you left your backpack at the back of the room today. Do you actually think someone from the class put it in there? I know it's a stretch, but what if someone followed you on the way to yoga? Someone who's smooth, like a pickpocket, and had a chance to slip it in while you weren't looking. After all, you do carry it on your back. It might not be that hard to do."

"Maybe, but highly unlikely. I think I would have felt

something."

"Not necessarily. The streets are busy on Saturdays. There's lots of crowding and jostling —but maybe you're right. That only leaves yoga, unless..."

"Unless what?"

Julie was giving her a pointed look. The implication of that look hit Dana. Her head swiveled to stare at the house. "Are you saying someone in the house did it? That's ridiculous. There's only Mrs. MacGyver and Philip, and they would never —" She shook her head, rejecting the suggestion as absurd, and turned way from the house. "Besides, there's no way they could have managed it."

"Why? They have keys. Did you have a shower or change in your bedroom while your backpack was in the living room? It could be done if someone was determined. They'd be taking a huge chance, but maybe they'd think it was worth it. Besides..."

Dana interrupted her friend. "No! Don't even go there. It wasn't Mrs. MacGyver! Or Philip. No way."

"Maybe not Mrs. MacGyver," Julie conceded. She stared at the sidewalk, avoiding Dana's angry look.

"No, I refuse to believe any of that," Dana insisted. However, yet another seed of doubt had been planted. *At this rate, I'll soon have a frigging garden of suspects*!

"Keep an open mind, Dana. There is another remote possibility. What if whoever put the rat in your bed came back? He could have a key and come up those back stairs."

Dana's horror at this prospect must have been evident. Julie quickly backpedaled. "On second thought, no. You're right. It couldn't have happened while you were at home. It would be too dangerous for anyone to try that. My money is on the fact it happened sometime when you were out, but not yoga class. Someone clever slipped it into your backpack. Like a pickpocket, only in reverse."

For some perverse reason, Dana found this theory more comforting. The idea of a stranger, rather than someone she knew, slipping the bow into her bag was far more palatable.

Although Dana was stronger than when they'd left the pub, she decided she didn't want to be alone. Affecting a lighter tone, she said, "Come on up, Julie. Maybe there's a good movie on. We can phone for Chinese, if you'd like."

"You're on!"

It was always easy to read Julie's open face, and Dana, seeing her obvious relief in the change of subject, determined not to burden her any further with her troubles.

To the relief of both women, they were able to enter the house and go up to Dana's apartment without meeting either Mrs. MacGyver or her nephew.

I couldn't have faced either of them tonight. I don't have the energy to explain this latest thing, and I couldn't explain it anyway! It's all too much! Tomorrow, I'll insist the master locks are changed, but I might have to find another place to live anyway.

That last idea was overwhelming in her present state of mind, so she turned on the television, hoping to find sufficient distraction there.

Chapter Thirty-Three

Television proved to be the perfect distraction. Dana curled up at one end of her couch while Julie relaxed at the other. Their shoes remained in the middle of the rug where they'd kicked them off. One empty pizza box, two almost-empty bottles of Chardonnay, two brimming wine glasses, and an assortment of used napkins littered the coffee table.

The friends were so absorbed in a Katharine Hepburn-Spencer Tracy Festival on the Classic Movie Channel that they barely moved, except to occasionally adjust the cozy afghan draped over their bare feet. Since the film wouldn't end until past midnight, and the wine was causing eyelids to droop, it was decided that Julie would sleep on the couch. All she needed was a pair of Dana's pajamas.

*****

Laying in bed, Dana attempted to keep her mind distracted by analyzing the Tracy-Hepburn films. They produced some easy laughs, and the simple plots were not too intellectually demanding. However, something about their style irritated her slightly. Who on earth ever talked that fast all the time? Was there ever a real-life couple whose exchanges were so quick-witted? Highly unlikely. The snappy repartee was entertaining but unrealistic. So, what was the great attraction? What made them popular?

And speaking of attractions, what about the two stars' famous (or infamous) real-life romance? For all those years Tracy was Hepburn's lover, he and his wife refused to divorce due to religion. Of course, their fans didn't know this at the time. If they had, it would have killed both of the stars' careers.

Back then, everything was all smoke and mirrors in an attempt to hide the truth. Now, stars can have affairs and live together and almost no one cares. We think it's different and more open now, but is it? How much do most people know about the celebrities they idolize? Usually, only what a celebrity's publicist wants their fans to know.

Never mind famous people, she suddenly thought. What about the people around us every day? We have no way of knowing if they're wife beaters, ex-cons, child molesters, or sex offenders. We take most people at face value.

Am I making the same mistake? I don't know anything at all about Philip, or even Mrs. MacGyver's past. And what about Bud? I met him less than four months ago. These were dreadful thoughts, but she told herself no matter how nice everyone seemed, she couldn't let her guard down until this was over —if it ever was.

Despite her earlier musings about Julie's unknown past, tonight she was grateful for her presence on the couch. She only hoped she wouldn't come to regret it.

Chapter Thirty-Four

A persistent ringing sounded somewhere in the distance. No, not in the distance, in her backpack. Dana rolled over in bed and grabbed the bag off the floor, reaching in to answer her phone. Philip's phone, she reminded herself. Got to get a new one–oh, no. She can't today. It's Sunday, so the local store will be closed.

"Hello?" She wondered if the same woman might be calling back for Philip.

"Dana? Is that you?"

Bud.

Swinging her legs over the side of the bed, she sat up and forced her still-sleepy mind to focus. "Bud? Is everything okay?" *Please, let everything be okay!*

"No! It's definitely not okay!" His strident tone increased. "It's Shirley. Oh, my…" Bud stopped to cough a couple of times and clear his throat.

"Shirley?" The name repeated itself several times in her mind. Searching her memory, she couldn't recall a Shirley. Perhaps it was a family member of Bud's. The name sounded familiar, though. *Wait!* It was Shirley who found the rat in the coffee pot. The memory jolted her to her feet.

"What's happened to Shirley?" she demanded, her voice sounding strangled due to her rising panic.

"She's dead," Bud voice broke. "I'm sorry to tell you

over the phone like this. It's just… She was…Oh, Dana! She was murdered!"

"Murdered?" Dana's legs gave out. Collapsing onto her bed, she repeated in a frightened whisper, "Murdered? How? Where?"

A frantic Julie rushed bare foot into the room. She came to a stop inside the door, her eyes wide as saucers. Her matted hair formed a hive of wayward strands, and her colour almost matched the white pajamas Dana had forgotten she'd loaned her. In fact, she'd momentarily forgotten Julie had slept over. The sight of someone else in her clothes was disorienting.

"Who's been murdered?" Julie demanded.

Before Dana had time to answer, Bud responded to her own question, "She was found at the church. It must have happened not long after we were there."

Fear and confusion paralyzed her thinking. "Shirley…" she mumbled into the phone. "Shirley…" Then, rousing herself, "Bud? You'd better come over right away."

"Hold on. I'll be there in fifteen."

As Dana turned off the phone, she turned to Julie as she took a fearful step forward into the bedroom. "Dana? Who's been murdered?"

"Shirley," Dana whispered.

"Shirley who? Do I know her?"

Dana's voice sounded hollow and dull as she explained, "Shirley who found the rat. In the coffee pot. At the church… she's been…" she couldn't finish the sentence.

Julie slumped to the floor beside the bed and laid a cold hand on Dana's arm. "How can this be? In the *church*? Why?" She shivered, then hugged herself for warmth, and rocked back and forth on her knees.

"Bud's coming over to tell us what happened." Dana looked around the room as if not quite sure where she was.

"I'd better get dressed."

"Me, too. It might be better if I left," Julie said, still rocking. She made no move to get up.

"Why? You don't have to rush off."

"Thanks, but I don't think Bud likes me much. I wouldn't be comfortable staying with him around."

Dana sighed. "I'm sorry. I know he can be pretty serious sometimes, but I wouldn't take it too personally. Please stay. I'd like you to be here, if you don't mind."

"Okay," Julie conceded, but her face displayed her reluctance. "Can I make some coffee? I need something strong to handle this… murder!" She shivered. "How about you?"

Dana stood. "Thanks for staying. And coffee's a good idea, but I'll make it."

She needed to do something —make coffee, get dressed, tidy up —anything to keep her mind from dwelling on Bud's words which, ultimately, was an impossible task.

Shirley! Murdered! Dear Lord, what's happening?

Chapter Thirty-Five

Dana sat in wait on the stairs where she had a perfect view out the window in the front door. She needed to watch for Bud's approach and let him in before he could ring the bell. There was no need to alert her landlady or her nephew. Not until she spoke with Bud. Only then would she consider worrying them more than they already were.

True to his word, Bud arrived fifteen minutes after their call. Dana ushered him in. His appearance alarmed her almost as much as his phone call had. From his bleary-eyed, unshaven face to his unkempt, buttoned-down shirt, which looked as if a cat had curled up and spent the night in it , to a strange, grimy patch marking his slacks, Bud's distress was evident.

She closed her apartment door behind them. No one spoke. Bud, for once, was without words. This unnerved her so much that she moved forward to hug him. "I'm so sorry."

He wrapped his arms around her and held on tight. "I'm sorry, too. I shouldn't have told you on the phone. It's so awful."

"Tell me what happened." She took his hand and led him to the couch.

It was only then that he noticed Julie, standing in the kitchen doorway. "Oh, you're not alone."

"Hi, Bud," Julie said. "Nice to see you, too."

Ignoring the remark, Bud turned to Dana. "Elvis called this morning. He's a basket case. The police contacted him as next-of-kin."

"Poor guy. What did he say? What happened?"

"I guess the janitor found her yesterday afternoon." He shook his head in disbelief. "A few hours after we were there."

Dana placed a comforting arm around him. After a quiet moment, she asked the question which had been uppermost in her mind ever since his call. "Was she…? Do you think she was there when we were? I mean, we looked all over the building. We couldn't have missed her, could we?"

Bud seemed to hear the deep concern in her question–almost a sense of panic that they'd had some part in what happened, or at least missed an opportunity to help Shirley in some way. He embraced her, stroking her back in a comforting manner.

"I don't think so," he reassured her. "They're pretty sure it happened not long before she was found."

Dana experienced a deep sense of relief. She couldn't bear the gruesome thought that Shirley might have been dead or worse, injured and dying —while she, Bud, and Philip had been in the same building with Officer Green.

"How…how did she die?" she whispered, laying her head on his shoulder.

"Struck from behind, though I'm not sure with what. Elvis didn't say."

He wiped his forehead with both hands, then ran them through his hair and looked off for a moment. "Poor Shirley."

Julie, who had been standing there taking everything in, spoke up. "But why was she there? There wasn't a rehearsal. And why was she alone? How did she get in?"

Bud looked at Julie as if he'd forgotten her presence and sighed. "So many questions! She had a key from

Audrey. Sometimes the wardrobe people meet there to sew and iron the costumes. Elvis spoke to Shirley that morning. She told him someone had volunteered to help work on the costumes, and they were meeting later that day to go through the costume cupboard. She didn't say who, but that's probably who did it."

Julie didn't reply but appeared to be considering this conclusion. Dana shivered. "Someone from the crew?"

"I don't know!" Bud's anguish was clear. "I sure hope not. What an awful thought. Someone we know!"

"It doesn't have to be," Julie said. "It could have been someone pretending to be part of the crew."

Bud gave her a grateful look. "It's possible, I guess. Not that it makes any difference to Shirley. But it might make the rest of us feel better if it were a stranger." He shook his head in disgust, adding, "I can't believe I said that, as if it would make any difference."

"It's okay. I know what you meant," Dana soothed him. And to her chagrin, she did.

Chapter Thirty-Six

Officer Green slumped on Mrs. MacGyver's couch. He no longer bore the bright-eyed appearance of a new recruit. Instead, his weary eyes betrayed a new reality. This was his first murder case, and he was taking it hard. Dana surmised he was assuming some of the blame, thinking that if he'd taken the dead rats more seriously, he might have prevented Shirley's death. She didn't believe that for a minute. Besides, no one had mentioned the possibility of a connection between the events. How could Shirley's murder have anything to do with the dead rats?

Although he held his notebook and pencil in his lap, Officer Green was not asking any questions. That was being done by Detective Small, the diminutive and dapper-looking detective who had accompanied him. Dana thought this was an unfortunate example of the name suiting the man, which probably led to a fair amount of ribbing, both good-natured and not-so-good. This might explain his tough persona, probably developed as a defense mechanism.

She guessed he was in his late thirties or early forties. His unusually erect bearing projected a military air.

Perhaps this was to compensate for his short stature, or maybe he was simply ex-military. His designer jacket and jeans were expensive, and he sported a neatly trimmed mustache, which he caressed with one finger from time to time. Dana was reminded of Agatha Christie's famous detective, Hercule Poirot. Not that Poirot had ever dressed in designer jeans. It was this detective's dapper air and mustache-stroking that brought the fictional one to mind.

Detective Small grilled Mrs. MacGyver about her tenants. When she explained that Dana was currently the only one, he asked about past renters. The landlady seemed surprised by the question.

"Oh, my. You don't think...? No, that's impossible. I've always had nice tenants. Mr. Syms, who was here before Dana came, was a retired teacher who lived on the third floor. He was here for five years, and he seemed fine to me, but his daughter started worrying about his being alone and didn't think he should be climbing the stairs anymore."

"We have to check into everything, ma'am. Now, besides this Syms, who else have you rented to in the past few years?"

"There hasn't been anyone on the third floor since Mr Syms moved out, nor has there been anyone in Dana's apartment for a while." She paused, frowning. "Though, the last young lady who rented it out was a bit of a problem, I admit...."

"In what way, Ma'am?"

"Oh, dear!" Flustered, Mrs. MacGyver thought about her answer. "Well, I had to chase her all the time for her rent, and sometimes she had friends over who seemed a little rough. They could be pretty noisy, too, but it wasn't anything terribly serious. I wasn't comfortable about it, so I asked her to leave."

Dana had the impression her landlady was downplaying the situation and she couldn't help but to wonder why.

"And how did the young lady seem to take that?"

"Not well, I'm afraid. I was concerned she might get nasty and take me to court or something. As you know, renters have a lot of rights these days. So, I made up a story." Embarrassed, she dropped her head and looked down at her hands, twisting in her lap. "A little white lie," she continued, "I told her I didn't want to rent that apartment anymore. I said my nephew might want to use it from time to time when he comes back home from Africa." She looked up at Philip, giving him a nervous smile.

"We'll need a name for this young lady and forwarding addresses for both tenants."

"She left in a huff, so I don't have her address. Her name was Sabina Wright."

"Was she a student, or did she have a place of work where we could check?"

"She waitressed. I can't remember the name of the café where she worked. It was downtown. I need a minute to think… Oh, dear! I'm sure she had nothing to do with any of this."

"We need to be certain. Call us when you remember the name. We can take it from there." He handed her his card and turned to Dana.

"Both rats were found on Friday, and the phone call also came that same day. I take it you haven't heard anything more from whoever it was that phoned you?"

When she shook her head, he took a deep breath and continued. "Okay, so now we have this murder, which we don't know for sure is related to the other stuff, and it's been more than twenty-four hours without any more phone calls or dead rats."

Now was the time to mention the ribbon in her backpack, a moment she'd been dreading. *Why?* she wondered. *Why should I be uncomfortable mentioning it? I've done nothing wrong. But I've been afraid all along that they'll think I'm crazy. Now, in light of Shirley's death —murder —it seems almost inconsequential.* Still, she knew she had to say something.

"Actually, there is something else...," Dana described what had occurred at the Beach Arms. "It was a small thing, at least, nothing as horrible as poor Shirley or even the rats."

"Don't take it too lightly, Miss Williams. It may seem small, but it could be important."

Officer Green finally spoke. "It also means that whoever is responsible for the rats isn't finished. What's more, he —or possibly she —has easy access to you."

His words hung in the air, forcing everyone to acknowledge the truth.

"Oh, dear," repeated Mrs. MacGyver, clearly distressed. "I'm glad Julie stayed with you last night, dear. This is so upsetting. I don't know what to make of it." She turned to Philip, who nodded in agreement but made no comment.

"Do you have the ribbon?" the officer interrupted with a sudden, hopeful light in his eyes.

"No, I left it at the restaurant. I couldn't bear to look at it, let alone touch it. Should I have kept it?"

It might have been useful. We'll check with the place and see if it's still around. You never know, someone on staff might have picked it up for some reason. If not, there's always the garbage bins again."

This was said with such a look of disgust, Dana was sure he was recalling the process of going through the garbage at the church to find the second rat's body, which must have reminded him of the original one she'd found in her bed. With a shiver, she wondered if that was just yesterday morning? So much had happened since then that it felt like ages.

"You said the first rat is still in your freezer?" Green asked Mrs. MacGyver. When she confirmed this, they went downstairs to retrieve it.

"It'll go to the lab," Small said. "We probably won't get anything worthwhile off it, but we can check for rabies, just to be sure."

With that, the two policemen departed, and Philip went off to buy new locks. Mrs. MacGyver insisted Dana stay while she put the kettle on. Dana, as always, found it hard to refuse her landlady. She had a full day of freedom ahead of he,r and she didn't want to be alone for any of it.

*****

Now I've probably got them all confused! What a bunch of clowns! They'll be trying to figure out how in the h-e-double hockey sticks that ribbon got into her backpack. Soon, they'll all be suspecting each other. No one will know who to believe or who they can trust. Or is that "whom" they can trust? Pardon me, O Grammar Police! Who cares? What I want to know is whether she'll move out of that apartment. Have you got the guts to stay, Dana, or are you gonna run? There are plenty more surprises for you where those came from, just wait and see. Yes, sirree! Just wait and see. Hey, that rhymes! And speaking of rhymes, "Three blind mice/ See how they run...."Ah, who cares about mice? Rats make so much more of a statement, don't you think?

Chapter Thirty-Seven

As Dana tidied up the bedding Julie had used, she contemplated on what was left of the day. Normally, a free Sunday with no obligations was a sweet pleasure to anticipate. Except, any sense of normalcy had vanished the morning she woke up to find that first disgusting rat in her bed. On top of it all, Shirley had been murdered! She squeezed her eyes to stop the tears that threatened to flow.

The growing desperation to get out of the apartment reminded her of the need to shop for her mother's upcoming birthday, and that she had promised to call her sister. *Well, now's as good a time as any, I suppose. It's Sunday, so she's probably home. The best thing to do is get it over with. Maybe, with luck, she won't be there, and I can at least say I tried to reach her.*

Caroline was home. It was an awkward conversation, to say the least. Dana always felt as if she had to walk on eggshells because she never knew what would make her sister take umbrage at something and flare-up. She had to admit, she didn't fully understand what lay behind this other than their two distinctly different personalities.

"Are you going up for Mom's birthday next week?"

"I don't know. Are you?" Caroline's reply was like a predictable challenge. Dana read between the lines: *if you're going, I won't.*

"Probably. I haven't been home since February, and it's the holiday weekend. I'll rent a car." She paused, then suggested, "We could drive up together if you'd like."

"I'll think about it. The traffic's always bad on long weekends, and the bugs will be out in full force. There's some good stuff going on in the city, too, minus the traffic and bugs. A couple of outdoor concerts."

"I guess your friends will be going to those."

"Some of them."

Dana hesitated before taking the plunge. *Okay, Mom, this one's for you!* She tried to sound light and breezy. "Are you seeing anybody lately?"

"Why? Did Mom tell you to ask?"

"I just wondered."

"What about you? You over that Dave yet?"

"As a matter of fact, I am, and I heard he's getting married." She was amazed at how easy that was to say and how good she felt admitting she was over him.

"I thought he wasn't the marrying kind."

"Yeah, that's what he said."

A long pause ensued. There seem to be little else to say.

"Well, as I said, I'll be going up north, and I'll have a car. I'd love your company if you change your mind." *A little fib never hurt once in a while.*

"Sure. Bye."

Well, wasn't that fun? I wish things were different between us. It would have been nice to share with Caroline what had been happening recently and to pour out her concerns. Perhaps she could've received sisterly advice or some comforting words in return, but she knew better than to expect that. *At least I can tell Mom I called her.*

To fill up the rest of her afternoon, Dana decided to take advantage of the mild, May weather and go for a long walk along the boardwalk. The breeze off the lake would still be quite cool, so she bundled up and headed off.

Chapter Thirty-Eight

The boardwalk was perennially popular, but a spring day full of promise brought out all those who'd avoided the winter winds. Dana enjoyed the variety of people walking their dogs. She noted proud parents and grandparents pushing tots in strollers; some even ran behind cutting-edge jogging strollers, giving their little ones a ride in the fast lane.

Not everyone was young and energetic. Several older folks progressed at a slower pace, sometimes arm in arm, and occasionally with the aid of a cane or walker. Plentiful park benches supported people-watchers of all ages, and, not surprisingly, the combination of fresh air and sunlight had even induced one or two to doze off.

Gray waves thrashed against the concrete breakwaters, spewing plumes of icy water on a few daredevils standing too close. Despite the frigid water temperature, three or four hardy kayakers paddled parallel to the shore. Most of the bigger boats wouldn't be launched for a week or so, but every marina along the lakeshore would be buzzing with eager boaters polishing decks and checking sails and engines, ensuring all would be shipshape for the season ahead.

Dana loved living near water; she craved this proximity. It must be in her DNA, or maybe it was due to years spent at the family cottage on a lake in Muskoka.

Even if she never went in it, as with Lake Ontario, simply absorbing the sights and smells filled her soul with peace. She wondered idly if being born under a water sign had anything to do with it. Although she was not inclined to take astrology and horoscopes seriously, sometimes the interpretations caused her to wonder if there was more to reading the heavens than she thought.

Approaching the tennis courts, she caught sight of Julie among a small group and waved to catch her attention. "Julie!" No response. She called again, louder. Maybe she was wrong, and it wasn't Julie, but no, she was certain that it was. Julie, laughing and absorbed in conversation, must simply not have heard. Deciding not to interrupt her friend's fun simply to say hi, Dana turned away. Still, some sense compelled her to look back over her shoulder. Just as she did, one of the men turned. *Brad!*

Julie and Brad? Is this simply a coincidence or something else? Suddenly, she heard Philip's voice in her head, cautioning her to be careful about whom she trusted.

Oh, for heaven's sake! Now I'm definitely getting paranoid. There's no reason why Julie and Brad, or anybody else, shouldn't meet at the tennis courts. Still, it makes me wonder if they planned to meet or if it was a chance encounter?

Stop being ridiculous! Next time you see her, you can simply ask. Now, it's a beautiful day, relax and enjoy it. By the time she left the boardwalk, she had run into two other acquaintances and enjoyed chatting about pleasant topics with people who were unaware of the recent traumatic events in her life. Walking back up to Queen St., she shook her head at her reaction to seeing Julie and Brad together.

Paranoid! Get a grip, girl. Get a grip!

Chapter Thirty-Nine

In the foyer, a large, black toolbox lay open in front of the door to Mrs. MacGyver's living quarters. Dana noticed that the original lock set had been removed and a cardboard box containing its replacement sat on the floor.

As she started up the stairs, her landlady stepped into the hall to ask if it would be all right for Philip to come upstairs and change her locks.

"I don't want to disturb your Sunday afternoon, Dana, but I think we need to get this done as quickly as possible, just in case."

The 'just in case' hung in the air like a suspended sword ready to slash and cut down anyone in its path. Dana felt a rush of sympathy for the woman. Even though she hadn't known Shirley, news of her murder had hit Mrs. MacGyver hard, and it brought the police back to her home. Dark circles under her eyes indicated she still wasn't sleeping well. The creases in her face seemed to be deepening daily.

"Of course. I'm sorry about all of this. I know it's been hard on you."

"It's not your fault, dear. You certainly don't need to apologize, and, by the way, I think it's about time you called me Iva, don't you? 'Mrs. MacGyver' seems much too formal for us."

Dana was touched. 'Thank you, Iva. That's awfully

sweet."

"Well, you've become much more than a tenant, dear. I think of you as a friend."

"I hope so. You've been awfully kind to me since I moved in." She instinctively moved back down the stairs and gave the woman a hug. "You can tell Philip to come up whenever he wants. I'm not certain if I'll be staying in or going out again."

As she turned to go, Iva grasped one of Dana's hands in a grip so tight she almost lost all circulation. "Is there any word on that poor woman … Shirley something?"

"Shirley Fox? Not that I've heard. I hope it doesn't take too long, though. Poor Elvis. The whole cast and crew are grieving, too. Shirley was well-liked."

Dana didn't want to say anything more like how freaked out they all were, wondering if the killer was one of the cast or crew or if he would strike again.

Back in her apartment, she flopped onto the couch and thought about the day. She wasn't sure whether or not she wanted to be there when Philip came to work on her locks. Somewhat refreshed and restored from her outing, she felt reluctant to be drawn back into discussions about the events of the past two days. On the other hand, she was well aware she couldn't stick her head in the sand and pretend all was well with the world because it definitely wasn't.

Choosing avoidance, she picked up Philip's phone and punched in the numbers of two old friends from her former neighbourhood, arranging a get-together for dinner and a film.

Chapter Forty

Meeting up with her friends, Dana was reminded of how much they'd always enjoyed each other's company. She felt guilty for not having kept in close touch since moving away more than six months ago.

When chided about this, she blamed it on being absorbed in finishing her play but realized she'd also been avoiding reminders of Dave Mitchell. Now, she was able to mention the subject of his upcoming marriage in a light-hearted manner that she hoped would announce she was over him.

The best part of the evening was spending a few hours with friends who were unaware of her bleak circumstances, which distracted her from any thoughts about rats or murder. It also felt good to catch up with what was happening in their lives, and she resolved to do a better job of keeping in touch.

Arriving home around eleven, she entered a quiet house. Mrs. MacGyver —no, *Iva,* she reminded herself — must be in bed already. Upstairs, light from the wall sconces reflected off the shiny new lock on her apartment door. Tucked into the doorjamb was an envelope that contained her new key and a short note.

Dear Dana,
Here is your new key. I'm going to keep the master

in a safer place now, so please don't worry.

Philip has moved his things into the third-floor apartment after all, so don't be alarmed if you hear movement up there. He seemed to think he was getting underfoot here with me, even though I assured him he wasn't. He'll be there for the next few days and maybe whenever he comes to Toronto in the future. Obviously, I'm pleased about that..

Have a good night.

Iva

Well, that was interesting. She didn't know how she felt about having someone, anyone, living above her, which was silly because Iva could have decided to rent that space at any time. She'd been accustomed to being the only tenant. *Spoiled!* It shouldn't make any difference to her. All it meant was that she might hear Philip moving around from time to time.

Letting herself into her dark apartment, a flicker of apprehension gripped her, and she chided herself for not having left a small light on. Or had she? She couldn't remember and that added to her unease. On second thought, maybe there was an extra measure of safety in having that upper apartment occupied, even if it was only to be occasionally.

The new locks, combined with Philip's presence on the third floor, produced an unexpected effect: Dana slept soundly for several hours until the early birds sang her awake.

*****

First thing that morning, Dana tried to return Philip's cell phone as she was on her way out to replace her own. Neither he nor his aunt were home, which surprised her as she hadn't heard anyone leaving the house. She also realized she hadn't even heard the anticipated movement from the third floor.

Entering the phone store, the overwhelming display of choices was almost too much for her, and, for a brief moment, she considered turning around and leaving. This reaction stunned her. *What's going on? This should be simple, just picking up a new phone, for heaven's sake. It's not like some major life decision. I don't need anything fancy. No complicated payment plans. What's wrong with me?*

She was relieved when a young woman in a bright t-shirt bearing the store's logo asked if she could help. Pulling herself together, Dana forced herself to concentrate on the task at hand and pushed the disturbing thoughts away. Still, she realized they stemmed from her current situation, and until that changed for the better, if it ever did, they were highly likely to return.

Half an hour later, as she left the store mission accomplished, the utter relief of having her own number again struck her. Such a simple thing brought a sense of returning to normal.

Although her late morning yoga class was diminished by several absences, which included Julie, Brad, and Anna, it nonetheless energized her, and the rest of the day passed uneventfully. Allowing herself to relax somewhat, she could even consider the possibility that whoever had been attempting to terrorize her might have been frightened off by the fact that the police were now involved in an investigation.

That evening, hearing movement above, she climbed to the third-floor landing. She'd never been up there, although she'd been curious. She hadn't wanted to take a chance on Mrs. MacGyver hearing her moving about and thinking she was a snoop. Now that a legitimate opportunity presented itself, simple curiosity impelled her to look around for a moment before knocking. There, on her left, was the servants' staircase leading down to the kitchen.

What an old-fashioned feature, but how convenient, too. Not only would it serve to keep servants out of sight, but a busy mother could climb up to peak at sleeping children —or deal with misbehaving ones —without going through the main rooms, especially if she had guests. Pretty clever!

When Philip answered her knock, she held out his phone and thanked him sincerely.

"I hope I haven't inconvenienced you too much. Although, there's only been the one call for you since you gave it to me Friday night."

"Yes," Philip frowned. "Sorry about that one. I guess it sounded pretty rude."

"You don't need to apologize. Whoever it was seemed to be taken aback that it wasn't you answering. I don't think she expected to hear a woman's voice, and I tried explaining that you'd loaned it to me, but..."

"It wouldn't have mattered what you'd said," he began and then became silent.

After an uncomfortable pause, Dana continued, "Well...thanks again. Good luck with your appointment tomorrow. It is tomorrow, isn't it?"

He nodded. "You haven't had anything else...unusual happen?" he asked hopefully.

"No. Fingers crossed."

"That's good. Heard anything further from the police?"

"No. They must be pretty tied up investigating Shirley's death, of course. That's way more important than the stupid rats. I guess the only thing we might hear from them someday is whether or not the bloody things were rabid."

"Right. I'm sorry about Shirley." He smiled ruefully. "I'm afraid the cupboard is bare or I'd offer you a coffee or something. I haven't even got a can of pop."

"That's okay," Dana rushed to say, suddenly awkward. "It's getting late, anyway. I wanted you to have your phone. Thanks again." She turned and took the stairs back down to her own apartment.

*****

In the confined space of the third-floor apartment, Philip paced restlessly. Time hung heavily on his hands, and his mind overflowed with thoughts and conjectures. He had assumed his return would be routine: visit family, find a job and a place to live, take up more or less where he left off three years ago —with one major exception —he thought. At least she hadn't called back if it was her. Who else could it have been?

His assumption had been wildly wrong. This homecoming was anything but routine. There seemed to be so many decisions and unexpected circumstances like the whole frigging business of the rats. Now, a murder! It was almost beyond comprehension. And Dana... he'd only just met her, but he couldn't stop thinking about her, and worrying about her safety, too.

In need of a distraction, he considered going downstairs and watching a game with his aunt. Normally, he wouldn't have minded not having a television in his room as it had never been important to him. However, at times like this, it would have served a useful purpose such as forcing his mind to concentrate on other topics. No, he'd put his mind to meeting with Guneer Sharma in the morning, then crack open a book and get to bed early. Guneer had mentioned the possibility of a research project overseas, but did he want to go that route again?

His pacing continued.

Chapter Forty-One

Chaotic dreams, populated with familiar faces from her yoga classes and the cast of her play, interrupted Dana's sleep. She woke several times, either drenched in sweat or shivering with cold as Bud pushed her off a building, or Julie ran her over with a streetcar, or Brad dumped her overboard from a sailboat into icy Lake Ontario. In another dream, Detective Small restrained Philip from attempting her rescue.

The morning sun creeping into her bedroom caused her to abandon any further attempts to sleep. She rose and put the kettle on instead. Exhaustion settled in with the hot, soothing drink, and finally her eyes closed once again. An hour later, she woke feeling significantly less tired.

Iva MacGyver caught her on her way out of the house. Dana noted an improvement in the woman's appearance; she seemed more rested.

"Good morning, dear. I don't want to keep you, but if you've got a moment, there's something I wanted to talk to you about."

"Is anything wrong?"

"Oh, no. Everything is fine. As you know, Philip hasn't been home to see his parents yet, and they're quite anxious, of course. He suggested the two of us drive down maybe Thursday or Friday. After what happened last weekend, I'm concerned about you being on your own here."

"Oh, please. Don't worry about me. I'm planning to go home for the long weekend, anyway."

"Oh, well, then. If you won't be here–"

"Go and enjoy a nice visit with your sister. I'll be fine."

"Thank you, dear. I hope you have a lovely weekend, too. I'm sure your parents will be glad to see you."

"Yes. I'm on my way out to find a birthday present for my mother. It's this Sunday. That's my main reason for going."

The woman's face had relaxed with relief on hearing that Dana wouldn't be staying in the house alone. Now she smiled. "Oh, how lovely. Well, good luck."

Dana opened the door and stepped out into a beautiful day. "Thanks. I'll see you later, Iva. Enjoy your day."

*****

Dana first stopped at the library, where she'd ordered some records for an article she was researching for *The Star-Telegram*. Much depended on this, as the new editor she'd been in contact with wasn't easily impressed.

Unfortunately, many types of library records are only available on film and fiche files, and after three hours of speed-reading dozens of them, her over-worked eyes begged for a break. Handing in the material, she packed up her notes, planning to return the next day.

By noon, her rumbling stomach indicated it was time to grab a salad at one of the many sidewalk cafes that had blossomed like early spring flowers almost the minute the snow melted. Sipping a cup of green tea, she was contemplating the menu when a man's voice startled her. "Hey, teacher, would you mind if I joined you?"

"Oh, my goodness, Brad! You made me jump! I was so absorbed in the menu that I didn't see you come in."

"Sorry I startled you. Are you waiting for someone?"

"No. Please, sit down."

"Thanks. So, what are you up to this beautiful morning, or should I say afternoon now?" He glanced at his watch.

"Oh, a little research at the library, and then I have to find a birthday present for my mother."

Brad smiled. "Not always easy, shopping for mothers. I once heard an older woman say that at her stage of life, there was nothing she needed, but if someone felt they wanted to give her a present, it should be something she could eat, burn, or read."

Dana laughed and was amazed at how marvelous that felt. The laughs had been few and far between lately. And no wonder, she thought.

"That's great advice. I'll keep it in mind this afternoon. Food, candles, or books. Hard to go wrong there."

"I agree. It would work for almost anybody, I suppose, not only mothers." As the waitress approached, he asked, "Can I buy you a drink, Dana?"

"No, thanks. I'm fine with this tea, but you go ahead."

When the waitress had brought Brad a dark ale and disappeared with their orders, they sat comfortably people-watching for a few minutes, which was always a relaxing pastime for Dana. As a writer, she often made notes of observations she thought might be useful someday.

"This would be a perfect spot if it weren't for the traffic noise and fumes," Brad commented. "I've never quite got the fascination with eating outdoors on a busy street. You have to wonder what you're inhaling with your food."

"I guess so," Dana said. "I imagine it's supposed to make you think of Paris and their sidewalk cafes, but nothing can ever compare to actually being in Paris and that whole ambience."

"I agree. Even though there's heavy traffic in Paris, too, it seems part of the experience and not an intrusion like it does here."

"I think it's my favourite city, though I haven't exactly seen the world yet. Do you like to travel?"

"I do, but I haven't had the time lately. I did a lot of backpacking after university. Seems like a long time ago."

"Head-hunting keeps you pretty busy?" Recalling the phrase made her smile. His own smile in return was almost sheepish but definitely charming.

"Yeah. The hours are kind of irregular. Lots of stuff comes up last minute, despite the best-laid plans. Can't complain, though. It's all good; business is improving nicely."

"That's great!" Dana suddenly thought about the group at the tennis courts. Should she mention it or not? Why not? she decided and took a deep breath.

"Do you play tennis? I saw you at the courts Sunday. I was on the boardwalk."

"I play *at* tennis. I wouldn't say I *play* tennis." He smiled modestly. "You should have said hi."

"I didn't want to interrupt. There was a group with you, and I didn't know any of the others... except Julie," she paused, waiting.

"I don't know the others, either. I was just passing by when I spotted Julie. Thought I'd see what was up with the club," he paused. "Funny thing, nobody else called her 'Julie'. They all call her 'Joan'. I couldn't figure that one out. You must know why, since you're good friends."

Dumbfounded, Dana asked, "Joan? Are you sure? I've never heard anyone call her that."

"No? I thought you would, being old friends."

"We're not really 'old' friends. I met her about six months ago and have only ever known her as Julie."

They both seemed to contemplate this anomaly for a few minutes. Then Dana recalled, "I had an 'honorary' uncle, if you know what I mean."

Brad nodded his understanding, and she continued, "His wife was my godmother and an 'honorary' aunt. Anyway, all my life he was Uncle Harry, until my godmother died. When he remarried, we were all shocked to hear his new wife call him 'Bill'! It turned out that for all those years he was known to family and friends as 'Harry', he was known as 'Bill' in business! I never figured that one out. There doesn't seem to be any connection between 'Harry' and 'Bill'. Since then, I've heard one or two similar stories about people using two different names. So, it does happen."

"Yeah, it does," Brad conceded. "Some people decide to use their middle name instead of their first. You'd think they'd want some consistency. I mean, I'd want everyone to call me the same thing. It would get too confusing, otherwise."

Dana smiled, "Well, you've piqued my interest! I must ask her about it sometime. Now, I guess I should get on with shopping for something to 'eat, burn, or read'."

"Good luck. And, Dana, do me a favour? Please don't mention to Julie that I'm the one who told you," Brad said. "I wouldn't want her to think I was gossiping about her."

"No problem. It was nice seeing you. I'm glad you spoke to me."

"So am I."

Yes, that certainly is a charming smile, Dana thought, as the waitress appeared with their bills. She reached into her bag for her wallet as Brad pulled his from a back pocket. As he extracted his credit card, something caught her eye. It was so tiny that, at first, she was sure she was seeing things, but when Brad tucked it back in, she knew she was right. Black ribbon. Lace-edged black ribbon!

Chapter Forty-Two

Dana sprang to her feet. She stood immobilized, unable to take her eyes off Brad's wallet, which held the appalling piece of black, lace-edged ribbon. Her face must have revealed her utter panic and fear, for Brad also stood up. "Dana? What is it? You look ill." He leaned forward and reached for her hand. Terrified, she yanked it back.

"What's wrong?"

She looked at him, too stunned to speak. *Brad? Brad and a black ribbon? Brad and the rats? I've got to get out of here!* Her legs betrayed her, and she stumbled, nearly falling as she sank into her chair.

Brad's stricken expression showed his alarm. Dropping to his knees beside her, he repeated his question. "What's wrong?"

Dana couldn't look at him. "You!" she hissed. "You!" She inhaled deeply. It was still difficult to breathe.

"What about me? What did I do?"

"In your wallet!" she whispered hoarsely. "I saw it. It was you! You've got the black ribbon! You put it...you put it...," shaking, she could say no more. She needed to escape, but he was blocking her from going anywhere. "Get out of my way!" Her raised voice drew nervous looks from nearby tables.

"Black ribbon? Oh, the one from Saturday at the Beach Arms? I picked it up after you left. I couldn't figure out why you suddenly got so freaked out. There must be some significance to it, for you to react like that. You're totally spooked again. Why? What does it mean?"

Dana shoved him aside and raced off. She fought her way past the other tables, unaware of the other diners taking in the scene with confusion, just as she was unaware Brad had thrown down money to cover the bill.

"Dana! Wait! Wait!"

She ran along Queen St., not caring which direction she was heading in. The only clear thing in her mind was that she had to get away from Brad. She faintly heard him calling her name, but soon that stopped. She didn't dare look behind to see how close he might be; she had to keep running. Where could she hide? How long could she keep going? Fear pumped adrenaline through her body and gave her strength.

As she approached the next intersection, a streetcar came to a stop and opened its doors. A few passengers descended from the rear doors, but no one was boarding. Dana cut in front of a car that came to a stop on the side street which formed the intersection. Ignoring the blast from its horn, she focused on those open doors and a clear path to them. Right before they closed, she leaped on board and, grabbing onto an upright pole, bent over to suck in big gasps of air.

"Geez, lady!" the streetcar driver gave her an insulted look. "I saw you coming. I would have waited. The light's red, anyway. You're gonna give yourself a heart attack."

Dana could only nod in reply as she gasped for breath. Reaching inside her bag, she pulled out her transit card and flashed it for him.

Collapsing into a seat, Dana tried to gather her wits when she realized the car was heading in the opposite direction to home. At the second stop, she got off and stood on the other side of the street, praying another car would come along soon. She hoped Brad hadn't seen her board and followed her.

An old bank building nearby provided a recessed entrance in which she could hide. From her vantage point, she could watch for the next approaching streetcar and scan the opposite side of the street for Brad.

When the next car arrived, she searched the crowds for any sign of him before bolting from her hiding place and into the car at the last second. She grabbed hold of an overhead bar for balance as the car lurched forward, nearly pitching her off her feet. Rather than take a seat, she remained standing so she could scan the area for any signs of trouble. When she got off close to her street, she ran until she had reached the safety of Mrs. MacGyver's front porch and slammed the front door shut behind her.

Brad! It's Brad! I have to call the police right away!

Chapter Forty-Three

Safely back in her apartment, Dana paced and paced as she tried to calm herself, but her heart refused to slow down. She was thankful no one appeared to be home downstairs. When she had raced inside and slammed the door, there'd been no response and, therefore, no need for explanations. *Lucky!*

The clock on her iPod dock read two-thirty. *Shoot! I've got a class at four. I can't possibly do it. I'm way too shaky. And what if Brad shows up? He will. I know it. There's no way I can go.*

She called the studio. On the first ring, a low, gruff male voice answered, "Yoga." *Valery!* Her boss. Although Dana had never spoken to him on the phone before, she recognized the impatient tone. "Valery? It's Dana Williams. I'm sorry, but I can't make my four o'clock class. I hate doing this to you last minute, but I'm not well. Do you think you could get one of the others to cover for me?"

"No way!" he yelled. "Whatsa matter with you? You couldn't let me know sooner? You getcha sorry selfin here— now! No way I can get replacement this late."

Dana couldn't believe he was yelling at her. *What's the matter with you, you jerk?* "I'm truly sorry, Valery, but it simply is not possible. Can you please try to find someone? Otherwise, maybe Nora or someone can make some calls to cancel. She could probably reach most of the class if she started now."

"Nora's a no-show. She didn't call. Why you think I'm here? What is this, an epidemic? I got better things to do than answer phone." Anger made his accent more pronounced, but his message was clear. "You want keep job, you come here!" He slammed the receiver.

Darn! Now what? She couldn't afford to lose this job. She'd have to go. Maybe if she could reach Detective Small in time, he could find Brad and bring him in for questioning before she got to the studio. She realized this was highly unlikely, but it was worth a try.

Dialing the detective's number, Dana prayed, "Please, please, pick up." She couldn't imagine what she'd do if this didn't work, and Brad came to the class looking for her.

*****

"Good. You're here." A scowling Valery stood by the picture window in the reception area. He peered at her. "You don't look sick. What you trying to pull, eh?" Valery's anger was a frightening thing to see. Dana, already shaky, was thoroughly freaked.

Scurrying past him, she tried to explain, "I may look okay, but I'm not."

"Good enough to teach class. You smart girl. You came in. I catch that Nora, she's fired. You try this again, you fired! Got that?" he thundered. Dana turned around to look at him. "I got it, but I'm not well," she insisted, perhaps unwisely.

Through the window, something across the street caught her attention. She observed Detective Small getting out of the passenger side of a parked car and stopping a man on the sidewalk. The man turned to face him. Brad!

"What you staring at? You got class. Go! Go!" Valery growled as he turned to look, too, but he didn't know Small or Brad, so he didn't catch on.

"Hold on a minute," she said with remarkable bravery and continued to watch as Brad got into the back seat of the cruiser. Relief flooded over her. That took care of him —for a while, anyway.

"Go!" Valery yelled.

Dana turned and walked to her locker, none too steady on her feet, and swayed momentarily. *I hope this is the end of it. What the heck was Brad up to, anyway? I barely know him. Why would he have it in for me? Maybe he's just one of those sick stalkers, and there's no rhyme or reason to it. I simply happen to be the lucky one he's fixated on, that's all. If that's what it is, though, I'm going to have to move. I can't stick around and put up with any more of this.*

She was truly unwell now, but for the sake of keeping her job, she put on a happy face and prepared for her class. *I'll have to find a new job, too.* This was disappointing; she had liked working here and the people she'd met. Well, most of them, anyway. She could cross off Brad and Valery!

*****

At six o'clock her phone rang. "Hi, Dana, I didn't get a chance to talk to you after class. You took off like a bat out of hell!"

"Hi, Julie. Sorry, I'm not feeling well. I tried to call in sick, but Valery threatened to fire me if I didn't 'get my sorry self' down there. His exact words. Such a nice guy!"

"What a jerk! He creeps me out. I don't like being around him at all."

"Yeah, well, at least he's hardly ever there. He said Nora didn't show up today. Didn't even call in sick, and that's why he was in such a foul mood. Maybe she's sick, too."

"Is it a cold? Do you need anything? Can I pick up something for you?"

"Oh, no, thanks. I need to get to bed early. I should be better tomorrow. Talk to you later." Dana was anxious to cut the call short. She didn't have the energy to be evasive with Julie, and she couldn't bring herself to get into the whole story about Brad at that moment.

"Well, call if you need anything. Hope you feel better soon."

Dana wandered into the kitchen, feeling at loose ends. Eating was the last thing she felt like doing, but she found herself taking a can of soup out of the cupboard. As it simmered on the stove, she inhaled its delicious aroma of tomato and basil. Maybe she did need to eat, after all. It would soothe her stomach, if not her nerves.

Thinking of food brought back the disaster with Brad at the restaurant. As her mind replayed that movie, she watched herself running off, terrified.

I wonder what's happening with him and Detective Small? I hope they can keep him there for a long time. What if they can't find any evidence against him, though? What do I do next?

She was so fearful that just thinking about Brad made her nauseated. The tomato soup didn't sit well with her, so she put it in the fridge and turned on the television for a distraction. In a straw basket beside her chair lay a quilt block that she hadn't picked up since moving in. It was the last remnant of her relationship with Dave Mitchell, during which she'd passed through a domestic phase and thought she'd enjoy learning how to make a quilt. The very idea was laughable now. Idly, she picked up the block in its frame, a threaded needle still attached, and made a few uneven stitches before putting it down again.

On her television, the weather forecaster scribbled

numbers and arrows on a map. She was an extremely animated young woman with long, slim legs. Her enthusiastic smile was misleading; she was predicting a rainy, long weekend. Then, as though she'd suddenly realized this was not good news, she allowed herself a pretty frown. Dana sighed. Well, that figured; sunny days during the workweek and rain for the holiday weekend. It wouldn't be much fun up north with her parents. *Mom's birthday present*! She'd completely forgotten, especially after Brad.

The ringing phone made her jump. She leaped up and grabbed it from a small table by the door, where she had dumped her bag.

"Dana? Detective Small here. Thought you'd want to know about Brad Wallenski."

"Wallenski? Is that his name?"

"You didn't know?"

"I guess I must have seen it on the class list at one time, but I'd forgotten."

"Does it mean anything to you?"

"No. I don't think I've ever known anyone with that name...if that's his real name. I guess you would have checked that out, though."

"Yeah, we checked him out all right. He's clean. We let him go."

"You let him go?" she shrieked. "How could you do that? I saw the black ribbon in his wallet! It has to be him!"

"We don't believe so. We ran a thorough background check on him. He's clean, and he is who he says he is. His only mistake was picking up that ribbon when you left the restaurant. He's not even sure why he did it, except it was obvious that something about it had upset you."

Dana couldn't believe what she was hearing. She'd been so certain. "Are you sure? What if he's fooled you somehow, sucked you in? Isn't that possible? Couldn't you search his house?" *Desperation talking here*, she realized. At the same time, she couldn't completely accept what Small was saying.

"There's no valid reason to search his house. We'd never get a warrant. No, as I said, he's clean. I know it's not a comforting thought, but whoever did these things is still out there. I'm sorry."

"I'm sorry, too, but thank you," she added, dejected.

"You did the right thing. It's good you called. Keep in touch, okay?"

She noted the change in tone. She'd come to expect Small's usually brusque manner, but he was trying to be reassuring. She thanked him again, more sincerely this time, and promised to keep in touch. She hoped there would be no need to keep her promise.

Chapter Forty-Four

Well, that stirred up some excitement! Well done, Brad! I couldn't have planned it better if I'd tried. Looked good on you, boy, sitting in that cruiser. Well, maybe not good... you were totally pissed off. Kinda spoiled those pretty boy looks a bit. And that detective! Thinks he's pretty sharp, the loser. Looked so full of himself, like he'd nailed the biggest criminal since Jack the Ripper. What a joke. Wish I could've seen the look on his ugly mug when he had to let you go. What a jerk!

Now that you're out, I guess Dana's pretty spooked again. Probably thought she was good to go with you at the cop shop. No, not quite so fast, Dana. There's more fun to come. You wait and see. Unless you decide to "get out of Dodge," of course —or get out of Toronto, in this case. LOL. I'm a little surprised you haven't yet. Maybe you need a little more incentive. Yeah, that's what you need, a little more incentive. Let's see, what would be fun?

*****

A knock at the door roused Dana out of her reverie. She'd been channel surfing but not paying attention. *Now what?* She was annoyed, almost indignant, at the interruption. Suddenly chagrined, she worried it could be Iva. Something had to be wrong for her to knock.

Philip stood on her threshold, wearing an uncomfortable expression and not quite looking at her, like a little boy sent to apologize for throwing a ball through a neighbour's window. Despite this unusual demeanour, the rest of him looked rather appealing. She liked the easy way he carried himself in his neatly pressed khaki slacks, light blue shirt, and navy jacket. He looked freshly shaven and ready for a business meeting or special occasion. He smelled great, too; a hint of citrus and something else she couldn't identify tickled her nostrils.

"Sorry to bother you. My aunt insisted I come up," he explained in a rush, then halted as his eyes came to rest on her face. "What's wrong? Something's happened, hasn't it? Dana, tell me!"

Boy, I must look like crap to get a reaction like that!

"Just a bad day," she tossed off. "Nothing to worry about."

The way he twisted his mouth and brow, along with the obvious doubt in his eyes, made it clear he didn't believe her.

"I'm sorry. It's obviously not a good time." He turned to leave as if relieved to have an excuse to escape.

"No, wait," she said. "You said something about Iva. Is she all right?"

Philip stopped to answer, "She's fine, but she's tired. I took her out for dinner, and we were supposed to go to the Jays' game, but she said she wasn't up to it. She wants to go to bed early. That's why I came up, and...well, I can tell it's not a good idea."

"Do you need help? Is there something I can do?" She felt terrible. All of this drama in her life was taking its toll on Iva.

"It's just that she bought these tickets as a surprise for me, and now she can't go. She thought maybe you'd like to take her place. In fact, she insisted I ask you, but I can see you're not doing so great, either. Besides, it's already started, and we'd miss at least two innings by the time we got there, not that it matters much."

Something in his expression told Dana that it did matter; Philip would like to see the game. *Oh, what the heck! If it'll make Iva happy, too, I'll go. I owe it to her. I might be able to salvage a miserable day.*

"Give me ten minutes, and I'll meet you downstairs," she said, attempting a smile. "I think I'd enjoy that. Please tell Iva thank you."

It was as if the sun had burst through the dreariest of days. The look on his face was one of such joy that she thought if nothing else good happened that day, his happiness at that moment would be enough to redeem it.

*****

Dana changed out of her yoga pants into a decent pair of jeans, a cotton shirt, and a warm jacket. The days might be warming up, but the nights were still chilly. In less than the promised ten minutes, she was downstairs where Philip waited by the front door, truck keys in hand. As soon as she appeared, he opened the door for her, and they were on their way.

"This is great," he said. "Thanks for coming. Aunt Iva is pleased her ticket isn't going to waste, and I'm pleased to be going to a game. It's been years, and it's always more fun watching with someone else."

His excitement was almost endearing. "I'm glad I could make everybody happy," Dana replied. "I'm looking forward to it, too. I have to warn you, though, I know next to nothing about the game."

"That's okay. I think you'll have fun anyway. There's a great ambience at a game that you can't get from television. You know, the hometown crowd and the fans around you, the mascots, the hotdogs, the Jumbotron. I could go on, but I don't want to bore you when you were nice enough to come."

"About all I know is the hot dogs...and The Seventh Inning Stretch," she smiled, taken with his boyish enthusiasm. "Maybe you can teach me some of the finer points."

It was a short drive to the stadium, and most of the parking lots were full. They drove up and down one-way streets before finally locating a spot several blocks away in an underground lot beneath an office tower.

Philip said, "I can't believe this. Most of the lots I remember parking in before are gone! We should have taken public transit." They jogged to the stadium, and by the time they dropped into their seats, breathless, it was the middle of the fourth inning.

With the evening fair and dry, the roof was open to the stars. Dana craned her neck to take in everything. She had to admit that with the enormous flashing screen, the excitement of the announcers, the high-decibel level of the cheering fans, and the tantalizing aromas of beer and hotdogs, the air hung with a sense of magical expectation.

The Jays were up, and she and Philip settled in to follow the action. Dana already felt lifted from the traumatic effects of her afternoon. She was glad she came.

Chapter Forty-Five

Even the hotdog Philip bought her from the vendor tasted especially flavourful. When he realized she hadn't had dinner, he'd been remorseful and bought not only the most enormous hotdog and a beer, but also a tray of gooey nachos piled high with sticky cheese. Then he grabbed some decadent ice cream bars from another vendor for dessert. He kept asking if she'd like another dog or another beer, as if he felt obligated to fill her up.

They shared the nachos, which were not easy to eat. All that gooey cheese became stringy and hard to separate, making their mouths and fingers a sticky mess. At one point, Philip took his napkin and delicately wiped cheese from Dana's cheek. The tenderness of his gesture touched her deeply and brought a smile to her lips. How long had it been since she'd felt a man's gentle touch? Too long, she thought, struck by how much she missed that intimacy. His eyes lingered on hers for a moment, and his smile made her wonder if he could read her mind.

During the Seventh-Inning Stretch, an enthusiastic and fit duo in tracksuits led the dance moves and the Jays' song from the roofs of the teams' dugouts. Dana and Philip laughed as they joined in on the boisterous fun. The screams of "Let's go, Blue Jays! Let's play ball!" were deafening. The Jays had a slim lead, and the beer had emboldened many of the fans around them.

As the shouts and cheers died down, Philip mentioned the upcoming holiday weekend. He was looking forward to seeing his folks at last and checking out his weekend place on a nearby lake. "I've missed it these past three years. It's nothing fancy, but it's peaceful," he said with an unmistakable wistfulness. "There's something about trees and water that restores me. I didn't find that in Africa, so it must have to do with home."

"And memories, too, I think," Dana replied. "I have great memories of my family's cottage. My sister and I practically lived in the water. We didn't come out until we were dragged out, and by then our bodies would be shriveled up like prunes. We loved being in the water so much, we'd go swimming in the rain! I remember feeling so… joyful! There was a sense of complete abandon, sticking my tongue out to catch raindrops. That used to seem so special." She shook her head at the memory and fell into her own wistful moment.

"And it doesn't anymore? Does your family still have the cottage?"

"Oh, yes! My parents live there year-round now, but it's not the same. Don't get me wrong, it's still wonderful, but in a more grown-up way, I guess. It's a long time since I went swimming in the rain."

Philip smiled. "I remember doing that, too. I guess a lot of things change when we grow up. Life becomes so much more complicated."

"I almost forgot!" Dana interjected. "Today was your interview at the university. How did that go?" Then, embarrassed at her forwardness, "I'm sorry. I shouldn't have asked. It's none of my business."

"No, no. Don't apologize. It was fine. They had a couple of things to offer. There's another posting overseas if I want that kind of project again, or there's one that would have me commuting between Guelph and Toronto. Two days there and three days here, or vice versa. Pretty flexible."

"That's great." Suddenly emboldened, she asked, "Which one do you think you'll take?" She held her breath as she awaited an answer. As soon as he'd said 'overseas', her heart had dropped into her stomach. She realized she'd be more than a little disappointed to see him leave.

"I'm not quite sure, but I don't think I want to turn around and go overseas again so soon."

She couldn't help grinning. The rest of the game was enjoyable, even though the Jays lost. Spirits remained high among the eternally optimistic fans. Dana decided, not for the first time, that baseball was long and slow. Maybe these days the extra hoopla, contests, and gimmicks were necessary to keep the stands full. While admitting the finer points and strategies of the game were lost on her, she understood that for a real student of the game, they would be what made the watching worthwhile. Philip had occasionally pointed out some of those strategies during the evening, but not to the point of overwhelming her or becoming a bore. He seemed more than happy just to have her company.

They grabbed coffee and tea and joined the crowded masses jostling their way out of the stadium. Everyone seemed in a desperate rush to get to their cars. Dana wondered why because once in their vehicles, there was an interminable wait to get out of the parking lots. She and Philip had time to sip their drinks leisurely in the truck while waiting in their own lineup for the exit.

Cruising along the expressway, she found herself thinking how cozy this was, two people discussing upcoming plans for a pleasant long weekend. In the comfortable space of the truck's cab, she felt insulated from the rest of the world whizzing past on the fast track, heading to who-knows-what job or party.

She was reminded of many such times when, after a long winter, simply getting into a car on a spring day made her long for the open road, for the exhilaration of just taking off, not caring where she was headed. It was the lure of adventure combined with the sense of freedom brought on by shedding winter coats and boots. Add in the unmistakable scent of fresh earth, newly released from its heavy covering of snow, and the pull was irresistible.

She believed if Philip were to turn to her at that moment and say, "Let's forget about going home. What would you think about taking off for the east coast? Nova Scotia, Peggy's Cove, Cape Breton? Right now, no strings, no looking back!" she would have said, "You're on!"

As they parked the car in the drive beside the house, that sense of magic lingered. Opening the front door as quietly as possible, they entered without speaking and listened a moment for sounds of activity in Iva's apartment. There were none; she must be asleep. Smiling at each other like co-conspirators in some college prank, they tiptoed up the stairs.

Dana put her key in the lock. Philip leaned over and whispered, "I know this sounds mean, but I'm kind of glad Aunt Iva passed up the game." He smiled as he added, "I wonder if she ever did intend to go? This might have been her little scheme all along. I wouldn't put it past her."

It occurred to Dana that he could be right. She could imagine Iva MacGyver plotting something like this. "Well, if she did, I'm glad. It was a wonderful night. Thank you."

Philip brought his hands up to cup her face and brushed her lips with the softest of kisses. "No, thank you!" he whispered, before swiftly turning to take the stairs up to the third floor.

Dana stood as still as a stone, watching him go until she heard his door open and close above her. Then, she turned her key and went inside, knowing sleep would prove elusive that night as she tried to make sense of the myriad of tangled thoughts and emotions weaving through her heart and mind.

Chapter Forty-Six

The predicted rains came Wednesday morning, not as a gentle spring mist, but a deluge. The wind picked up, too, turning umbrellas inside out and rendering them useless. Dana left the house early, determined to find that elusive birthday present for her mother and spend more research time at the library. Since the story she was working on involved events in the same neighbourhood one hundred years earlier, the local branch's historical collection was proving invaluable.

Bundled up against the weather with rain boots, umbrella, and windbreaker, she carried her laptop bag over one shoulder and hoped to keep its contents reasonably dry. For this reason, she hopped on a streetcar and rode the ten blocks. The streets were fairly deserted. School was in, most people were at work, and it wasn't a day for window shopping or outdoor patios.

When the rear doors opened for her to step off across the street from the library, Dana noticed a newly-opened shop. She was reasonably certain it hadn't been there the previous week. *High Tea* the freshly painted name on the squeaky-clean window proclaimed. A display of antique teapots, cups, and saucers made a colourful display behind the glass. Intrigued, she entered and was instantly assailed by exotic, spicy aromas of the teas displayed in identical glass jars whose labels read like the itinerary for a trip around the world: Darjeeling from India, Chinese Oolongs, Rooibos from South Africa. Then there were the blends: Blueberry, Strawberry, Earl Grey, Lady Grey. Herbal tisanes of every possible flavour and mixture abounded. Inside an old-fashioned glass display case, the most enticing selection of fancy cakes and cookies Dana had ever seen sat on paper doilies, next to Melton Mowbray meat pies and Cornish Pasties.

"Good morning," greeted a friendly woman behind the counter. "Lovely weather for ducks."

"It sure is," Dana replied, dripping all over the newly tiled floor. "I don't think I've noticed this shop before. Have you just opened?"

"We have. Saturday was our official grand opening! Are you looking for something in particular?"

"I was just curious," Dana said truthfully. "But now I see you may have exactly what I've been looking for. Do you have gift boxes, or could you put one together?"

"Absolutely! We have gift certificates, too, and we have a menu for tea and scones or sandwiches." She pointed out a few small tables with pretty cloths and fresh flowers, which Dana had not yet noticed.

"Perfect! I'll remember that. Right now, I'll choose a selection of teas, if you'll show me what you can recommend."

Twenty minutes later, Dana had purchased a pretty box bearing an interesting assortment of teas she thought her mother would enjoy. She was pleased with her choices. The woman carefully wrapped the box in a sturdy bag, and Dana thanked her for her help. "I'm sure I'll be back, and I'll mention you to my friends."

As she turned to leave, the shop's door opened and Anna Novak blew in, brushing water off her shoulders and her smart rain hat.

"Dana! Hello!" she smiled. "Isn't this a great place? I was in on Saturday, and I had to come back."

"It's lovely. I bought a gift box of their teas for my mom."

"That's nice. Listen, I came in for a cup of tea and one of their amazing scones. Will you join me? You've never tasted anything like their cranberry-lemon scones! My treat."

There was something insistent in Anna's manner. Dana couldn't put a finger on it, but she felt as if the woman was almost pleading. Maybe she simply wanted company on a dreary day.

"Sure, that'd be nice. I'm actually headed for the library to do some work, but I got sidetracked coming in here."

"Great! I'll place our orders. What kind of tea would you like? I love their Lady Grey."

"I'll have the same then. The scone sounds good, too. Thanks, Anna."

She took a seat at one of the small tables, placing the bag containing her mother's gift and the one holding her laptop on an extra chair beside it. A moment later, Anna joined her, removing her coat and hanging it on a hook by the door.

"Can I hang yours up for you?" she asked. Dana hadn't planned to remove hers. This would be a quick cup of tea and she'd be off, but the room was warm and might get stuffy, she realized, so she removed her coat and handed it to Anna.

Pointing to the gift box of teas, Anna said, "I think your mother will love those. Are they a late Mother's Day gift or some other occasion?"

"Her birthday."

As if someone had flipped a switch, Anna's mood changed. Her face seemed to darken with a slight scowl. "You're lucky to still have your mother."

"I know. It sounds like you don't. Has she been gone long?"

"Several years now. My father, too."

"I'm sorry."

"It's okay. You get used to it, but I think it's harder when you're an only child."

Dana didn't know what to say.

"Do you have siblings?"

"One sister."

"You're lucky. Are you close?"

Dana squirmed. For some reason she couldn't define, Anna's questions were making her uncomfortable. Nodding her head in answer, she changed the subject. "I missed you in class the other day."

"I was out of town, but I'll be back. I enjoy yoga," Anna replied in a monotone. Dana thought, something seemed off and wondered what was going on.

"That's good. It's a nice group of people in that class." She immediately thought of Brad. *Oh please, don't let him come back. He could still be the one, despite what the police think. I couldn't handle it if he showed up. If it turns out he's not the one, I'd be so embarrassed. He'll know I had to be the one who called the police.*

Their order appeared on a silver tray with doilies, and Anna seemed to snap out of her strange mood. There was a pot of tea to share, along with small jugs of cream and milk, a dish of lemon slices, and another holding colourfully decorated sugar cubes. Two plump scones full of cranberries with pats of butter on the side sat on plates with lacey paper doilies. As the waitress placed cutlery and two dainty china teacups before them, Dana smiled at her.

"Thank you. It's a long time since I've been served anything this nicely. It sure beats take-out in a paper cup!" To Anna, she said, "It feels like a special occasion!"

"It does, doesn't it? That's why I wanted to come back today. By the way, I enjoyed that night at the Beach Arms, too. Getting to know Elaine and Julie, especially. It was fun." Her look became more sober. "Until you took ill, that is. What do you think happened? It seemed to be so sudden. Do you think it was the food? Or your drink?"

"I don't think so." Dana didn't want to say more, but Anna persisted.

"So, it had to be something to do with that piece of black lace ribbon. I assumed as much the minute I saw Julie's face. You both looked stunned, and you didn't want to touch it. The way you reacted, you'd have thought it was a poisonous snake or something!"

"It's not a big deal, Anna. I was tired, and I overreacted."

Anna clearly did not believe her but, thankfully, changed the subject. They tucked into the scones, which were indeed as remarkable as promised.

Eventually, Anna mentioned the upcoming long weekend. She was thinking about going somewhere but said much depended on the weather forecast. Dana said that no matter the weather, she'd be going to visit her parents. "Where do they live?"

"Up north in Bracebridge."

"Bracebridge? I love that whole Muskoka area! It's so beautiful. Are you going up alone?" Dana's surprise at the question must have been obvious. Anna apologized, "Sorry, that's my awkward way of asking if there's someone in your life, but it's none of my business."

Dana hesitated to respond, and Anna rushed on. "I didn't mean to be nosey. It's just that I saw you with a great-looking guy the other day at the pizza place. I had the impression you were together."

"Well, we're not. He's my landlady's nephew. He was doing me a favour that day."

"Really?" Anna sounded doubtful. "I saw the way he was looking at you. I thought there must be something between you."

Dana noted an almost imperceptible change again in

Anna's tone. It was hard to define but again made her uncomfortable. She also noticed a slightly hard edge to the brilliant smile. "Where were you sitting?" she asked. "I didn't see you there."

"Oh, I wasn't at the restaurant. I was waiting for the light at the corner. You were at an outside table, so I just happened to see you."

Dana thought about that. The corner with the light was close to the restaurant, but not that close. Anna likely saw her with Philip, but it would have been impossible to notice how he was looking at her from the corner. If indeed, there *was* a "way" he'd been looking at her!

"As I said, he's my landlady's nephew and just a friend." She took the last sip of her tea and rose to gather her things. "Thanks for the tea, Anna. I enjoyed it, but I must head over to the library and get to work. I'll see you at the next class. Have a great weekend."

Her sudden departure flustered Anna, who spoke rapidly. "Oh, that's too bad you have to rush off, but I understand. What are you working on?"

Dana struggled to get into her still-wet raincoat, which remained chilly and damp even on the inside. "It's an article that has a bit to do with the history of this area," she replied. Gathering her bags, she left the shop and waved at Anna who stood to watch her cross the street.

Chapter Forty-Seven

Once Dana was settled in at an empty library table, she spread out her laptop and papers across the surface. Before diving into her research, she sat back for a moment and thought about the scene in the tearoom. Something was definitely a bit off about her interaction with Anna, but Dana was unsure what it was. She had a knack for reading people, but now she felt unsure of her initial assessment.

Anna was an attractive, sociable person. The others would agree with that —especially Brad. But was there something else, something deeper and perhaps darker that Dana had caught a glimpse of? It was an unsettling thought, and perhaps she was reading more into it than she should.

Later that afternoon, Dana arranged with an agency to rent a car for the weekend. She'd pick it up and leave Friday after her late-morning class. Next, she texted Caroline to remind her sister that if she changed her mind, they could head up north together. Taking the coward's way out, she also texted her mother. She wasn't in the mood to be quizzed about how her earlier call to Caroline had gone.

Checking for messages, she noticed she'd missed a call late the night before. The timestamp read after midnight when her phone was off, and she had been lying awake thinking about Philip.

The voice mail began with a chirpy, *"Hi, Dana!"* She froze. The same tinny, mechanical voice continued. *"Good game, wasn't it? Too bad the Jays lost, but you looked like you were having fun, anyway. Sorry I missed you. You enjoy the rest of your evening, now. Oh, rats! How could you when I've gone and spoiled it for you? Goodnight, Dana."* The last words were followed by a chuckle, then the line went dead.

The phone slipped out of Dana's grip and landed in her lap. She stared at it as if it might suddenly spring to life and bite her, or at the very least ring again. *This creep is still watching me. Why? And how does he have my new number?* Furious, she punched in *69. *Great! A blocked number. I should have known.*

*****

Detective Small answered Dana's call. He took note of the message she'd received but also made it clear how low of a priority it held on his list. "We're up to our eyeballs with the Shirley Fox case right now.

"Of course, I'm sorry, but I thought you'd want to know. Have you made any progress in Shirley's ... case?" She'd almost said Shirley's murder but couldn't form the words. Nor could she stop her stressed-out mind from conjuring up frequent, gruesome images of how the unfortunate woman died.

"It's still early days. Are you going ahead with your rehearsal tomorrow night? If so, we'll swing by. We still need to interview most of the cast and crew."

Since no plans had been announced for Shirley's funeral that week, Bud had decided to carry on with the rehearsal. She supposed there hadn't been a funeral yet because the body hadn't been released to the family. *I guess that's Elvis. Poor guy.*

"Yes, we're carrying on. If there had been a funeral this week, we'd have cancelled, of course, but Bud thought it might be good for us all to be together. It's supposed to be kind of therapeutic, I guess." She paused before pressing further. "Have you learned anything at all? Any clues?"

"Nothing conclusive. But there's always a chance someone in the cast may have seen or overheard something without realizing its significance."

Dana prayed he was right. She didn't think she could hold on to her dwindling sanity much longer. Going up north for the weekend was looking more and more appealing. She couldn't wait for Friday morning to roll around.

When her phone rang, she decided not to answer it. *Let the creep leave a message again. I'll save it for the police.*

An hour later, curiosity overcame her repulsion. She plucked up her courage to listen to the crazy rant. "Dana, it's Bud. Look, if you're up to it, we might as well carry on with dinner at Trattoria tomorrow night. I made the reservation last weekend and with everything that's happened, I forgot to cancel. I could pick you up at five. Let me know if that works for you. Take care."

Bud! She'd completely forgotten. He'd mentioned Trattoria when they met Officer Green at the church on Saturday. *Oh, drats!* Dana ran her fingers through her hair. The last thing she felt up to was having dinner with Bud, but she didn't want to let him down, either. What could she say? She'd try suggesting next week or ask for a rain check. By then, this nightmare could be over. She prayed it would. *Please, let it be over.*

Bud's disappointment was obvious when Dana returned his call and begged off dinner. However, he was somewhat mollified when she suggested they make plans for the following week.

"I've had a crappy day, Bud, and you have to admit it's been a horrendous week. Plus, I'm leaving Friday morning to see my parents. I hope you understand."

"Well, naturally I'm disappointed, but I understand. We'll plan on it for next week. See you tomorrow night. Seven o'clock. Take care."

If she'd thought she would be relieved after making the call, she'd been proven wrong. Somehow, she felt even more stressed. Throw in a truckload of guilt, too. A completely useless emotion but almost impossible to avoid.

She wasn't used to praying, but if ever there was a time for it, this was it. The police needed all the help they could get Thursday night, most of all for Elvis's sake, but for everyone else, too. There had to be an end to all this uncertainty, even if Shirley's killer didn't turn out to be someone in the cast or crew. No one would be able to breathe easily until this was over.

Chapter Forty-Eight

The rain continued into Thursday, which didn't help Dana's mood. She spent most of the day at home working on the historical article she was assigned. For the first time, it was a relief not to have a class at the yoga studio, something she'd always enjoyed. How had it come to pass that she was now so uptight around a couple of her students? It wasn't only Brad she was nervous about now; she'd added Anna to her list. Realistically, however, she knew her tormentor could be anyone.

Around five o'clock, when she was preparing to leave for rehearsal, there was a knock on her door. Dana opened the door to see Iva's merry eyes sparkling as she held out a long, narrow white carton tied with a jaunty red bow. Her excitement was palpable.

"This is for you. Florist's delivery."

"For me? I can't imagine who. It's not my birthday or anything."

"I'm sure there'll be a card inside. Maybe you have a secret admirer! And good luck tonight. I hope all goes well." Her face turned more somber as she added, "After everything that's happened."

"Thanks. I hope so, too. It should be fine. That detective is going to be there to talk to everybody."

"That's good. I feel better knowing that. Good night."

"Good night. Oh, Iva! I meant to say thank you for thinking of me last night. I enjoyed the Jays' game. It's too bad you weren't up to it after all of your planning."

Was it her imagination, or was Iva looking a bit sheepish? "Oh my, you're welcome. I'm glad you were able to go. I'm sure watching the game with someone younger was much more fun for Philip."

Dana thought Philip's surmising might be correct, and Iva had carried off a little scheme. Thanking her again, she closed the door and carried the florist's box to her coffee table where she puzzled over it. Her sense of unease returned, and with it, a reluctance to open the box. *You can't sit and look at it forever. It's not as if you haven't seen a dead rat before. Take a few deep breaths and steel yourself. How bad can it be?* Loathe to touch the box any more than necessary, she retrieved a pair of vinyl gloves from the kitchen sink, then felt foolish putting them on. *It's probably from Bud. It's the thoughtful kind of thing he'd do after rehearsals got off to such a terrible start last week.*

The red bow slipped off, and Dana lifted the lid. A dozen salmon-pink roses lay resplendent amongst delicate baby's breath and some feathery greenery. She gasped in delight and relief. *I was right!*

She peeled off the gloves to open the envelope. Good gravy, vinyl gloves! Talk about paranoia.

Dana,

Thanks for being such a good sport. I hope we can do it again.

Philip

Philip? The message was so unexpected that it took a moment for it to compute. *Philip!* Dana smiled and sat back to absorb it all. *Roses from Philip. How sweet.*

She couldn't wait to thank him and hurried to the window to see if his truck was in the driveway. When it wasn't, her disappointment was profound. She'd have to catch him later.

Arranging the slender stems with their delicate blooms in her only vase was the perfect antidote for her disappointment. By the time she was on her way to rehearsal, her mood was so light-hearted she almost skipped down the stairs and danced out into the rain.

Chapter Forty-Nine

In the church's dimly lit vestibule, Dana shook the rain from her umbrella, removed her boots, and left her wet raincoat hanging alongside other soggy gear belonging to the cast and crew. She hesitated a moment before entering the auditorium. So much had happened since she'd been there Saturday morning. Shirley's body being found later that day was at the forefront of her mind.

The contrast in the atmosphere to that of the first rehearsal was striking. That night, the buzz of excitement and anticipation had been thrilling; tonight, everyone was subdued. The previous boisterous talk and laughter had morphed into strained whispers. People were frightened and in mourning. The news had been an overwhelming shock to everyone. Frankly, she was surprised to see so many had returned.

Bud walked out from stage left and spotted her. With a wave, he made his way down a set of steps and hurried over to her.

"Welcome back!" He kissed her on both cheeks. "We're in good shape backstage. I don't foresee any problems. Everyone's here and ready to go." Despite this hearty greeting, there was a tautness to his face and solemnity in his eyes, which betrayed the fact that behind his encouraging words lay a great deal of worry.

Before she could reply, Dana caught a glimpse of

Detective Small and another man she didn't recognize going through the kitchen doors. Bud noticed her look.

"He brought along a sidekick. They promised to be discreet if that's possible," he explained with a shrug and a grimace to indicate his doubt about this. "The plan is to interview a few people in the kitchen and poke around. I doubt they'll learn anything from this group. I only hope they don't freak anyone out."

"I'm so sorry about all of this, Bud. I hope it's all over soon."

"No need for you to apologize," he said, distracted by something across the room. "You had nothing to do with Shirley's death." He turned to her with sudden concern. "Nothing else has happened to *you*, has it?"

She shook her head. There was no point in telling him about the most recent phone call or the black ribbon at the Beach Arms. He'd become more adamant that she move out of her apartment or find a way to protect herself.

"Well, thank heaven for that. We should get started."

*****

Shirley's absence was most notable during the coffee break. Another crew member had taken charge of refreshments and set the coffee and treats out on a table. People grabbed a coffee with barely a word spoken, then disappeared in groups of two or three into the far corners of the auditorium. They whispered to each other and glanced around at the others, as if sizing up who among them might be a killer.

Bud, conversing with a crew member, stopped mid-sentence to glare across the room at someone. Following his gaze, she was surprised to see Philip by the door. His eyes searched the crowd until, spotting her, he grinned and walked over.

"What's he doing here?" Bud demanded.

"I have no idea," Dana replied, concern filling her with dread. "I hope nothing's wrong. Maybe it's Iva."

"Bud," Philip reached out to shake hands. "How's it going?"

"Fine. What brings you here? You're too late if you're looking for a part." Bud's half-hearted attempt at humour was painful to watch. His stiff manner as he shook hands indicated his annoyance at Philip's presence.

"Is anything wrong?" Dana asked.

"No. Everything's fine. I thought you might like a ride home. It's pretty nasty out there."

She and Bud replied at the same time, interrupting each other. "Dana always has a ride home. You could have saved yourself a trip," Bud growled, while Dana thanked Philip, "That was thoughtful of you." *He truly is kind of wonderful.*

"Besides," Philip continued. "I'm interested in seeing your play, if that's all right? I don't want to spoil anything, so I'll be sure to stay out of the way. If you'd rather I didn't watch, I can wait outside."

"Of course, you can stay and watch. I hope you won't be bored."

"Oh, I doubt I'll be bored."

The two of them stood there, smiling at each other in a goofy kind of way, oblivious to everyone else around them. Bud placed a protective arm around Dana's shoulder and said, "Come on, Dana. Let's get back to work."

She glanced back at Philip, giving him what she hoped was an encouraging smile. At the same time, she stepped slightly sideways and slipped out from under Bud's arm. He frowned as she put a small distance between them but said nothing.

Chapter Fifty

Detective Small strolled up to Philip, stroking his mustache, eyes narrowed with suspicion. "Surprised to see you here. You're not part of the cast or crew, are you?"

Philip sighed. "No. I thought I'd stop by and offer Dana a ride home. It's pretty wet out there."

"I thought she and that Bud were together. You're interested, too?" Small's eyes seemed to narrow even more as he contemplated this idea. "Could be trouble," he offered with a dark, warning look.

Philip bristled. It was none of this cop's business whether or not he was interested in Dana. "I don't see why. Dana's a free agent." Then it occurred to him that maybe the officer was onto something. Bud was definitely worth looking into as a potential suspect. From Small's point of view, so was he!

"I told you," he repeated, "I'm only here to drive her home. Besides, I'm interested in her play. I thought I'd sit and watch for a bit."

When that drew a loud snort, he changed the topic. "How's it going with your interviews?"

"There are some interesting people around here. They're so absorbed in what they're doing, they probably wouldn't have noticed a streaker run across the stage. Some of them have pretty vivid imaginations, too. They conjure up something they might have seen, hoping it will make us happy and we'll go away. But for every one of those, there's somebody else who shoots it all down."

"Did you get a lab report on the rats?"

"Not yet. There's a big backlog at the lab, and this isn't exactly top priority."

"How about Dana's old phone. Get anything off that?"

"No, she got the second call on her new phone, but it was a blocked number. Whoever's behind these calls probably used a throw-away, or a stolen phone."

"She got a second call? From that creep?" Philip's outrage was white-hot. "When?"

"Yesterday afternoon." Small studied Philip's reaction to this latest information for a long minute before pointing across the room to where a petite young woman stood apart from the others. "Do you know that one over there, the blonde?"

"No. Why? Is she a suspect?" Other than her somewhat unhappy expression, she looked incapable of swatting a fly, let alone rounding up rats, and he couldn't begin to imagine her committing murder.

"Everyone's a suspect at this stage. I wondered if you knew her, that's all. She sure seems to have it in for Dana. I thought you might know why."

"I have no idea. I haven't been around here long, remember?"

"That's right, I almost forgot. Kenya, wasn't it?" The detective gave him an appraising look before wandering off in search of his partner.

What the heck was that all about? 'Kenya, wasn't it?' He knows very well it was. But something else the detective said was bothering him even more. *Dana didn't say anything about another phone call! She's either taking this all much too lightly or for some reason, she doesn't want to talk about it.*

Philip was unable to believe she'd be so cavalier about things at this point. He could only surmise she might be afraid to say anything. But why be afraid to tell him? Did she think that making him aware of the call would bring some kind of retribution? She hadn't been afraid to tell the police, so that couldn't be it. He could only think of two possible reasons: *she's either trying not to worry Aunt Iva, or she's not sure she can trust us. Well, not us... me!*

This last thought was a deep cut. If Dana didn't think she could trust him, he'd have to convince her she could. Except, wasn't he the one who'd warned Dana not to be so trusting of the people around her? He hadn't thought she'd paid attention— or that she'd include him!

*****

Philip watched the on-and-off-stage activities with a modicum of polite interest. No matter how great Dana's play might turn out to be, rehearsals were deadly dull if you weren't involved yourself. He paid more attention to those milling around the auditorium. At one point, he caught sight of a girl they called Julie backstage. Could this be Dana's friend, Julie? He'd never met her. Since he'd arrived at the end of the coffee break, he hadn't yet seen any other backstage, lighting, or sound people, either.

In Philip's opinion, there were too many unknowns. Too many unknown people around Dana and too many unknown reasons or clues as to why she was targeted by someone determined to terrorize her with those rats. Was someone trying to get her to move out of the apartment, or leave town, or just scare the wits out of her? What would be the reason for any of those scenarios? Had she witnessed something she shouldn't have? Was she in someone's way, for some reason?

If those were the reasons, and she didn't take the

hint, would it escalate into something far more dangerous like what happened to Shirley? The idea was chilling. Could there possibly be a connection between the insanity with the rats and the even greater insanity of murder?

He didn't believe Dana had a stalker. This didn't seem like classic stalker behaviour. From the little he knew on the subject, stalkers were usually enamoured with their subject and, misguided as they were, wanted to become a part of that person's life.

They don't normally want to scare them away, but that's what usually happens. The person they're so obsessed with gets frightened and moves away.

No, he kept coming back to the idea that Dana knew, or had seen, something she wasn't supposed to and was completely unaware of the fact. *But if that's the case, where did this happen? At work? Highly unlikely at a yoga studio.* He didn't know anything about the restaurant where she occasionally waitressed, or the people who gave her writing assignments.

Looking around the auditorium, he thought about this place and Dana's play. What could possibly have happened around here? They'd had only one rehearsal, so far, and despite that being aborted, things appeared to be going smoothly tonight.

Before he knew it, people were packing up and preparing to leave. It seemed everyone wanted an early night on the eve of a holiday weekend. "Have a great weekend," several people called out. Someone said, "I'm heading to the lake right now. Don't want to get caught up in Friday's traffic."

Philip was glad Dana would be heading north, too. It would put her out of reach of whoever was behind this craziness and give her a much-needed break. He could relax and enjoy his own weekend, knowing she was out of the city.

Dana walked towards him, closely followed by Bud

who seemed to hover whenever she moved or spoke to anyone else.

"Ready to go?" Philip asked.

"Yes, thanks. It looks like we're having an early night."

"I could easily have taken you home, Dana," Bud said. "I assumed you knew that."

"I know, Bud, and thank you, but since Philip is here, there's no need for you to go out of your way. Have a great weekend."

"Yeah, you, too," Bud grumbled. "You still going up north?"

Dana nodded. "In the morning. I don't know if my sister is coming with me or not. I haven't heard back from her, so probably not. What about you?"

"I'm staying in the city. Lots to do."

"Dana!" called Julie, scurrying across the vast room. "Wait up!"

Face flushed, she caught up to the three of them. "I wanted to say goodbye. Have a great weekend. I guess you're all right for getting home tonight?" She gave Philip an evaluating look.

"Sorry, Julie. I forgot you two haven't met. This is Philip Marshall. Philip, Julie Chen."

Philip reached out to shake Julie's hand. "Nice to meet you, Julie."

Dana smiled to herself; it was clear Julie was sizing Philip up. "You, too. I guess you're going to take Dana home?"

Philip nodded. "Can I give you a lift, too?"

"Thanks, but I have a ride." Julie seemed satisfied with her appraisal. Turning to Dana, she said, "See you next week," and left to catch up with a dark-haired young woman Dana didn't recognize. She must be another member of the stage crew.

Leaving a thoroughly ticked-off Bud, she and Philip

headed for their coats.

Chapter Fifty-One

The door to the auditorium burst open, and a man with his head lowered like a bull rushed headlong through, not even noticing he'd nearly knocked them over.

"What the ...?" Philip cried. "Watch where you're going!"

"S-s-sorry!" apologized Elvis Fox, coming to a halt. Frightened by Philip's anger, he appeared to cower and shrivel into himself.

"Oh, Elvis!" Dana said, putting an arm around him. "I'm so sorry. We're all terribly upset about Shirley. I guess everyone's nerves are a bit on edge."

"Thanks. Is Bud still here, or Audrey?"

"I'm here!" Bud came up to them. "I didn't expect to see you tonight. Are you okay?"

"I'm fine," Elvis replied, although he clearly wasn't. His exhaustion was obvious, from the dark pouches under his eyes, to his even paler than usual colour. "I wasn't going to come tonight, but I found this in the trunk of Shirley's car, and I thought it might belong here. I think it's for costumes."

He held up a medium-sized red suitcase with a smiley face sticker on one side.

"I don't recognize it, but Audrey might." Bud caught Audrey's attention and called her over.   He turned back to Elvis. "Shirley had a car? I didn't think she drove."

"She had her licence, but she didn't drive. Too nervous."

Bud shook his head in confusion. "Then why keep a car?"

"It was her dad's. She didn't want to sell it after he died. I was checking it out, deciding whether or not I'd keep it." He looked almost apologetic. "She left everything to me; even the house. I can't believe it. It was her parents' house. My aunt and uncle's." He shook his head, and his voice dropped to a whisper, "Everything is so unreal! Shirl was supposed to live there a long time, and now she's gone."

"I'm so sorry, Elvis," Audrey said as she embraced the young man.

"Thanks." He hoisted the suitcase. "I wondered if this is yours? It was in Shirl's car, and I thought it might be costume stuff." He looked away for a moment, attempting to control his emotions. "I'm surprised she even had a suitcase. She never went anywhere." He wiped away a tear.

"It's not mine, but is it all right if I have a look inside?"

"Sure."

By now, a small group had gathered, and Elvis was overwhelmed by well-intentioned hugs and condolences. Bud laid the case on a nearby table and opened it. A slight frown creased Audrey's forehead as she sifted through a few pieces of clothing.

"It has nothing to do with the costumes. I don't recognize anything." She picked up a small white plastic bag. "What's this?" As she opened it, a pair of fabric shears fell out, hitting the wooden floor with a thud and bounced a few feet away.

"I'll get them," Philip offered and bent to retrieve them. When he stood back up, Audrey was pulling out the remaining contents. Dana gasped. Several metres of lacy black ribbon tumbled to the floor, forming a long loop.

"Well?" Bud quizzed Audrey. "Is it costume stuff or not?"

"No. It must be Shirley's."

"Stay here!" Philip ordered the small group. "I've got to catch that detective before he gets away." He took off like a runner who'd heard the starting gun, slamming through the doors into the outer hall. Raised voices shouted, "Hey, watch where you're going!" and "Take it easy! What's your hurry?"

"What' the heck's going on?" Bud demanded, his voice rising. "Has everyone gone friggin' mad?"

Chapter Fifty-Two

An hour later, a now miserable and muttering crowd was trying to sort out boots and umbrellas in the entrance hall. Philip had managed to flag down Detective Small, who had returned and resumed his questioning, thereby detaining everyone. No one was pleased, and the unending rain didn't help the general mood. Shirley's murder was uppermost in everyone's mind, and any lingering hopes for an early wrap-up and improving weather for the holiday weekend had long vanished.

At last, they were all on their way. Outside, reflections from streetlights danced off the multitude of puddles. Some cars ploughed through them without slowing down, drenching the few scattered pedestrians scurrying along. As Dana and Philip huddled under his umbrella, she had the passing thought that those dancing reflections might have seemed festive under different circumstances, but not tonight. Her raincoat had a hood, and she didn't need the umbrella's protection, but it was comforting to squeeze together out of the rain. She needed that right now.

Philip had managed to find parking two blocks away, right in front of a coffee shop that was still open.

As they approached his car, he asked, "Feel like a coffee?"

"It's tempting," she replied honestly. "But I have to

pack for the weekend and take care of a few other things. Thanks, anyway."

While that was the truth, Dana had to admit that needing to pack wasn't the real reason why she declined. Although part of her desperately needed company after the shock and confusion of seeing that black ribbon in Shirley's suitcase, another part of her was more frightened and wary than ever.

She was inhabiting a nightmare and didn't know what to believe or whom she could trust. *Shirley! What did she have to do with all of this? Did she put the ribbon on the dead rats? She couldn't have! She was as terrified as I was when she found that one in the coffee machine. She nearly fainted! Unless....*

An uneasy thought wormed its way into her mind– unless she was an exceptional actress! It was a theatre group, after all. Maybe Shirley had acting experience. Dana didn't know anything about her, only that Bud said she had "issues". Maybe those issues were more serious than anyone realized.

Another thought occurred: had someone suspected Shirley, or found proof of her guilt, and doled out their own justice? That prospect was equally terrifying. Who would go that far? Bud? She knew he was falling for her, but would he kill for her? *Stop it! Don't go there!* Dana wanted to scream out loud at the insanity of it all.

She was aware of Philip's eyes on her and struggled to keep her composure, but the crazy ideas wouldn't stop. Was this man capable of such vigilantism? Could he have taken it upon himself to stop Shirley once and for all? *No!* Her mind rejected the idea immediately.

She trusted her feelings for Philip, even though they'd met less than a week before, and things were moving much too quickly for her comfort. Was it simple proximity? After all, they were living in the same house. Maybe it was the sense of shared danger, almost like

Stockholm Syndrome, where some hostages came to sympathize with their captors? She warned herself to keep her guard up.

A glance at Philip's downcast face revealed his disappointment, so she added, "Sorry. Maybe another time?"

"Sure," he said, unlocking the car door for her. "I just thought you might need to talk."

"Thanks, but not right now."

When he got in, she noted his grim look and decided to deflect him from the obvious topic. She wasn't up to analyzing the night's events. Assuming a light-hearted tone she did not feel, she asked, "So, I've been wondering about something. Does anyone ever call you Phil, or is it always Philip?"

He gave her an odd, assessing look before replying. "I get Phil occasionally, but it doesn't seem to stick. I always got Philip at home."

"Is it a family name?"

He must have sensed her need for diversion and decided to play along. As he started the truck, he gave her an embarrassed look. "No. My mother's a bit of a monarchist. She named me after Prince Philip."

"Wow! That's kind of cool. I guess naming kids after the Royals is still popular. I've met a couple of guys named Will, after Prince William. But you're the first I've met named after Prince Philip."

He didn't reply, concentrating instead on pulling out onto Queen St. Traffic was lighter now, and Dana couldn't see a single remaining pedestrian. It was a good night for staying warm and dry at home if you could. At the next corner, she spotted a homeless man tucked into a doorway. She would never become accustomed to such sights. Her heart ached, and like many, she despaired at the current lack of suitable solutions in an affluent city.

Philip interrupted these thoughts. "Your turn. How'd

you get your name?"

Grateful he was playing along, but still distracted by the homeless man, she replied in a somewhat subdued manner. "It's not nearly as exciting as your story. Mom was reading a novel with a character named Dana in it, and that was that. She liked the name."

"Your mom has good taste. I like it, too." He turned to smile at her. "So, are you looking forward to going home tomorrow?"

"I am. What about you? I was there three months ago; you've been gone three years!"

"Yeah, it'll be nice." Philip sounded relaxed and happy as if truly anticipating a great time. "I probably shouldn't have stayed away so long. I'm not sure my mother will ever forgive me!"

"But all in all, you're glad you went to Africa?"

"Absolutely. No regrets. Glad I went but glad to be home. And especially glad I stopped to visit Aunt Iva for a few days." He gave her a long look that ended in a slow smile.

Dana couldn't believe how such a simple comment, accompanied by that smile, made her stomach flutter. Her face felt warm, and she sincerely hoped she wasn't blushing. Embarrassed, she admonished herself to stop acting like a love-sick fifteen-year-old!

She didn't respond to his flirtatious comment and was thankful when they reached the house a few minutes later. They dashed through the downpour to the safety of the front porch, shaking the excess water off their coats and boots before entering. In the foyer, the play-by-play of a ball game could be heard from Iva's living room.

"I should go in and talk to her about tomorrow," Philip said, looking into Dana's eyes, but he made no move to do so. It was clear he was reluctant to leave her.

Grabbing the opportunity to make a quick escape, Dana hurriedly thanked him for picking her up. "Safe trip!" she called over her shoulder as she ran up the stairs.

Unlocking her door, she was greeted by the heavenly scent of the flowers he'd sent and remembered she hadn't yet thanked him. Turning, she looked back down the stairs to find his searching eyes still upon her. The effect left her breathless.

"Thank you for the flowers. They're beautiful," she managed to blurt out before fleeing inside.

Closing her door, she stood still, waiting for her thundering heart to return to normal. Would it ever feel truly normal again? *Not as long as he looks at me that way!* Closing her eyes, she pictured Philip's expression as he stood in the hall gazing at her. Then, shaking herself out of this reverie, she attempted to turn her mind to packing. Instead, she was overwhelmed by the vision of the black ribbon tumbling out of that plastic bag from Shirley's suitcase.

"Help me!" she cried out to the empty room in despair, overwhelmed by all of her conflicting thoughts.

As she gathered some weekend clothes, Dana continued rehashing the past week's events. To her surprise, a new train of thought emerged from the tangled morass of emotions, and with it, the stirring of slight hope that if it was Shirley who did all this, did that mean it was over? Could this inexplicable horror be finished?

Chapter Fifty-Three

Dana discovered it wasn't easy getting Philip off her mind. Her new hope that Shirley Fox's death would mean this nightmare of dreadful events might be over allowed other, more pleasant thoughts to surface, and Philip ranked first among them.

Although Shirley's killer remained to be found, Dana was confident the murder investigation had no bearing on the one into the dead rats that had terrorized her. The only connection was the black lace ribbon in that suitcase Elvis found. Dana wanted to believe it was Shirley's and that the dead woman was behind the episodes with the rats, because then she could put it all in the past and move on. The fact that she couldn't come up with a plausible motive didn't bother her. Shirley had problems and probably acted irrationally.

Last night, Bud had defended Shirley, dismissing the idea that the lace could be hers. He had insisted to Detective Small there must be black lace ribbon in stores and sewing kits all over the city. It was a common enough item. Maybe someone had given the suitcase to Shirley, contents and all.

While she found Bud's attempts to defend Shirley admirable, Dana thought he was stretching credulity with his theories. Detective Small's reaction was difficult to read. He said little as he kept stroking his mustache. The other detective, whose name she struggled to remember (*Moffat, was it?*) concentrated on taking notes.

As she packed for the weekend, she allowed herself to feel some relief from the past week's tensions. Philip's fascinating face kept swimming in and out of her thoughts, teasing and distracting. In her sleep, she had dreamed of Prince Philip. She chuckled to herself about that one. Even on the streetcar ride to the car rental agency that morning, the crush of commuters failed to distract her. He remained uppermost in her mind.

To be honest: it wasn't only his face, it was the total package! She was unable to resist dwelling on all his fine, physical attributes and became so warm she opened the window a crack, drawing a frown from the woman seated beside her.

*****

Philip and Iva had pulled out of the driveway half an hour before Dana left. She wondered if they were still sitting in rush-hour traffic or if they were past it and sailing down the highway. They were fortunate to escape before the real logjam of people on holidays attempted to leave the city later in the day. It hadn't been easy finding a replacement instructor for her yoga class that afternoon, but she managed to convince someone to cover for her.

Now, as she drove out of the city, mid-morning traffic required her total attention while satellite radio provided a channel featuring relaxing music based on the sounds of nature: crickets, frogs, soft winds, and gentle rain. It was a prelude to what she hoped for: time in the woods and on the lake, soaking in the transformative powers of nature, even if constantly slapping at black flies was a requirement in May.

An hour later, the crush of cars dissipated, the sun made an appearance, and Dana relaxed into the sense of happy anticipation that driving to Muskoka always elicited. She believed Muskoka was a state of mind as much as a physical location.

For some, the area represented the elite arriving by private plane at their lakeside mansions the size of small hotels. At least, that was what interested most of the lifestyle magazines and how the media often portrayed the region. However, countless others like Dana had come to know the cottage life from a small frame building at the lake's edge and a silent canoe. In those less glamorous dwellings, a child could lie in bed, windows wide open, listening to chipmunks scurrying through the bush, and the rapping of a pileated woodpecker attacking a tree.

Loons sometimes allowed a canoe's careful approach, and the child would hold their breath in wonder as the awkward and dramatic prehistoric bird rose to display its wide black and white wingspan, trumpeting one of its many thrilling calls.

Dana was grateful not only for those early experiences but for the fact that she could still return to this enchanting place with its power to restore the weariest spirit. She seldom gave thought to children of her own, but if there were any in her future, she would find joy in introducing them to the lake and woods.

Two hours later in the village near the cottage, she pulled in beside the liquor store. She'd been overtaken by a craving for sangria, so along with picking up some red wine and orange liqueur, she would need to make another stop for fresh fruit and soda. On the main street, she cruised a foodie shop for a few specialty items her parents might enjoy. At the ice cream stand next door, she indulged in her first cone of the season, a salute to good things to come.

With a light heart, Dana pulled out of town and turned onto the narrow winding road that led to the lake. Ten minutes later, she crested a hill and turned into the driveway. The familiar vista of rocks, trees, and sun-dappled water spread itself before her. She remained in the car for a moment, absorbing this perfection. When she stepped out, a pine-scented breeze whispered, "Welcome home!" Then the cottage door opened, and her parents stepped out, smiling their own welcome.

Without warning, her eyes filled with tears. Pretending to blow her nose, she wiped them away. Her raw emotions must be much closer to the surface than she'd imagined. She'd have to take care not to alarm her parents with emotional displays over the weekend. She wasn't usually a weepy person, so tears would be difficult to explain.

Once Dana had dropped her bags in the familiar pine-paneled bedroom with its ancient bunk beds, she joined her mother in the kitchen. A pot of freshly brewed tea and three cheerfully coloured mugs sat on a tray next to a plate of her favourite cookies.

"Dana, you couldn't have found anything nicer than this assortment of teas," her mother smiled. "I've made the Earl Grey. Let's take it out to the screened porch. It's warm enough today, and Dad's already out there."

"Sounds great!"

Dana carried the tray out to the porch, where the same frisky breeze that had whispered its welcome now tinkled the wind chimes. Sunlight sparkled on the quiet bay, and a canoeist's paddle flashed in the distance. She inhaled the fresh air like a long-needed tonic and smiled.

"This is heaven! It's so peaceful."

"Caroline is coming up by bus on Sunday morning," her mother related. "It's too bad you couldn't have come up together, but maybe you can drive her home."

Surprised, Dana said, "I tried to get her to come with me, but she said she had plans with her friends."

"Never mind," her father said. "It will be good having the two of you here together, even for a short time."

"Now that summer's finally coming, you'll probably see too much of us and be glad when we leave!" Dana joked.

"Never!" her mother said. "Now, I'm going to start lunch. That pie you brought looks delicious, but maybe I should save it for Sunday when Caroline's here?"

"No way," her father protested. "I haven't had a good pie like that in ages. If we want more when Caroline gets here, we'll buy another one!"

Dana laughed, "I guess that's decided!" While she was pleased for her parents' sake that her sister was coming, she couldn't help wondering what had prompted Caroline to change her mind.

Chapter Fifty-Four

His mother's tears surprised Philip. He couldn't remember ever seeing her cry before, not even when his brother died. She'd remained stoic and dry-eyed then, at least in his presence. It occurred to him now that she'd likely had private moments when the tears flowed. Odd that he should only think of that today, after so many years.

She held Philip as if she didn't dare let him go —like she feared he might take off again to some other remote part of the known world. He had to bend down for the hug. He'd been doing that for years, but today his mother seemed tinier than usual. Could she be shrinking like some people did as they aged? He had never thought of his parents as getting old.

From the moment they had stepped out the front door to greet him, their old dog, Bo, had been frantically barking with excitement, running in circles and making joyful doggie sounds. While attempting to intervene in the human hugs to receive her own, she'd managed to poke her head in between Philip and his mother, nudging Philip's knees for attention. When his mother finally released her son, Bo jumped up, placing her paws on Philip's chest. Her long, wet tongue hung out as she panted.

Philip burst out laughing. "What a welcome!" he

exclaimed, rubbing the beloved creature behind her ears. Bo almost moaned with happiness.

His father stood behind his mother, impatiently waiting to greet his son. Philip could read his father's excitement on his broad, open face. Although it would never be expressed in so many words, he also felt his father's love.

"Welcome home," his father said, embracing his son after Bo finally calmed down. Philip noted new lines around his father's eyes and a few more gray hairs, but little else had changed. He had no idea how gray his mother might be because she kept a blond tint on her hair like her sister, Iva. Some fresh laugh lines had appeared, but Philip thought they suited her.

"It's great to be back," he said to both of them, and he meant it.

After Iva received her round of hugs, the two returned to the car for their bags, Bo running circles of joy around them. Philip grabbed the suitcases while Iva gingerly handled several fancy boxes filled to the brim with her baking.

"Oh! You shouldn't have," said his mother like she did each time Iva brought treats.

"But we're glad you did!" was his father's predictable response as he reached to relieve Iva of some of her load.

Philip laughed. "Some things never change!" *And thank goodness for that.*

He held the door open for the three excitedly chatting older folks and one ecstatic dog, and as he followed them into the familiar sights and scents of his old home, he silently repeated, *Thank goodness for that!*

*****

Philip had asked his aunt not to mention anything about Dana and the strange episodes with the dead rats. Although she had agreed, it was not in Iva's usual chatty nature to keep things to herself, and he prayed it wouldn't slip out before the weekend was over. There was no way of explaining those events, and he didn't want to try.

"I thought I'd take a run out to my place," he announced after lunch. "Just to check on things. Have you been out there lately?"

"Not since last fall," his father replied. "We made sure it was ready for winter, but you know Joe always does his neighbourhood watch out there. He'd call if anything needed seeing to."

"Right. I'll pick up a case of beer and stop by his place."

"That's a nice idea, dear," his mother said. "But don't be late for dinner. We'll hold it till seven."

"Don't worry, Mom. I wouldn't miss it." He kissed her on the cheek, something he couldn't remember doing since he was a boy. She seemed startled but pleased and reached up to give him a tight hug.

Philip had been glad to turn in his rental earlier that morning and looked forward to hopping into his truck for the first time in three years. It was the first vehicle he'd bought brand new, and he took a certain pride in it. His dad had driven it occasionally in his absence to keep it running, but he hadn't put much mileage on it.

Still looks great, he thought as he stood for a moment in silent admiration. Its fire-engine red shone like a mirror. His father must have taken it through the car wash and gotten it waxed.

Climbing behind the wheel felt instantly familiar, as his old room had. He adjusted the mirrors and seat for his taller frame and turned on the radio. In between the front seats sat a stack of his old CDs he knew he hadn't left there. That had to be his dad, too. He smiled to himself. Like the wash and wax job, this was one of his father's frequent, thoughtful gestures that had a way of making people feel special. Slipping an early *Prairie Oyster* CD into the player, he backed out of the driveway, humming.

Chapter Fifty-Five

On the highway where passing farms were starting to green up, Philip noticed a new crop of windmills. Wind farms were making some local farmers prosperous, but not everyone favoured of them. Protest signs dotted the fields of many of their neighbours.

Driving through a few small towns, he thought about how much he had missed their distinctive architecture, their sense of history and civility, and orderly streets lined with ancient trees and well-tended gardens. Philip noticed a few in-ground sprinkler systems and thought about how people took an abundant, clean water supply for granted.

The image of clean water turned his mind to the lake. He admitted to being excited about opening up the place again and enjoying his weekends there. He was considering living there for a while, since he'd had to let his apartment go when he left for Africa. In time, he might rent another one but not until his job offer was firm. Thoughts of the lake brought to his mind Dana in Muskoka, and he wondered what she was doing at that very moment.

Would she be out in a boat, relaxing on a dock, or hiding indoors from the blackflies? Philip pictured her lithe body lazily paddling a canoe or lounging in a Muskoka chair with her long, bare legs stretched out to catch an early tan. No matter what he imagined her doing,

Dana looked tantalizing in his mind's eye. Philip shook his head. Man, he was in deep trouble.

He wanted to be with her, put his arms around her, and draw her close. He could imagine the sweet scent of her hair and those lips that had a way of pursing a certain way when she was thinking and made him long to taste them. If she were to call right then and say, "Drop everything and come on up!" he knew he'd turn his truck around in a heartbeat and head directly north. He wouldn't even think twice about not seeing his place or about disappointing his parents, who had waited so long for this visit, and that fact said everything about his state of mind when it came to this mesmerizing woman he'd only met eight days ago. Yes, he knew he was in trouble, but it was the kind of trouble that made his heart race with anticipation.

Philip thought back to the measly brush on the lips he'd given her after the ball game and wished he'd had the guts to kiss her deeply and thoroughly. He imagined her responding to him with the same intensity and felt a physical ache that almost made him moan. Shifting in his seat, he took a swig of coffee from his thermal mug.

He had to pull himself together, or he'd end up in a ditch! Still, he couldn't help smiling.

Romance of any kind had been the furthest thing from his mind for a long time now, and this intense attraction to Dana had taken him by complete surprise. His previous relationship had turned into a nightmare. Within the first few months, he'd realized he was dealing with an unstable personality. Caught in her web of lies and manipulations, he'd tried to end it, but the increasingly erratic woman had refused to accept it was over. In the end, part of the reason he'd taken the job offer in Africa was the hope that by putting an ocean and continent between them, she'd finally get the message.

However, the call Dana had taken on his phone last

weekend from that mysterious woman had him troubled. It had to be Susan —no one else would call his number and react that way when another woman answered. He swore. Was she going to start things up all over again? He wondered if she was still in the area but didn't want to upset his parents by asking.

If it was Susan, at least she hadn't called back. Maybe that was a good sign. On the other hand, he should reconsider his idea of moving back to Guelph; it could stir up the hornet's nest again. Besides, Dana was in Toronto, where he wanted to be.

Dana! He certainly wouldn't want Susan to learn about his interest in Dana. Talk about a disaster waiting to happen! There was enough scary stuff going on in Dana's life without adding "Scary Susan" to the mix.

Philip thought back to the first time he'd laid eyes on Dana—he had seriously questioned *her* sanity that morning. He remembered prodding Aunt Iva for information about her. Two days later, he'd caught a look on Officer Green's face that suggested he considered her a suspect as well. As if she might, in some sick way, be planting the dead rats and pretending to receive threatening phone calls to attract attention to herself.

Munchausen Syndrome.

Philip recalled watching a documentary on the topic. Munchausen Syndrome was the name given to those who craved attention to the extent they purposely made themselves sick or feigned symptoms of illnesses to undergo tests and even be hospitalized. Some even feigned psychological trauma.

Philip's mind balked at the thought Dana herself might be responsible for the dead rats. At the same time, he realized his attraction to her could easily be clouding his judgment. As if that hasn't happened before! he thought. When it came to thinking clearly in such circumstances, lust frequently defeated logic.

He knew his developing feelings towards Dana were much more than simple lust, however. He reminded himself it was important to remain clear-headed until the bizarre events in Toronto were either solved or ceased. He lapsed into a somber, reflective mood.

Half an hour later, he caught sight of the familiar sign indicating his turn off the highway lay straight ahead. His heart lifted, as it always did, whenever he approached this special place. Three years' absence made his anticipation even sweeter, and he felt like a little kid about to open a Christmas present from Santa Claus.

Since Joe had been keeping an eye on things, he wasn't concerned about facing any big maintenance problems. As long as his pump was still in good shape, he could turn the water on. If any mice had found their way in, Philip would have to clean up after them and look for signs of where they entered, but those were the usual tasks when the place had been closed up for winter. There might be some leaf-raking to do, but he'd enjoy the physical activity and being outdoors. If there were time, he'd get the canoe out for a short paddle. Philip corrected himself out loud. "Not *if* there's time! I *am* going for a paddle! Boy, I've missed this place!"

Chapter Fifty-Six

Philip turned into his gravel driveway and pulled up behind his cottage. Everything looked exactly as he'd pictured it all the time he'd been away. Home, Sweet Home!

Climbing out of his truck, he strolled around the perimeter of the house and noted a neat pile of firewood by the back door. Joe had been expecting him. The property looked good, and when he stood on his dock, the scene was as soothing as ever—not a soul could be seen or heard on the water. In the profound quiet, only the rustling of chipmunks through the underbrush reached his ears, and a faint breeze stirred the lake's surface. Philip's heart soared. This place was what he'd dreamed about, even amid all the exotic environments he'd enjoyed in the past three years.

Joe had done a great job with the leaves last fall, and Philip couldn't see anything that required immediate attention. He returned to the truck for a bag of supplies he'd brought to stock up for his next visit and, grabbing the house key, hoped he could get the water turned on without any problems. Most of all, he hoped he wouldn't find mice. He was anxious to get that canoe in the water.

Bounding up the steps, he put the key in the lock and entered, then smiled as his nostrils were hit by the familiar scent of a wooden building that had been closed up and unheated for several months: a nostalgic combination of wood, dampness, and residual fireplace smoke. That would disappear in time after he put some heat on and as the coming days warmed up. Closing his eyes for a moment, he relaxed and absorbed the joy of homecoming.

His senses were immediately assaulted by something else when he opened his eyes: smashed kitchen dishes everywhere, slashed cushions on his ancient sofa and chairs, chunks of foam stuffing littering the old carpet which shone with globs of something sticky like syrup or honey. Philip dropped his bag of supplies right where he stood, stunned and immobilized. *What the…?*

*****

In a corner, the screen of his small television displayed a gaping hole. That tv was the only thing of any value in the place, yet whoever did this hadn't bothered to take it. On a hunch, he moved over to the cupboard where he'd left a small supply of liquor; the bottles were still there and intact. Whoever had trashed the place hadn't been interested in stealing the television or liquor. They'd been hell-bent on sheer destruction.

He'd have to call the police. Deciding not to proceed any further into the chaos, Philip rightened a wooden chair that lay overturned on the floor and sat. Removing his ball cap, he scratched his head, leaned forward with his elbows on his knees, and absorbed the shock of the scene before him.

Local teens might have done this, but he thought they'd also have taken the television set and the liquor, or at least drunk some of the alcohol. It didn't look as if there'd been a party. If they'd been looking for money or something to pawn to buy drugs, they must have been mighty disappointed. Maybe that explained why they'd trashed the place: they were taking out their anger.

He shouldn't leap to any easy conclusions and assume it had been teenagers. There were plenty of disturbed adults around. Frustrated and angry, he prepared to call the police and the insurance company. This was not how he'd planned to spend his afternoon.

Finding the local number, he placed his call. There was no point in calling 911 since this wasn't an emergency. There was no telling when the trashing had happened. A hundred thoughts swirled in his head, but one in particular kept circling and nagging at him. He tried to bring it into focus; it was something he'd said to himself only a moment ago, something about not leaping to any easy conclusions about teenagers and that there were plenty of disturbed adults around. Disturbed adults ... like Susan? No!

Philip's brain rebelled at the idea. Susan had only come to mind because he thought about her on the drive over. Why on earth would she do this? They hadn't had any contact for three years. He found it profoundly disturbing that someone he had been involved with was capable of such mindless destruction, and yet, she must know he was back in the country. After all, the only person who could have been the mysterious caller Dana had taken on his phone last weekend would be Susan.

Waiting for the police to arrive, Philip decided to check out the rest of the cottage after all. Skirting the living room, he proceeded down a short hall to examine the vindictive destruction in the other rooms, which was chiefly slashed comforters. However, in one bedroom, a blast of cool air hit him, and he discovered the obvious point of entry: a smashed window. How had he missed that when he walked around outside earlier?

He was thoroughly ticked off. It wasn't the value of the damaged goods that bothered him; the place was largely furnished with cast-offs and second-hand pieces. No, the invader had violated something Philip treasured far more.

Missing that paddle in his canoe and cleaning up the mess that faced him were minor annoyances; it was the possible loss of his idyllic sense of peace and sanctuary here that disturbed him most. Whoever had done this would probably never get caught, either.

Although he was careful not to touch anything in case there was any evidence, Philip held little hope that would make the slightest difference. In his discouraged state, his thoughts returned to Susan. If she was responsible, he had much bigger problems than a trashed cottage!

Chapter Fifty-Seven

Philip hated lying to his parents, even if it was a small lie to protect them. However, he wouldn't tell them over the phone what had happened at his cottage —make that "to" his cottage.

"It's only a maintenance thing, Mom, but I can't leave until it's taken care of. I'm sorry. You go ahead and start dinner without me."

He was grateful his dad hadn't answered, or he'd have faced tougher questions. He wasn't going to tell either of them that he was in the middle of dealing with the local police. Heaven only knew how long that was going to take.

The officer who arrived asked him several questions and took photos of the scene, but Philip had the impression the man wasn't too hopeful about solving the case. As the policeman moved about almost laconically, he informed Philip that there had been half a dozen break-ins along the shore.

"Have to say most of 'em were obvious attempts to find booze or money," the officer told him, as he scribbled a few notes. "Far as we know, they've only taken a laptop and a TV. Nobody else has been trashed. Nothin' more than a broken lock or window for most of 'em."

"Lucky me," Philip said. "But the booze is still here, and it doesn't look like anything's been stolen. So, if this is the only place that's been trashed, maybe it wasn't done by the same people. Maybe this is a separate case." He watched the man's thought process playing out on his face.

"Could be," the fellow was slow to agree. "But usually what looks like the obvious answer is the answer. Unless we find somethin' more concrete that indicates what you're suggestin', for now, we have to go with this bein' just the latest in a string o' break-ins."

After the officer left, Philip taped cardboard over the broken window and took a call from his insurance agent, who promised to meet him there the following morning. By the time he'd locked up the best he could and headed home, a dark and threatening sky had obliterated the sunny day, presaging a severe storm. It suited his mood perfectly.

His parents and aunt were understandably dismayed about the vandalizing. As he had more time to mull things over, Philip began to wonder if he was the crazy one for thinking it could be Susan. "I can't believe it! Joe was just there the other day checking on things," his father railed. "This must have happened in the last two or three days."

His mother was indignant. "It simply infuriates me! People have no respect for private property these days! And just when you were so looking forward to enjoying it, dear," She was close to tears.

"I know, Mom, but it's nothing that can't be cleaned up and repaired," he said, trying to appease her. "At least there wasn't any water damage or anything structural. It can all be fixed." The pep talk was as much for himself as for his mother.

By the time they all went to bed, Philip had convinced himself that what had happened was just another local job. Thinking about Susan had made him paranoid, that was all. Then, that stubborn niggle of doubt crept back in. He wanted to be wrong about her, but could he afford to ignore this persistent gut feeling?

*****

I'm here! I'm there! I'm everywhere! You see me, then you don't!

Well, now, that was cool! Have to do that again! I've never trashed a place before. It's kind of therapeutic. It's a wonder the docs don't recommend it. What a rush! Releasing all those fantastic endorphins might be the cure for all sorts of conditions. Not that I have a condition! No, no, no. Wish those docs would get that through their empty heads.

It would have been perfect if I could have seen his reaction! But then, I seldom stick around for people's reactions. That place was a dump to begin with. I probably did him a favour. He's the kind that'll have insurance, and they'll clean it all up. Yes, sir, it'll be better than ever...until the next time. Yeah, until the next time.

Chapter Fifty-Eight

Bo's frantic barking made Philip's hair stand on end. His bleary eyes fought to read the clock on the nightstand: two thirty-five a.m.! "What is it, old girl?" he muttered, even though the dog was nowhere in sight. He heard his father shouting down the stairs. "Bo! Knock it off! What's the matter with you?"

Philip found his father wrapped in an ancient, faded robe in the hall. His sleepy mother half-stumbled out of their room, calling, "What is it? What's got her going? Something's bothering her."

"Oh, you know, Bo," his father replied. "She's getting old; she reacts to everything. It's probably some wandering tomcat." He resumed shouting, "Bo, knock it off!" The dog gave a low yowl of protest, followed by a few more subdued barks.

A worried and rumpled Iva had now joined them.

"Shouldn't you check and see, in case there is something out there? She seems upset."

"I'll go down," Philip said. "I'll turn on the outside lights."

"Be careful!" his mother called after him.

"This isn't Toronto," he heard his father mutter. "We don't have car-jackings and stuff like that around here. It's probably a tomcat, like I said. That'd be enough to set any dog off."

Philip switched on the porch lights and stepped outside. Chilly air slapped him in the face, banishing any remaining sleepiness. He was wide awake now. Standing barefoot on the lawn, he shivered. The icy dew soaked the hems of his pajama bottoms. He swore under his breath. *There's nothing here. No tomcats or anything else. Not that I expected to see one, anyway. It would be long gone.* He looked over at his truck. In the dark, it looked black instead of red. Other than that, it appeared to be all right. *'No carjackings around here', Dad said. Guess he was right. Old Bo's just getting old.*

*****

As Iva and his mother chatted in the kitchen after breakfast Monday morning, Philip managed a minute alone with his father.

"Do you ever see or hear anything about Susan?" He tried affecting a nonchalant manner. If his father saw anything more than a casual interest in the question, he didn't let on. "We heard she moved, possibly to Toronto, but we don't know. You knew she spent some time in a psychiatric hospital after you left, didn't you?"

"No. I never heard anything. Where?"

"Pretty sure it was the old Clarke Institute in Toronto. I think it's called CAMH or something now. Anyway, I believe she was there several months."

Philip absorbed this information. In a way, he was not surprised. Still, it was disturbing.

"You're not going to look her up, are you, Philip? I think that would be a mistake."

"No way! That's the last thing I want!" He moved to pick up Iva's bags to put in the truck.

"Good. Glad to hear it!" Then, with sudden alarm, "Philip, you're not thinking Susan might be connected to the break-in, are you? Good Heavens, son..."

"No, no!" Philip protested. "Being back here made me think about her, that's all. No, I don't think even Susan would go that far." He almost crossed his fingers behind his back, the way he'd done as a kid whenever he told a whopper.

"That's good." His father's expression relaxed as his smile returned. "Now, safe travels. I hope it won't be too long before we see you again. Coming home meant a lot to your mother."

Philip hugged his dad, knowing what his father meant but couldn't put into words: the visit had meant a lot to him, too.

Out in the driveway, it took a minute for what he was seeing to sink in. *Four tires! All four? At the same time?*

Chapter Fifty-Nine

Dana and Caroline left Muskoka on Monday afternoon and joined the long stream of traffic heading south. Caroline fell asleep almost immediately, her pretty head lolling against the window.

Dana thought it was just as well. They had both put forth an effort for their parents' sake, but they'd also pretty well exhausted most topics of conversation in the past twenty-four hours. Dana felt a great sadness that she and her younger sister had drifted apart. How had that happened? She racked her brains for an answer but was at a loss.

Dana loved Caroline, but somewhere along the line, their relationship had shifted from what she thought was reasonably close —despite the gap in their ages —to one of a distinct coolness on Caroline's part. Dana couldn't think of anything she might have done to bring this on, and it was impossible to approach the topic.

It couldn't be jealousy. Caroline was the one with the brains and looks. People were always surprised to learn that she was in her third year of engineering at the university. In some quarters, the idea that pretty women weren't supposed to be that brainy remained alive and well, despite all the advances women had made.

Caroline woke up stretching and yawning as Dana pulled off the highway for gas. "Sorry," she mumbled.

"Guess I was tired. Exams and everything."

"It's all right. I could use a coffee. How about you?"

"I'll get it while you gas up. Regular, right? Want a muffin, too?"

"That'd be great, thanks."

Back on the road with the steaming, aromatic coffee working its magic, Caroline punched in a light rock station and hummed along. Dana smiled and joined in. Before she knew it, they were singing along to the next song and the one after that. Caroline laughed when Dana didn't know a couple of lines and made some up. "You don't know that one? When did you get so old?" she teased.

"Hey, I'm not that much older than you!" Dana smiled. "I haven't heard that one for a while, that's all."

"Where've you been? In a cave somewhere?"

Dana thought about that. "Pretty much, I guess," she admitted. "Most of the time, I'm either working, taking a course, or writing. Doesn't leave much time for anything else."

"At least you're not involved with Dave anymore. What a total jerk he turned out to be."

The vehemence in her sister's words shocked Dana. Before she could summon a response, Caroline jumped in. "I'm sorry. I didn't mean to put it quite that way. It sounded harsh. I know you were in love with him."

"It's okay." Dana reached over to give her sister a reassuring tap on the knee. "He is a total jerk." There was still a shock of relief in acknowledging the truth and being able to speak it out loud.

Glancing over at Caroline, she offered a wide smile, and received a grateful one in return. "I just wish I'd realized that a lot sooner, but you know what they say, 'Love is blind'." She paused. "I did fall hard for him, though."

"I know. I'm sorry. But to be honest, it's not

surprising. Old Dave is pretty smooth. He knows how to lay on the charm when he wants to. He had me fooled, too, with all his joking, and that cool law-student persona, and you have to admit, he is pretty good-looking…" Caroline's voice dropped off.

Oh, good gravy! Was it possible Caroline had fallen for Dave, too? Dana wondered. The idea had never occurred to her, but if her sister had, even just a little, it might explain some of the distance that had developed between them.

For a moment, she contemplated asking, just putting the question out there, "Did you fall for him, too?" But really, what good would that do? It would only embarrass Caroline, just when there seemed to be a thaw in their relationship. She didn't need to know if her little sister had had a crush on her boyfriend. Ex-boyfriend, she reminded herself.

Caroline had been staring out the window. A loud honk from a passing truck broke her reverie.

"At least he's not taking up all your time anymore," she said. "You have to admit he could be pretty possessive, too. He didn't seem to leave you any spare time. I thought after you broke up, you'd have a bit more."

Was that it? Dana wondered. "I guess I buried myself after that. I had to stop dwelling on him and everything that happened. I kept going over and over it, and it wasn't doing me any good, so I started spending every spare moment on my play."

"I remember that play. You've been writing it for years."

"You remember it?" Dana was impressed. She didn't think Caroline would. "It was one more thing I put on the back burner while I was with Dave, but I made myself get back to it."

"Good for you."

"Yeah, good for me," Dana laughed. "Did I tell you it's in rehearsal? It's only a neighbourhood theatre group that's doing it, but they're pretty good."

"No kidding? You finished it?" Caroline sounded impressed. "I always thought it was-something you fooled around with. I didn't know you were that serious."

Dana couldn't help being pleased that her sister appeared interested. "Well, maybe I didn't let on how serious I was. I didn't believe it would ever happen, so I guess I downplayed it a bit."

"That's kinda cool. A real play! What's it about?"

"It's a romantic comedy."

"So, it's autobiographical?"

Dana glanced over at her sister and laughed out loud at the mischievous look in her eyes. "Darn right, it is."

An idea was forming that she hesitated to share for fear of rejection. "Actually," she said at last. "Performances begin at the end of next month. I could get you tickets. I mean, if you think you'd like to come."

"Absolutely. I wouldn't miss seeing your romantic life on stage!"

Dana reached over and playfully punched her sister. "Hey, keep your hands on the wheel!" Caroline laughed. "Seriously, Mom and Dad must be excited. They're probably telling anyone who'll listen."

"They don't know yet. I wanted to see how things go before I surprise them."

"You're kidding, right? You haven't told them anything?"

"Nope. You're the first in the family to know."

"Cool."

"Well, it still could all fall apart. We didn't get off to a good start with our first rehearsal, but I'm hoping for the best."

Caroline, distracted by a new song, was singing along again, which left Dana to her thoughts. She reflected on their conversation, pleased by the slight softening of Caroline's tough surface. It was a start. She decided she'd make more time for her sister. Maybe Caroline was lonelier in the city than she let on. There might even be a way to get her involved with the play... if she was interested.

Reflecting further, Dana realized that flying down the highway, singing songs with her sister after a weekend in Muskoka was like living in a different world—one of pure and deliberate escapism. As the city drew nearer, so did the sense of dread she had been trying to push away. Somehow, she'd managed to compartmentalize things over the weekend, partially setting aside the horrors of the past week, and above all, Shirley Fox's death. Not death — murder! Cold-blooded murder.

But surely, the worst was over? It had to be. Several days had passed without any more of those sickening rats or black ribbons. How much worse could things get than murder? Not wanting to go any further down that depressing path, Dana tried turning her mind to the details of the next rehearsal and soon felt a building excitement, which she knew wasn't all about the play. She'd be seeing Philip Marshall soon.

Chapter Sixty

The next day, a puzzled Dana headed off to her Tuesday morning class at the studio. She hadn't seen Philip the night before or that morning. The sound coming from the apartment overhead confirmed he was back, but neither he nor Iva had made an appearance. She told herself there wasn't any reason for them to seek her out, but that didn't lessen her disappointment.

In the driveway, a bright red truck shone in the sunlight. She assumed it was Philip's. What was it about guys and red cars or trucks? Usually, the clichéd purchase of a little red sportscar meant a mid-life crisis. But Philip was far from middle-aged, and this was no sportscar!

Lost in thought, Dana didn't notice the group clustered outside the yoga studio until she was upon them. Angie rushed up to her. "Dana! How could this happen? Did you know?"

"Know what?" She realized everyone was looking at her, including Anna, who stood among the group gathered on the sidewalk.

"You honestly don't know?" Elaine asked. She pointed to a sign on the door that read: *Closed by Order of the Sheriff's Office.*

"Look in the window," Julie said. "There's nothing there. It's empty."

"The sheriff's office?" Dana was stunned. "What

does it mean?"

"I think it means they've gone bankrupt," someone said.

"Well, that stinks!" Elaine said. "Now, what?"

"I guess it means it's over," Anna chimed in. "We look for another studio. It would have been nice of them to let us know!"

"Oh, Dana!" Julie sympathized. "What will you do? Here we are complaining, but this means you're out of a job!"

That reality of it was dawning on Dana. She wondered why she hadn't seen any warning signs. What had she missed? On the other hand, how would she know why the business closed? *All I did was show up to teach my classes and take my pay. I don't know the first thing about how to run a business. I should have been paying more attention.*

Dana's students remained on the sidewalk, uncertain what to do next. All eyes rested on her, as if she might have an explanation or solution to offer.

"I'm sorry. I have no idea what's going on," she said. "I'm as surprised as you are."

"It's okay. It's not your fault, Dana," Elaine said.

"Of course, it's not!" Julie's eyes flashed, as she came to her friend's defense. "If Dana had known about this ahead of time, don't you think she'd have tried to let us all know? Look at her! She showed up just like we did, and you can see she's stunned by this, too."

Julie finished by placing an arm around her friend's shoulder. Dana attempted a smile of appreciation, She had a sudden need to sit down.

"Julie, could we go somewhere, please? I need some tea and time to think."

As the others dispersed, one by one they expressed their regrets.

"I enjoyed your classes. If you start again somewhere

else, please let me know," Angie said.

Elaine, having calmed down somewhat, nodded in agreement. "You're a good teacher, Dana. This stinks what they've done to you. "

At last, only Anna remained.

"I'm so sorry," she said, placing a hand on Dana's arm, her eyes full of concern and her voice soft and comforting. "I mean, it's terrible. You're probably out of a job. Can I at least buy you a coffee? I don't quite know what else to do at the moment."

"Thanks," Dana attempted a smile. In all this confusion, it was Julie's company she wanted. However, it would be rude to refuse Anna's offer.

Now that the others had wandered off, Dana noticed a petite young woman she didn't recognize standing close to Julie. She appeared distinctly uncomfortable and hadn't spoken once as the others voiced their theories.

"I'm sorry," Dana apologized. "Were you here to join, or…?"

"Oh! No," Julie interrupted. "I'm sorry, this is my friend, Sue Choi. I invited her to class today, not knowing, of course. Anyway, Sue, this is Dana."

"Hi, Sue," Dana said. "That's too bad you came all this way for nothing. The studio closing is a real shock. I had no idea anything was wrong." She gestured helplessly towards the storefront.

"I'm sorry for all of you," was the shy reply. "Joan was always going on about how great your classes were."

"Joan?"

"Oh, that's me!" Julie gave a slightly embarrassed shrug. "I was always Joan growing up, but when I got older, I decided I'd rather be Julie. I was Christened Julie Joan, so it's no big deal. It's just hard for kids I grew up with to make the change. And don't get me started on my mother's reaction!" Her rueful smile explained that particular situation well.

"Sorry, Julie!" Sue blushed.

Here was the simple answer to the mystery Brad had brought up when he'd heard Julie being called Joan at the tennis courts. And Dana admitted to herself that it was a relief. Julie was exactly who she said she was, except when she was Joan! She smiled inwardly at her own little joke.

"Well, this is all very interesting," Anna said. "But maybe we should go and get that coffee we were talking about instead of standing here on the street."

Julie gave Dana a look which clearly asked: What's got her goat all of a sudden?

Dana walked over to the storefront window again. Pressing her nose to the glass, she raised one hand to shut out the sun's reflection and peered in as if expecting a sudden clue to resolve this bizarre situation. The bare room revealed nothing. The others gave her a moment to let the reality sink in, and then the four walked to the corner coffee shop in silence.

Chapter Sixty-One

There wasn't much to say. Sitting at an outdoor table, Julie and Anna speculated on several possible theories about what might have caused the studio to close, while Sue Choi, obviously uncomfortable, sipped at her cappuccino and focused her attention on passersby. Dana barely heard the conversation across from her. She was still in a state of shock over the sudden closure —and the fact she was now out of a job.

Finally, even Julie and Anna ran out of ideas about what could've happened and lapsed into silent commiseration. "When I get home, I'll phone Valery," Dana stated firmly. "He owes me some kind of explanation."

"Why not call him now?" Anna prompted. "I'd like to hear what he has to say, too. And I'm sure Julie would, right?" she added, looking to Julie for confirmation. "As clients, we deserve an explanation, don't you think?"

Julie nodded. "Whatever you think, Dana, but maybe it would be better to call now when you're with friends."

"Maybe you're right," Dana sighed and took out her phone to search for her boss's number on her contacts list. "He'll probably bite my head off," she said, recalling her previous call to him. "He's not all that approachable."

After a moment she reported, "It's ringing," and drew a deep breath, preparing herself to speak to the irritable

Valery. Then her face fell as she listened to a recorded message. "Guess what? The number is no longer in service!"

"Well, that's just great!" an angry Julie declared. "What are we supposed to do now? Is there anyone else you could call? What about that girl who was working at the front desk?"

"Nora? She probably doesn't know any more than I do. Besides, I don't know her last name. She was only there a couple of weeks at the most."

They formed a glum group until Julie brightened up. "I know! I'll call the Sheriff's office. Surely, they can tell us something." She looked hopeful until Anna said, "Do you think they will? Maybe they're sworn to secrecy or something."

"I'll call anyway," Julie declared. "Somebody has to tell us something!"

Dana attempted a smile. "Thanks, Julie. That'd be great. I think I'll go home now. I'm still in shock, and there's a lot to think about."

"Will you be all right?" Anna asked. Her concern was touching, but after remembering the woman's prying questions in the tearoom, Dana decided to be careful of what she said around her.

"I'll be fine, thanks. No need to worry. Julie, I'll see you at rehearsal on Friday, if not sooner. Goodbye, Sue, it was nice to meet you. Bye, Anna!" Jumping up from her chair, Dana almost knocked the teacups flying in her haste to get away. She needed time alone to think!

Chapter Sixty-Two

Turning the corner onto her street, Dana noticed there was no red pickup in the driveway. Neither were there signs of anyone in the house. She sighed with relief as she shut her apartment door behind her and flopped onto her couch. Closing her eyes, she felt a massive headache building and, using her fingertips, gently massaged her temples. A wave of nausea rolled across her stomach as she thought about her new circumstances.

What am I going to do? I needed that job. The rent! How will I manage that? At least I'm paid up for the next month. That gives me some breathing room. It might take a while to find another yoga job, though. I'll have to try to get more shifts at the restaurant. I should call right now. Instead, she continued to lie there, her mind a jumble of thoughts and theories about all the strange and worrisome occurrences that had recently taken over her life, beginning with that first horrible rat.

She was dreaming of a door closing and muted voices when a louder noise brought her fully awake. Momentarily disoriented, she concentrated on establishing where she was.

Her dry mouth was stuffed with cotton batting, and someone was tuning up a buzz saw behind her eyes. She had fallen asleep! She wasn't dreaming about the door or the voices —Philip and Iva must have come home.

Instead of being excited at seeing Philip again, Dana wanted to be alone and decided to lie low in her apartment. She wasn't up to talking to either of them, not that they would expect her to be home at this time of day. The buzz saw in her head ratcheted up a notch. *Oh, boy. I need something for this headache! She* rose to a sitting position with great care and waited for her head to stop spinning before she dared get up and search for whatever painkillers might be on hand. Moving like a stiff, old person, she managed to get to her feet just as her phone shrilled inside her purse. Bending over to retrieve it brought on another wave of nausea. She recognized Julie's number and debated whether or not to answer but remembered Julie had been going to call the sheriff's office. Maybe she had some new information.

"Dana? Is that you?" Julie sounded uncertain. "You sound funny. Have you been crying?"

"No, I haven't been crying!" Dana realized she'd sounded cross and shouldn't be taking her anger out on her friend. "Sorry, Julie. I fell asleep, that's all. What's up? Did you call the sheriff?"

"Yeah," Julie sighed. "They wouldn't tell me anything. It's an ongoing investigation. That's all they'd say, and I was lucky to get that much out of them. So, we're no further ahead. I'm sorry. I tried."

"That's okay. Thanks for trying. I thought there might be something in the local paper about it. Or maybe the landlord who owns the building could tell us something."

"I have an idea," Julie's voice brightened. "What about Anna? Isn't she in real estate? Maybe she could find out who the rental agent or owner is? It's a thought."

"You're right. I wonder why Anna didn't suggest that this morning?"

"Well, in her defense, we were all a little shell-shocked. Maybe she needed time to process it, like us."

"Maybe," Dana thought for a second. "Leave it to me, anyway, Julie. I might not have to bother her. There might be another way of going about this."

Later, when the painkillers were doing their job, Dana reconsidered Julie's suggestion, but she couldn't quite bring herself to ask Anna for any favours.

Rather than spend the remainder of the day inside moping about her lost job, she decided to tackle the one she still had. She'd head for the library, which would be open late that day, and with luck, complete her research.

There was no need to avoid Philip and Iva as she left, because the red truck still hadn't returned, which puzzled her. She was confident she'd heard them coming into the house earlier. She must have imagined it. She had been half asleep, after all. Or maybe they had come in and gone out again. But if that were the case, why hadn't she heard them leaving?

An uneasy sensation overtook her. If she had heard someone come in, and it wasn't Iva and Philip, who could it have been?

Chapter Sixty-Three

Dana's mind was set at ease when she arrived home from the library and saw Philip's red truck had returned. She was about to put her key in the lock when the heavy front door was yanked open. Philip stared at her.

"Oh!" Dana exclaimed. "You startled me!" She laughed, a little embarrassed.

"Dana." Philip sounded uncertain and hesitant. There was no return smile. "Sorry, I didn't know you were there."

"That's okay; I was daydreaming."

When he said nothing, she asked, "Is everything all right?"

Now, his words came in a rush. "Yeah, sure. Sorry, I'm just heading out. See you later." He brushed past without meeting her eyes.

Dana watched as he hurried down the walk to the driveway and climbed into his truck. As he backed out into the street and drove off, she remained mystified by his cool manner. The change from last week was puzzling and unsettling.

"Dana?" Iva MacGyver's voice called out. "Is that you, dear?"

"Yes. Sorry. Here I am holding the door wide open." She turned to go inside, closing the door behind her. "Philip seemed in a rush," she commented.

Iva's eyes looked away for a brief moment. "Yes, a little," was all she said. Then, with an obvious attempt at changing the subject, she brightened and asked, "How was your weekend? Did you have a good time?"

"Yes, I did. The weather was good, and it's always great to be at the cottage. How about you? Did you have a nice visit with your sister? I bet she was glad to see Philip again."

"She certainly was," Iva replied.

She's not her usual chatty self. Something's definitely up.

"It's nice to see Philip has his truck now. I love the colour."

"Oh…yes, the truck," Iva said in a subdued voice.

"Iva, is something wrong? Philip rushed past me with barely a word, and you're definitely not yourself. Is it his parents? Is your sister not well?" she asked with concern.

"Oh, no, dear! They're both fine. They're in perfect health," Iva hastened to assure her. There was a pause before she continued, "It's just… poor Philip! Some rather unfortunate things happened to him while we were there. It certainly spoiled his homecoming." With a sigh, she continued, "I've made a pot of tea. I don't want to worry you with our troubles, but maybe you should come in, and I'll try to explain what happened. Although, I don't understand it myself."

With that mysterious invitation, Dana shoved aside her worries about the closed yoga studio and listened to the strange account of Philip's bizarre homecoming.

*****

Later in her apartment, she attempted to sort out the many

conflicting thoughts racing through her mind. What the heck was going on in Guelph? Philip's cottage trashed, his tires slashed? It was unbelievable! It was frightening! Was it a coincidence that two awful things happened to him on the same weekend? Could it simply be random violence, or did someone there have it in for him? If so, why?

What could Philip have done to deserve such violent retribution? After all, he'd been out of the country for three years! If it was a grudge, it must be an old one. One thing was for certain, if someone was targeting him for any reason, he was dealing with a deeply unstable and vindictive person. She shivered at the thought of such malice, and a picture came to mind. A picture of a rat —in fact, two rats —tied up with lacy black bows.

An insidious thought wormed its way into her brain. Was it a coincidence that the same morning the first rat appeared, Philip did, too? What a horrible suspicion! Yet, she couldn't avoid it. He had also been there the night the second rat was discovered at the rehearsal. But he wasn't at the Beach Arms. It was Brad who had the piece of black ribbon in his wallet. And Philip couldn't possibly have trashed his own cottage. But, if he was mentally disturbed, he might have slashed his own tires.

Her head dropped into her hands. *I don't know what to think! I don't want to believe he's capable of any of this, but do I know him well enough to be certain?*

Chapter Sixty-Four

Philip strode along the boardwalk, trying to clear his head. A brisk wind off the lake whipped at his pant legs and blew his hair in all directions. So many conflicting theories were running through his tired brain. He hoped the fresh air would help him sort them out.

What on earth was going on? The question repeated itself in his mind. In the three years that he'd been in Africa, he hadn't had as many weird experiences as the ten days or so that he'd been back in Canada! Ever since his first morning, when that rat had shown up at Aunt Iva's. Well, actually, in Dana's bed.

Dana! Is it all a coincidence? She was also there when the second rat turned up at her rehearsal. Who could have planted those sick things? Surely not her? What did he know about her anyway? He acknowledged the strong attraction he was developing towards her could cloud any attempt at logical thinking. But Dana certainly wasn't in Guelph! She drove to Muskoka for the weekend.

"But did she?" a tiny voice asked. "Did she?"

Get a grip! For one thing, Dana couldn't possibly have known about the cottage!

Unless —unless Aunt Iva told her about it.

"That's ridiculous!" he muttered aloud.

What reason could Dana possibly have for trashing his place and slashing his tires? They'd never met before last week. No, it was more likely—but, no, his father said she'd been institutionalized. The Clarke Institute, he said. And The Clarke was in Toronto, not Guelph.

He walked on, wrestling with his contrary thoughts. He couldn't go back to his aunt's house or back to Guelph for that matter until he'd sorted them out. He didn't like to admit it, but he wasn't sure who could be trusted. An involuntary shiver caught his breath, and it wasn't from the cold.

*****

Philip entered the house quietly and listened. Nothing. Since he'd told his aunt he wouldn't be home for dinner, he hoped she'd taken advantage of the chance to go to bed early. Although she pretended all was well, he knew what had happened on the weekend had taken a toll on her nerves, and he felt tremendous guilt about it. He should call his parents, too, and see how they were doing. Like Iva, they'd put up a good front, but he was concerned.

He climbed the stairs quickly, hoping not to run into Dana. If she was still home, she didn't open her door as he passed. Maybe she'd gone out again.

After he left the boardwalk, he'd downed a coffee and sandwich in his truck, then put in a call for Guneer. Given the hour, he knew Ted likely wouldn't still be at the university but thought he might catch him on his commute. He felt a compelling need to discuss the positions he'd been offered.

He didn't want another overseas assignment; of that much, he was sure. However, now he felt uncertain about spending a few nights a week at his aunt's place if he were to take the Toronto job. He'd have to look for someplace else to rent; although, he knew it would be difficult explaining why to his aunt.

Maybe he should commute from Guelph and forget

about renting a place in Toronto entirely. He could certainly do that for a while until he found out exactly what was going on. If he ever did find out. There was a possibility he might not, and then what?

And something else— what if these crazy events escalated? How safe was he? How safe would Aunt Iva be if he stayed in that apartment? He didn't think he could assume whoever was behind everything was finished. And what about Dana? Yes, what about Dana?

*****

Dana had managed to rescue something good out of an abominable day by finishing the first draft of her article for the magazine. And, despite having lost her job, she'd decided to throw caution to the wind and reward herself for that achievement by having a late dinner out. Walking the few blocks to a new café relaxed her, but she was still vigilant enough to scout the customers inside before entering.

The waiter seated her at a somewhat private table in an alcove that allowed a view of the door. She didn't want to meet anyone she knew and be forced to talk about her non-existent job or anything else for that matter.

Fortunately, the evening passed without incident, and she returned home to the distraction of television. Some inane reality show featured well-dressed and toned women sitting around the pool of a pricey home screaming obscenities at each other. This was reality? In whose warped world? Then she remembered her own currently warped universe and clicked off the set. By eleven o'clock, she was in bed, hoping for sleep.

*****

Looks like everyone's a little spooked! Good! They deserve it. Why should everyone else float through life with no problems? Hmm? They shouldn't, that's all there is to it. Let's see how they handle my next little surprise! Will they finally fall apart? Or maybe they'll "all fall down", like in that stupid kindergarten song, "Ring-around-a-Rosie, A pocket full of posies?" That's it!

What they need is to have a great fall like that Humpty Dumpty nursery rhyme. Ha-Ha!

As for Dana and Philip—those two are getting entirely too cozy. And that annoying old witch of a landlady! Somebody needs a little reminding about who's in charge here. Well, they'll find out soon enough!

Here's one just for you, Dana!

"There once was a little girl,
who had a curl in the middle of her forehead,
And when she was good, she was very, very good,
But when she was bad, she was horrid."

Chapter Sixty-Five

Unable to sleep, Philip stared out of his apartment window that overlooked the street. He was shrouded in darkness, the whole house quiet and still. A glance at the illuminated dial on his watch showed that it was 2:30 a.m. Presumably, both his aunt and Dana were asleep; he had tried but was not able to rest.

He pondered his dilemma: would it be better to move out or stay? If he moved out, he assumed his aunt would be safer. After all, no one had targeted her. If he stayed, he might be able to protect her if something else did happen. But why should anything else happen in this house? Dana was the only answer. Either someone was trying to terrify her, or she was the one doing the terrorizing. He shook his head. That made no sense at all! But since when did any of this make sense? Leaving the window, he plopped down on the sofa, wanting to sit and give the matter more thought but promptly dozed off in an upright position.

*****

It was the sudden movement of his head snapping back that woke him from a deep sleep. After a moment of confusion, his head cleared, and he decided he should climb into bed now that he was finally sleepy. *I can't spend the night sitting here.* Except, he was too tired to move. *I've got to get up.* He tried to focus his eyes on the clock. *Three-thirty. I haven't been here that long. I should be able to get at least another four hours if I get into bed.*

Forcing himself upright, he passed through the living room into the bedroom and pulled the blinds. A slight sound made him pause. *What was that?* Holding his breath, he listened again but heard nothing. City noises, he told himself. I'm still not used to them. It might have been a car door— somebody's probably coming home late. However, he wasn't quite able to convince himself. Too many weird things had been happening lately.

Creak!

I know I didn't imagine that! Is Dana up, too? Or Aunt Iva? It didn't sound like it came from either apartment. It sounded more like the stairs.

He held his breath and tried to move across the small living room without making a sound, not an easy task in an old house. Pressing an ear to the door, he listened. Did he hear a whisper of movement? It wasn't coming from the main staircase, he was certain. It sounded closer, like someone was coming up the back stairs from the kitchen. *Could it be Aunt Iva? But why would she be sneaking around at this hour and on those stairs? Why wouldn't she use the main staircase?*

He opened the door, taking great care in case it squeaked. He'd expected the hall light downstairs to throw some illumination onto the landing, but he looked out into complete darkness. *Great! The bulb's blown. I'd better replace it in the morning.*

As he was about to close his door, a black shape morphed out of the darkness and hurled itself at him with tremendous force, throwing him off balance. Philip toppled backward, his head hitting the living room floor so hard he nearly passed out. He couldn't get his breath. His chest burned as if all the air had been knocked out of his lungs. The shape was on top of him. All he could see was a black balaclava covering a face, except where two holes revealed eyes full of hate. Bared teeth showed through the narrow mouth slit. The shape raised an arm above its head, and a streetlight below the window glinted off something shiny in its hand. A knife!

In horror, he tried to grab onto the wrist holding the knife, but his attacker was quick and evaded his grasp. The arm raised again. He tried to roll out from under the fellow's weight. He wasn't heavy, but his knees had a vice-like grip on Philip's hips. Philip kicked uselessly and reached for the knife again but missed. Instead, he grabbed for the mask and twisted it.

"I'll kill you!" a raw voice screamed as the knife came down. Philip managed to raise his knees enough to throw the devil slightly off-balance, and the knife slashed into his right arm, narrowly missing his chest.

"Die!" the strangled voice shrieked again, pulling the knife out of his flesh. Philip felt faint from the pain. His arm was soaking wet. *It must be blood!* Summoning his remaining strength, he jerked his knees again, and with his left hand, grabbed the assailant's wrist. They grappled for control of the knife, Philip getting weaker by the minute.

Suddenly, there were too many arms and legs. *I'm seeing double!* A hand grabbed hold of the knife arm, and yet another yanked his attacker's head straight back.

"Argh!" His assailant thrashed in an attempt to get free.

Philip couldn't comprehend what was happening. He felt himself starting to lose consciousness. From a distance, he heard a furious woman's voice scream, "Drop it, you creep!"

Dana? Where was she? He had to warn her. *Dana! Don't come in here,* he tried to scream. *Dana! Get away! Get Aunt Iva and get out of here!*

The voice was closer now. "Drop it!" One of the extra arms pulled harder on the balaclava. Philip wished he could clear his double-vision. Was it really Dana's voice? Where was she? "Dana…" he whispered.

"Hang on, Philip! Please, hang on!"

Get off of me!" his attacker screamed. "Let me go, you…I'll kill you all!"

Dana didn't respond. She was panting with exertion.

"Let me go, I said. Or I'll…" A frantic banging at the front door below interrupted the threat. "Police! Open up! Police!" a male voice shouted.

At that moment, when all three were caught off guard, the hooded figure twisted free, rolled to one side, and jumped up, heading for the door. Free of that bodyweight pressing on him, Philip tried to lunge after them but fell back, gasping with pain.

The room swam as his head dropped back onto the floor. Dana took off after the retreating figure.

No, don't go after him! Philip tried to yell, but no sound came from his mouth. *Dana, let him go!* Frustrated at his lack of voice, he pounded the floor with his fist. *Let him go! Let the police get him!*

He could hear someone ramming the front door downstairs. *Hurry!* his mind screamed.

A closer crashing sound arose as if bodies were falling down the stairs, hitting the walls. *No! Oh, dear God, please, no! Dana!* Abruptly, the crashing stopped, and the sudden silence that followed was even more terrifying.

Chapter Sixty-Six

"Police! Stop right there!" a male voice shouted. Philip heard Dana's shaky voice reply, "It's okay! It's okay! In here! –fell down the stairs. Please help me! He's not moving. He's not moving!"

Fell down the stairs? His mind panicked in a haze of pain. *Who fell down the stairs? Not Dana? Please, not Dana!*

"Raise your hands, ma'am!" came a loud, gruff command.

"Stand aside, please. Over there."

Philip could make out the shuffling sounds of many feet below but not the mumbled words. His intense frustration at not knowing what was happening was almost unbearable. Then he heard his aunt's voice.

"Philip? Where's Philip?"

"Here!" he whispered. "I'm here!"

"He's upstairs. He's going to be all right." Dana's voice. She sounded exhausted. He prayed she wasn't injured, too.

Heavy footsteps rushed up the stairs. Two uniformed officers entered his room, guns drawn as they scanned it, before one knelt to check Philip's wound.

"Hold on, buddy," he said reassuringly. "Help is on the way." He moved back to the door and yelled down the stairs. "Tell the paramedics there's another one!"

Another one? Who else is hurt? He needed to know, but there was so much confusion. People were moving around everywhere.

A familiar face! Detective Small pushed his way past the officer and bent down. After a quick examination of Philip's wound, he disappeared into the bathroom, returning a moment later with a towel which he proceeded to wind around Philip's arm.

"I think you're going to live," he said with a tight smile. "An ambulance is on its way. Should be here in a minute. Are you able to tell me what happened?" He tightened the towel, putting pressure on the wound.

Philip wet his lips. His mouth was so dry it was difficult to speak. "Who else is hurt? My aunt? Dana?"

"There's nothing to worry about. Try to answer my question. What happened?"

"He must have… been on the stairs. I…I heard a noise. Opened the door." He paused to catch his breath. "Hall light was out. He came at me. Out of nowhere. No warning."

"Got a surprise for you there: it's not a he— it's a she."

"She? A woman?" Philip was incredulous. He thought of the attacker's body weight pressing on him; the form hadn't been large, but it had been strong. He remembered the tight grip of the legs pinning down his hips and the raised knife. "A woman?' He was having difficulty comprehending this. "Who?" At the same moment he asked the question, his mind leaped to a conclusion: *Susan!* He rejected the idea immediately. *No, Susan was never violent!*

"She's out cold, so we lifted the balaclava a bit, but we aren't moving her. She could have a pretty bad back injury, maybe even a broken neck. Anyway, Miss Williams had a look at her. She's pretty sure it's someone she knows from yoga."

A woman! Philip shook his head. He couldn't absorb this piece of information. "Dana?" he asked again. "My aunt?"

"Both are going to be fine," Small assured him. "They got a bit knocked about, but they're pretty feisty women. Seems your aunt surprised your intruder in the back hall outside the kitchen and got knocked down. She said she passed out for a couple of moments, but when she came to, she got to the phone and dialed 911. Like I said, a feisty woman."

"But she's… all right? And Dana?"

Small nodded and smiled. "They make quite a pair," he said with some admiration. "Miss Williams got knocked into the wall, but she bounced back like a rubber ball. She's gonna have some bruises, but she'll be fine." In a more somber tone, he added, "It looks like you're all pretty lucky. Whoever this woman is, she wasn't here to pay a pleasant social call. She was dead serious."

An approaching siren sounded. The detective stood up awkwardly, rubbing his knees. "That'll be the ambulance. I'll need further statements later. We need to find out why you were attacked." He moved towards the door but paused, stroking his moustache while giving Philip a thoughtful look. "She wasn't after your aunt, or she'd have stayed downstairs and finished the job." Philip winced at the choice of words. "And she didn't head for Miss Williams' apartment. She came straight here. It would appear you were her intended target. As I said, we need to find out why."

Dana entered the room ahead of the paramedics. "Oh, Philip," she cried. "I can't believe this. Are you all right?"

He thought he'd never been so glad to see anyone in his entire life. Dana's face bore scratches, and a significant bruise was beginning to form over one eye. He wanted desperately to get his hands on whoever had caused them. At the same time, he was struck by how beautiful she looked, despite everything she'd been through in the past hour. She'd thrown a coat over her pajamas, but he caught a glimpse of blood spatters on her top.

"You're bleeding!" he cried, pointing to her chest.

She looked down, surprised. "Oh! I must have gotten splattered." Her nose crinkled with distaste. "I'm fine," she insisted. "Are you going to be all right? Does it hurt a lot?"

"I'll be okay," he grimaced as the paramedics set to work. A spasm of pain tore through his shoulder, catching his breath. When he could speak again, he apologized. "I'm so sorry about… all of this. But you saved my life!" he managed a smile. "I owe you big time." As the room began to spin again, he asked, "How's Aunt Iva?"

Tears were pouring down Dana's cheeks. Embarrassed, she tried brushing them away. "I don't know why I'm crying. I never cry. Iva's fine, except she might have a sprained ankle— she can't put any weight on it. But she was lucky. When I think of what could have happened–that knife! I can't stop thinking about that knife!"

As the attendants lifted him onto the stretcher, he reached out with his good hand and grabbed hers. His voice was hoarse when he spoke. "We're all pretty lucky. I'm just thankful you're all right."

Dana watched the men maneuver the stretcher down the stairs. Then she followed in its wake. *What the heck happened here tonight?* Why on earth had one of her students broken into *Iva's* house and attacked *Philip*?

In the downstairs hall, Iva sat on a chair and watched as Philip's stretcher arrived on the main floor. She wore a dressing gown over her nightgown, and Philip was immediately concerned with how drawn her face looked.

"Oh, my dear," was all she could manage when she saw him before tears bubbled up.

"I'm all right, It's only a scratch. But you need to take it easy now."

Dana put a hand on Iva's shoulder. "I'm here," she assured both of them. "We'll get someone to look at that ankle now." Trying for an upbeat tone, she added, "At least we know all this craziness is over."

As Philip was carried out onto the front porch, he heard his aunt say, "But we don't know why. Why did all this happen? What was that woman trying to do?"

That's the sixty-four-thousand-dollar question. Why would some woman Dana knows from yoga attack me? It doesn't make sense. What if Small's wrong? What if I wasn't the real target? Philip wondered if he had simply been in the wrong place at the wrong time. What if the woman had been after someone else?

Chapter Sixty-Seven

Dana was grateful for the unexpected quiet of the hospital waiting room. Apparently, there was often a brief lull at this early hour, which worked to their advantage. A technician had taken Iva into a room across the hall for x-rays. In the Emergency Department, a doctor was suturing Philip's arm. She was physically and mentally exhausted, but now that she had a few moments alone, she tried to sort through her jumbled thoughts.

The attacker was Anna Novak, of that much she was certain. Now, she was somewhere in this same hospital under police guard.

But why? Dana anguished over all the possibilities but couldn't think of any logical reason for such an attack. Yet she had to ask herself if there was ever anything logical about attacks like this? Was Anna simply insane? It was upsetting to think she'd never had that impression of the woman. Except for that odd conversation in the tea shop, nothing had seemed the slightest bit off about Anna. Still, she kept second-guessing all of their interactions. *Did I do something to antagonize her?*

She'd even thought something was developing between Anna and Brad. *Brad! Oh, dear heaven! I suspected him of all the weird stuff with the rats because he had that black ribbon, but it couldn't have been him.*

Unless... are the dead rats somehow tied up with this attack on Philip? Or are they something completely separate? Her brain was on overload. She felt a headache coming on and tried to make her mind go blank.

An orderly wheeled Iva back to the Emergency Department, and Dana walked behind them. There wasn't any conversation. Iva was as overwhelmed by the events as Dana and needed some quiet time for her own thoughts.

In the main waiting room, they settled into a corner, where Dana busied herself ensuring Iva was comfortable in her wheelchair. When she looked up, Detective Small was approaching.

"The assailant isn't up to questioning yet. She's in pretty rough shape, and it's not looking good for her. The docs think she might have fractured her spine. They'll be doing an MRI, etc." He paused to let them absorb this bit of news. Dana thought of the Anna she'd known practicing yoga and living an active life. What lay ahead for her now?

"We found her vehicle parked several blocks away, on Glen Manor. Forensics is going over it now, but we did find a backpack inside, so we got her drivers' license." He removed a notebook rom the inside pocket of his jacket and read aloud. "Full name: Susannah Anna Novak. 193 Spruce Crescent. You sure you never met her, before she came to your class?"

"Positive."

"What about you, Mrs. MacGyver?" He reached into his pocket and handed Iva the drivers' license with its photo of the blond woman who had invaded her home.

Iva looked at the tiny picture. "I don't think so."

"You're sure?"

She peered at it more carefully, then added with some hesitancy, "Oh, maybe... no, it couldn't be..." She shook her head. "No."

"What were you going to say?" Small prompted her. "It couldn't be who?"

"Well, I don't like to say because I'm probably wrong. These photos are never good, and I don't want to cause trouble for anyone."

"Ma'am…" Dana could tell the detective was exasperated. With a visible effort, he collected himself and continued calmly. "I understand what you're saying. But there's already been a great deal of trouble. Your nephew was almost killed. Remember that."

Iva looked chastened. "Of course. You're right. When I think of poor Philip…" She drew in her breath and continued. "The woman in the photo does bear a resemblance to a former tenant, but that woman was heavier, and she had brown hair, so I don't think it can be her."

"Her name, please?" Small prompted.

"Sabina Wright. She moved out about three years ago, and I have no idea where she went. All I know is she was working at a cafe at the time, but I can't remember the name." Iva gave the detective an apologetic look. "I'm afraid that's not much help, is it?"

"The name helps. Why did she move out? Did she leave town?"

"I'm afraid I had to ask her to leave. She and her friends were quite disruptive, but I tried to do it nicely. I told her I no longer wanted to rent that apartment. I said I was saving it for my nephew. It wasn't a complete lie. I knew Philip would come home eventually, and I did think he might stay there from time to time."

"We'll check into it. Sounds like a bit of a long shot, but you never know."

"I didn't want Sabina to leave angry. She could be a bit volatile, and I didn't want to stir up trouble." Iva looked stricken. "Maybe I did after all, but goodness, that was three years ago!"

Dana had been listening thoughtfully, but now she rushed to repeat the detective's words. "It does sound like a long shot. Try not to worry about it too much." She realized they sounded hollow; however, her mind was busy calculating. Whether the woman's hair was brown or not made no difference. It was easy to change hair color and losing a few pounds could make a big difference.

Is it possible? Could Anna and Sabina be the same person? The idea seemed unbelievable even fantastical. *But if they are the same person, why wait three years to take revenge? What could have made her act now, after all that time? And what in the world was she doing in my yoga class?*

Chapter Sixty-Eight

Philip stepped out of a room down the hall, his arm bandaged, his face white, and an orderly lending support.. He swayed somewhat as he approached, and Dana raced to take his good arm. As she did, he smiled at her, and in a flash, she had the answer to her question. Why had all this happened now? What happened three years after Sabina was asked to leave? Philip came home! But what did his homecoming have to do with this Sabina or Anna? Could it be as crazy as retribution against Iva, simply because he was now staying in that same apartment? How insane was that?

Detective Small approached Philip. "How're you doing? You going to be okay?"

"I was lucky. It's all superficial. There's no damage to the tendons."

"Good. I've got a photo I'd like you to take a look at to see if you recognize the face."

Dana was irritated. "Can he at least sit down first?" It had been several hours since the attack, and she'd just about reached the limit of her patience.

"I'm sorry. Sure, have a seat."

Philip lowered himself into a nearby chair. "Is it the woman you know from yoga?" he asked Dana.

"Yes. Anna. She joined my class a couple of weeks ago. Actually, it was the same morning I met you. After I found the rat." Dana shivered, remembering. "There were two new people that morning, Anna and Brad." She turned to the detective. "I thought Brad was the one. Remember? I called you and told you what I suspected. You talked to him, and you said not to worry."

"Yeah, I remember. He was clean."

"You're sure? I used to wonder if he was interested in Anna. Sometimes they talked together, and they both appeared to be on their own."

"I'm sure." True to habit, he stroked his moustache. "No reason I can't tell you now, I guess. Brad Wallenski is R.C.M.P., undercover."

"A Mountie? Brad's a Mountie?" This night was getting stranger and stranger.

"Yeah. He was investigating the yoga studio as part of an extensive money-laundering scheme. He was quite interested in your boss. In fact, that's why the studio is closed now."

"Money laundering?" She felt foolish, repeating everything he said. She thought of her boss, Valery, and his rough, furtive manner. It was all too much to absorb. "But that day at the café, Brad had that piece of black ribbon in his wallet, the same kind that was on the—I was sure he—"

Small chuckled. "Yeah, Wallenski felt bad about that, but he couldn't risk talking to you further. Things were starting to go down fast. He picked up that ribbon one night when you were all at a pub. I guess it was his cop instinct that made him hold onto it. He knew something was going on with the way you reacted to it."

Dana slumped against the back of her chair. Iva took her hand and patted it. Having taken in everything, Philip offered no comment. He was examining the driver's license Small had handed him.

"Your aunt says it reminds her a bit of a tenant she had a few years back, but she's not certain." He pointed to the license. "The name on that is Anna Novak.

Specifically, Susannah Anna Novak. Mean anything to you?"

"No, but it's strange; I thought there was a slight something about it, too." Philip looked at his aunt. "I didn't know your tenant, though, so I'm probably starting to imagine things, hoping to find an answer to all this madness. Sorry, I'd like to be of more help, but I'm positive," he concluded as he handed the photo back, "I've never seen her before."

The detective pocketed the photo. "Right. Thanks." He seemed about to leave but spoke again. "For a moment there, though, you did think of someone." As Philip started to protest, Small said, "I know, I know. You said you were wrong, but out of interest, who was it?"

"I was wrong," Philip declared. "She couldn't have changed that much. She has brown hair, and she's heavier."

"Just like Sabina!" his aunt told him. "That's exactly what I said. She had brown hair and was heavier."

"But women can change," Dana interjected. "More easily than men, I think. All it takes is a new hair colour and maybe a new cut. People do lose weight, too. Or wear clothes that change their shape, make them look slimmer."

"Care to give me a name?" Small prompted Philip.

"But…" Clearly, Philip was reluctant. "I don't want to stir things up," he said. "She's not…not all that stable. Last I heard, she was in The Clarke."

Small stared him down.

"Susan," Philip finally replied. "Susan Neilson."

"The Clarke, eh?" Small finished writing the name down. "There's something else. This Anna Novak, or whoever she is, had a notebook in her purse. Shirley Fox's address and phone number were in it."

He paused, waiting for a reaction. There was none, except for the stunned confusion in each pair of eyes. The weary trio looked as if they couldn't absorb one more bit of news.

Small continued. "If this woman happens to be connected to the rat incidents, and we're looking into that, she would have been in that church kitchen at some point. It's possible on the night Ms. Fox found the rat in the coffeepot, she'd seen someone in the kitchen earlier on, and that person might have been afraid she'd put two and two together and identify them."

Dana, close to tears, seemed to express what the others were thinking. "It all seems so unbelievable, so…preposterous!"

The detective snapped his notebook shut. "I'll be in touch. In the meantime, check that back door lock and be careful."

The three sat in silence, watching as the detective strolled down the hall and out a door leading to the parking lot.

Philip stood up on unsteady legs. "I'll call a cab," he said.

Chapter Sixty-Nine

It was a silent ride home, punctuated only by the occasional moan when the taxi hit a pothole. Once they'd managed to maneuver Iva on her crutches into the house, Dana and Philip's priority was ensuring her comfort. After easing her into bed and helping her place pillows and blankets the way she wanted, they set water, pills, and her bedside phone within reach. With promises to check in regularly, they let the exhausted woman sleep.

They climbed the stairs with heavy hearts, too tired to speak. On the landing outside her apartment, Dana was unsure what to do next. Invite him in? Offer coffee or a beer? He still looked pale, and from the way he leaned against the banister, she knew he was in great discomfort, despite the painkillers administered at the hospital.

There was something in his eyes, like a message he wanted to convey. Was it longing or pleading? She couldn't tell, and after an awkward moment he simply asked, "Will you be all right?"

"I'll be fine, thanks. How about you? Can I make you a drink or anything?"

"No, thanks. I just need to sleep. Good night."

"Good night. Be careful on the stairs!" As each of them retreated to their own space, Dana thought they were not unlike wounded animals seeking refuge in their caves, needing time alone to nurse their wounds and come to terms with the shock of all that had transpired.

Collapsing on her couch, she fell into a deep sleep. Sometime later, when a creak on the stairs broke through her consciousness, she shot straight up. Moving fast made her head spin, and she was forced to hold onto the furniture as she made her way towards the door. When she'd mustered enough courage to open it a crack, Philip was tiptoeing past.

Her overwrought mind immediately conjured up all the worst possible scenarios. "What's happened?" she whispered, afraid of the answer.

Looking back over his shoulder, he gestured down the stairs. "I'm checking on Iva."

She slumped with relief against the doorframe. "I'll come, too," she replied. "If she's awake, you might need help."

"No need. Go back to bed." He waved her off and carried on. Disappointed, she watched him go, thinking she should have insisted, but something in his tone told her to do as he said. *We're all overwrought. Don't take it personally.*

Still, his manner was unsettling.

*****

Oh, dear God, please help me! The pain! The pain! What kind of sick dope did they give me anyway? It's wearing off too soon. Shoot! Shoot! Shoot!

It wasn't supposed to be like this! Philip's the one who should be strapped down here with a broken back. He should be in pain, not me! Better yet, he should be dead!

All three of them should be dead. Yeah, him and his crazy aunt and that stuck-up phoney, Dana. I nearly did it! I almost got 'em all. If that raving lunatic_hadn't jumped me, I'd have taken care of Mr. Philip Marshall.

Oh, no! Mustn't try to move. Pain's getting worse. Everything hurts. Hurts to breathe, even.

I didn't want to do it. I still love him, after all. But he didn't give me any choice. Yeah, I plead not guilty, Your Honour. It's all his fault, 'cause he forgot. I told him we belong together. I told him over and over and over, and what'd he do? Took off for some God-forsaken place in Africa. Africa! Never even sent a postcard. He forgot. Well, no, Philip! It doesn't work that way. And now you know.

I can't feel my legs. Lousy doctors said I might never walk again. Well, I'll show them. Next thing you know, I'll be doing yoga again. Ha! Ha! Stupid Dana! It's her fault, too. She should have taken the hint and moved out. That's all she had to do, make room for me. I thought for sure the rats would do it. Any normal person would be long gone, but not Miss Dana, no!

Thinks she's Miss Perfect. Thinks she can get it on with Philip. Thinks she can write a play. Thinks she's the cat's pajamas! Well, guess I showed her, too. I pretty much wrecked her play. They won't be putting that garbage on, now. Well done, Susan! Well, done! Take a bow! Bravo!

That stupid woman in the kitchen almost ruined it, but I fixed her, too. Nobody gets in Susan Neilson's way...except maybe that dumb cop.

He said they found my car and now they're going over it with a fine-combed tooth. I mean, fine-toothed comb. Stupid drugs! Gotta keep a clear head. Cop's tryin' to scare me, but I'm not worried. Nope, absolutely not. Nothing to worry about at all. I don't think so, anyway. I hope not.

Oh, shoot.

Chapter Seventy

"VIOLENT HOME INVASION" the headline screamed. "Four Injured Including Assailant. Police Seek Motive."

Before noon, reporters and photographers appeared on the lawn, and Iva's phone rang so often that Philip disconnected it. Dana prepared breakfast for Iva, helped her get dressed, and then let her rest again. Philip drew the living room drapes against the scene outside, shaking his head.

"I guess we should have expected this," he said. "We'll have to lay low until they get tired of waiting and move on to something else."

Dana nodded. "It's almost too much to take in. Not only about Anna. I'm still thinking of Brad and my boss and the whole money-laundering thing. Why didn't I catch on to something strange there? I went in, taught my classes, took my paycheck, and didn't pay attention to anything else. There was always someone new on the front desk, but Valery was so miserable, I figured they kept quitting. Other than that…," She shook her head in resignation.

"Don't kick yourself, Dana. None of us could have predicted any of this, but in the end, it's my fault. I knew something wasn't right with Susan, but I thought putting some distance between us for a while would make a difference. I should have known better."

"Don't, Philip! You couldn't have known she'd react like this. She —" A buzzing in her pocket interrupted the moment. Taking out her phone, she recognized the number. "My parents," she explained. "Shoot! I should have called earlier, but I didn't want to frighten them first thing in the morning. Now, they've probably heard it on the news, which is exactly what I wanted to avoid."

On the next ring, she answered. "Hi, Mom."

*****

Dana's frantic parents had to be convinced not to come down to the city. "I'm fine, Mom. Honest! I truly am. There's no point in you coming down. You'd have to find a place to stay, and it's a crazy situation right now. There are reporters all over the place."

Her dad could see her point but had many questions. She answered what she could, then had an idea. "Look, how about I drive up there instead? I had a good sleep last night despite everything, and it would do me good to get out of here for a while. I need time to unwind, and the cottage is the best place for that."

They weren't entirely reassured but accepted her decision. "If you're sure," her mother said in a doubtful tone. "Maybe you should ask Caroline to come with you. She'd be good company, and if you get tired, she could drive."

Dana made no promises. "I'll think about it, Mom." If she was going to make the three-hour drive, she'd prefer being alone and having the time to think. It was not meant to be, though. Her mother must have made another call, because the next time Dana's phone buzzed, it was Caroline.

"Dana! Are you all right?"

"Hi Caroline. Yes, I'm fine. Don't worry."

"Oh, my gosh! I can't believe this. Who did it? Was it

someone you knew?"

Her sister's questions, though well-intentioned, were nevertheless overwhelming.

"I'll tell you later. I promise, I just finished talking to Mom and Dad, and they wore me out. It took a lot of convincing for them not to rush down here immediately. I know they only want to help, but there's nothing they can do. I finally promised I'd go see them as soon as possible."

"Which is why I'm calling... besides making sure you're okay, of course, and thank goodness, you are." There was a brief pause, and Dana thought she heard a slight sniffle. Was it possible her sister was crying?

Before she could ask, Caroline spoke again, "Can I go up with you? I know you're all right, and I'm glad, but I could help with the driving, if you get tired."

"Only if you want to. I know Mom probably put pressure on you, but I'm fine, and it isn't necessary."

"No, honestly, I'd like to go with you. It would be nice to have some time together again."

Dana was touched, and by the time the call ended, she'd agreed to pick up Caroline at the end of her afternoon shift, so they could drive up north together.

Chapter Seventy-One

"**Just watch me!**" Iva said as she displayed her newly acquired skill with crutches. Laughing, she moved around the kitchen, filling the kettle.

Dana laughed, too, pleased to see the positive changes in her landlady's disposition in the few days she'd been away visiting her parents.

"Watch it, young lady! Don't get too carried away," Philip admonished her, but he, too, chuckled.

Iva and Philip both appeared well-rested, and Philip used his injured arm as if nothing had ever happened. Despite these improvements, she was certain it would still take time for them to recover from the mental stress and anguish Anna or Sabrina or Susan had caused.

It wasn't simply a case of what had happened to the three of them, either —more importantly, there was Shirley Fox's murder. No one had heard whether charges would be brought against Susan for that, but Dana assumed they would.

She couldn't get her head around the idea of the woman she'd known as Anna being so insane as to commit such a heinous act, and yet, why not? She'd tried to kill Philip, for heaven's sake!

Would they ever learn more about why Shirley died? If Susan was to blame, was it because she thought she'd been spotted and had to make sure no one lived to tell the tale? Or had Shirley mentioned having seen her in the kitchen? But Shirley couldn't have known Susan, could she?

Wait a minute! Elvis said Shirley was meeting someone who'd offered to help sew costumes. Could that have been Susan? Dana's head was swimming with possibilities.

No one had come forward to say they'd noticed anything suspicious or that they'd recognized Susan in the auditorium, and there were no surveillance cameras. All these finer points remained a mystery to Dana. She'd have to leave the details to Detective Small. He was the expert, but she felt she couldn't put any of this behind her until she knew everything the detective did.

*****

As they sat at Iva's table, Dana filled Philip and his aunt in on her visit home. All things considered —her mother's tears, her sister's questions, her father's protective anger–it had gone better than she might have expected. She hadn't disclosed anything beyond the fact that there had been a home invasion. Such happenings were not common in the city, but they weren't uncommon either.

"I'm sure your poor parents were upset," Iva said. "They must wonder what kind of place you're living in."

Iva was right. Her mother had cried seeing Dana's bruised face. "I don't think you should go back to that place," she'd said. "It doesn't seem like a safe part of the city. And who are these people—Mrs. MacGyver and that nephew of hers? We don't know anything about them. You could go back to The Annex. Nothing like this ever happened there."

She'd paused to wipe her tears and catch her breath, but she wasn't finished. "And I never understood what happened with Dave, either. He was such a nice fellow, steady and ambitious."

Dana couldn't believe what she was hearing. Her mother had never said anything nice about Dave before. Annoyed, she had been about to make that point when Caroline spoke up.

"Speaking of Dave, that 'nice, steady' fellow," her sister said, with evident relish. "Remember he got engaged?"

"Of course," Dana sighed. "What's that got to do with anything?"

Ignoring the question, Caroline continued. "Well, it's off! Cancelled! Kaput! Fini!"

"What's off? The engagement? I just heard about it the other day. Are you sure?"

"Yup, I heard it on good authority. He always said he wasn't the marrying kind. I guess he was right."

Dana had no words.

"Thought that would perk you up a bit," Caroline said with a smile.

"I never liked that fellow," their father commented. "You were right to get out of that one, Dana."

For once, her mother had nothing more to say.

Chapter Seventy-Two

Philip was speaking, bringing Dana out of her reverie. "Your parents must have had a lot of questions," he prompted.

"They did," she nodded. "But I didn't think they were ready to hear about Anna, Sabina, Susan, and all the stuff about the rats. Not yet. They're still in shock about the attack." Closing her eyes, she sighed, "And I certainly wasn't going to mention Shirley's murder."

None of that had made the news. For the time being, the police were not disclosing anything beyond the break-in and attack. It seemed highly unlikely some keen investigative reporter might wonder if there was a connection to Shirley's murder. When the time seemed appropriate, she would tell her family more, but that time wasn't now.

"I think that was the right move," Philip said. "I called my parents first thing that morning before they had a chance to hear it on the news…,"

"Which is what I should have done," Dana interjected. "I could kick myself."

"I know. But hindsight is 20/20," he replied. "Anyway, they were like your parents and wanted to help Iva and fuss over us. We had a tough time convincing them not to. Aunt Iva said she was much too tired for company, and I told them if they came, they'd have to run the gauntlet of cameras and reporters and might end up in the headlines. That wouldn't have deterred them for a minute, but I tried. In the end, it was Aunt Iva who convinced them. She promised to call daily and said we'd come down the minute she felt up to the drive."

Iva added, "We didn't tell them any more than we had to over the phone, either. As you said, we can fill them in later. The less said now the better. Philip was right about those reporters, too. They haven't been around for a couple of days. I guess since there were no new developments, they lost interest, and then there was that huge gas explosion in Scarborough. They say the cause looks suspicious, so I guess that's where they all are now."

Philip got up to fetch the teapot and poured Iva another cup. Dana watched him carefully. Before she'd gone home, she'd been worried about a certain tension or strain between the two of them and hadn't been sure what to make of it. Maybe he'd needed time alone to get over the shock of everything and heal in his own way —that would be quite natural. She had felt the same way.

But what if he was trying to let me know he's no longer interested? Maybe he never was. After all, everything had happened so fast. Was it only two weeks since the night of the first rat, the same night Philip had arrived back in the country? Horrific events had thrown them together, that's all, and she'd probably misread some of his signals. As her mind tried to rationalize the situation, her stubborn heart rejected every point. *I wasn't wrong! Something definitely was happening between us. But what does that mean now?*

She observed Philip, who was laughing with Iva and appeared at ease. Surely, that was a positive sign? He was certainly being polite and hospitable to her. Though, he would be kind to anyone. She remained confused.

One thing she had to admit was that everything had been much harder for Philip. *He once believed he was in love with Susan, and now, he's probably questioning his ability to judge people. And he must feel a tremendous responsibility for what happened to Iva.*

Dana was certain this weighed heavily on him and likely would for a long time. She had an intense desire to console him but feared being rebuffed. Maybe she should wait for a signal from him first? If she took the first step, and he rejected her, would she have the courage to accept it?

All her doubts resurfaced. Had their attraction simply been the result of being thrust together in extreme circumstances? She'd been so convinced it was real. Overwhelmed by a sudden compulsion to know, Dana closed her eyes, said a silent prayer, and reached across the table to rest her hands on Philip's.

She resolved to wait as long as it took —a moment, a day, a week, a month, a year —as long as was needed for his answer.

Chapter Seventy-Three

In the crowded auditorium, a heightened sense of anticipation produced a low but audible hum and more than one *frisson* of excitement. When a door swung open with such force that it bounced off the wall, almost everyone jumped.

Amid gasps from the crowd, a man strode through the door onto the stage. Breathing hard, he came to an abrupt stop in front of a woman. She stepped back, the hesitant expression on her face revealing her uncertainty.

Everyone could see something was wrong. A quick scan revealed one or two buttons on the man's expensive jacket hastily pushed through the wrong holes, causing it to hang off-kilter. Smudges of dirt spoiled his white shirt. No tie! That was the most telling sign. This was not the fastidious GQ look they'd observed earlier.

The woman took her eyes off him for the briefest second and glanced at the oversized clock on the mantle. Four-thirty. There was definitely something unsettling about his behaviour and his appearance at this time of day. Fighting a growing sense of unease, she backed further away. "I wasn't expecting you 'til seven. What's going on?" When he didn't immediately answer, she added, "You're starting to frighten me!"

"Attila!" he gasped, having found his breath again. "I had to fight off Attila."

"Attila?" She sounded shocked. "But he's so small! What did he do?"

"He may be small, but he's fast! He snatched something important off my desk and took off with it. I had to chase him." A wide, self-satisfied grin crossed his too-handsome face. "But I brought him down, the little bugger!"

"Oh, my goodness! You tackled him? Did you have to go that far?"

"*I* thought it was important, but maybe *you* won't agree." He attempted to straighten his jacket and — looking her in the eye —moved slightly closer. She stood rooted to the spot, unable to look away. Suddenly, he tossed a small package at her. Despite her edgy nerves, she managed to catch it.

"Open it," he said. She stared at it for a long moment as it lay in her open palm. It was about the size of a small orange. Trying to ease the tension, she held it to her ear and smiled. "At least it's not ticking!"

He didn't return her smile. "Open it!" he insisted in a softer tone. This time it sounded less like an order and more like a plea.

"This wrapping paper's seen better days. It's all muddy."

"Yes, well. You can blame him for that."

"Poor Attila! Is he all right?"

"Poor Attila nothing! He's a thief. He never shows any remorse. He thinks it's all quite funny, a big game. If he'd made it any further, he'd have stashed it someplace where I'd never find it in a million years. But don't worry, I didn't hurt him. He'll live to steal another day."

Removing the wrapping revealed a velvet box in a familiar shape. With great care, she opened the hinged lid. What she saw was so astonishing that she fumbled her hold on the box and watched its contents roll across the floor and under a couch.

"I'm so sorry!" She immediately dropped to her knees to begin searching. "I'm so sorry.   It's …it's a beautiful ring! I don't know what to say."

With great gentleness, he lifted her to her feet. "All you have to say is yes."

Her stiff body softened as she finally relaxed. "Yes!" she said, falling into his arms. He wrapped them around her and buried his face in her neck, covering it with multiple tender kisses, before moving up to her ear and cheek, then finding her lips. After some moments, she leaned back and studied his face. "I think we could use Attila's help right about now, don't you?"

"You're absolutely right." He laughed and let out a long whistle. Within seconds, Attila appeared in the doorway with his head down, almost looking guilty. Almost, but not quite.

"Go find it, Attila. Go find the ring! She said yes!"

With a tiny bark, all five pounds of the intensely excited Shitzu scrunched under the couch. For a moment, all that could be seen was his rear end wiggling in the air until he backed out and, with twinkling eyes, held the diamond ring in his mouth, daring someone, anyone, to chase him for it. The game was on again!

Amid peals of laughter, the curtains closed, and the audience clapped with enthusiasm. "Bravo!" someone shouted. "Brava!" called another. The curtains reopened, and the cast stepped forward in a single line, holding hands and bowing. Their beaming faces revealed how much they appreciated the applause.

One of them held up "Attila", and a cheer arose for the talented pooch. Then, here and there in the audience, people got to their feet. A standing ovation! The actors looked at each other in disbelief, then grinned like children on Christmas morning.

From her perch on a stool at the rear of the auditorium, Dana heard, "Author, author!" and recognized her father's voice. A familiar whistle pierced the air. "That's Caroline!" she laughed.

Philip took her hand and pulled her forward. "They're calling for the author," he smiled. "And that's you. Congratulations!" He kissed her cheek, then taking her by the hand, led her down the side aisle and stepped aside, so she could climb up a narrow set of stairs onto the stage.

As soon as she walked on, one of the actors stepped forward to place a bouquet of spring flowers in her arms. After kissing her on both cheeks, he led the audience and cast in more applause. Surrounded by the excited actors who had spoken her written words on stage and in public for the first time, and looking out at the smiling people who were still applauding, Dana felt a rush of pure joy and soaked up her special moment. *It doesn't get any better than this.* Her proud family was sitting in the front row, along with Mrs. MacGyver. Philip stood beside them, wildly clapping and whistling, too. Her eyes caught his, and as they traded giddy grins, he winked. *Or maybe it does!* She thought her heart might burst.

Chapter Seventy-Four

"But what about the rats?" Philip's mother shivered with disgust. "Who was responsible for those rats?" She looked at her sister with compassion. "How horrible for you! I'm so sorry you had to go through all this."

Iva smiled and waved her hand as if to say it was nothing. "Dana can explain it better than I can," she told her sister.

Mrs. Marshall turned expectantly to Dana.

"That was Anna, too," Dana said. "I mean Sabina. No, *Susan!* I'm sorry. I keep mixing them up." She was flustered, not only by the recounting of what had happened, but by the circumstances she found herself in at the moment. She looked at Philip and his aunt for support.

They were sitting on the Marshalls' garden patio, enjoying the July first holiday weekend. Philip had insisted Dana and Iva come to his parent's home for a relaxing change from the turmoil of the past few weeks. It was relaxing, sitting around the glass table under its shade-giving umbrella. In this peaceful, leafy neighbourhood, only the chirping of birds interrupted the quiet. On the table, a vase of yellow roses cut from a bush in the garden provided a perfect centerpiece. Nevertheless, meeting Philip's family, as lovely as they were, was a bit overwhelming.

The police investigation was over. Iva was off

crutches, and Philip's arm was healing well. They had recently attended a Celebration of Life for Shirley Fox, at which Elvis seemed overwhelmed by the large turnout and sincere tributes to his cousin. Unquestionably, Shirley's murder and the other shocking events of the past few weeks had altered the lives of many people. However, Dana had begun to notice signs of life returning to that sense of normalcy for which all of them longed, and she was grateful.

She believed Bud's decision to carry on with the production of her play had helped several through the darkest period. Including herself. And it hadn't turned out too shabby, either. There had been four performances the previous week, ending on Saturday night with a cast party. Bud had done a great job directing, and most importantly, the audiences' enthusiastic reception had given her a satisfying sense of accomplishment.

All the busyness of extra rehearsals, including the dress and technical rehearsals, had not only filled her time but had also provided a space for both her and Philip to step back and consider where their relationship stood—whether they would proceed as friends or as something more. There was a tentativeness between them during those weeks, but by the closing night of her play, perhaps caught up in the general euphoria, it had become clear to both of them that they did indeed share something deep and precious.

*****

Now, she and Philip and his aunt were finally revealing the events of the past several weeks to Mr. and Mrs. Marshall. Well, at least they were attempting to do so. It was proving difficult to keep all the details straight.

Iva spoke up. "It's all right, dear. I'm still confused, too. I only knew Sabina, you only knew Anna, and Philip only knew poor Susan. No wonder we have trouble keeping it all straight."

"Poor Susan?" Mr. Marshall was indignant. "How can you possibly say 'poor Susan' after everything she's done? She almost killed Philip, and she certainly didn't care about you, the way she knocked you about. Or Dana!"

"It's my fault," Philip said, "for getting involved with her in the first place."

"Now, Philip…," Mrs. Marshall began, only to be interrupted.

"It's true, Mom. I should have had more sense, but I had no idea how disturbed she was, and I guess going away only made her worse. She knew about Aunt Iva, and she deliberately went there and talked her into renting that apartment to her, even though Aunt Iva didn't want to rent it to anyone. I suppose Susan thought if she was there when I returned, we could get together again. She's a classic stalker. Now you know why I called her 'Scary Susan'." He tried a wry smile to dispel some of his parents' tension. It failed.

"Scary is right," his father agreed. "But she won't be stalking anyone anymore." He was thoughtful for a moment before asking again, "But what about those rats?"

"Susan was trying to scare Iva's remaining tenant away. She didn't care who it was, she wanted them out of there. Unfortunately, it happened to be Dana."

As Philip leaned over to take Dana's hand, his parents glanced at each other, sharing a smile.

"But she'd done her homework," Dana added. "She'd gotten wind of the news that Philip was coming home, probably through phoning Professor Sharma, and she was watching Iva's house. She stalked me, following me around the neighbourhood.

"She's the one who made those frightening phone calls, too. The police found the phone in her car and were able to establish she'd called both my number and Philip's. I was sure it was a man because the voice sounded so weird, but evidently, she used a voice distorter." Dana shook her head in wonder. "She certainly is diabolical. She even joined my yoga class. And that night at the play rehearsal, when poor Shirley found the second rat in the coffee pot…"

A gasp escaped Mrs. Marshall. "In a coffee pot? How gross! I think I'd have fainted."

"Oh, not you," Philip joked. "You and Aunt Iva come from the same hardy stock, remember? You're both 'feisty women', as Detective Small would say."

"Nevertheless, there are limits," his mother replied. "I'm sorry, Dana. I interrupted you. Carry on."

Dana smiled. She liked Philip's parents. They were doing their best to make her at ease. "Well, Anna…sorry, Susan, followed me that night, too. I guess she wanted to see how I was reacting to the first rat, which I'd found that morning. She slipped into the lighting booth and told the guy there she was a new member of the crew. Neither Philip nor I ever saw her."

"How did she get the rat into the building?" Philip's father asked.

"Good question, Dad," Philip remarked. "Best guess is that she had it in her car and carried it in a gym bag or something. Since she still isn't saying much, we'll probably never know some things for certain. But we did hear that when the police went through her car, they found a tiny snip of black ribbon identical to what was used on the rats."

Dana said, "Elvis said Shirley told him the morning she was killed that she was meeting someone at the church who had volunteered to help with the sewing. If that was Susan, she might have befriended Shirley and gained her confidence. She could even have been to her house and found an opportunity to plant that bag of ribbons Elvis found in the car."

Iva added, "Maybe Shirley invited her for coffee or something and showed her around the house."

"Maybe," Philip said. "Or *if* she killed Shirley, she could have stolen the keys to her house. I guess we'll never know exactly, unless they suddenly show up, or the police track them down. Elvis has a set, but he never found Shirley's."

They were all quiet for a moment. "Would you like some more iced tea, Dana?" Mrs. Marshall asked. The poor woman was trying her best to be a good hostess and act normally. "Iva, how about you?"

After glasses had been refilled, Dana looked at Philip and said, "It's funny how many people I suspected: Brad, Bud, even Julie for a short while." She smiled. "Even you!"

Philip laughed, "That's okay. I had my moments when I wondered about you!"

"Philip, no!" his aunt admonished. "You never! Not Dana?"

"Well, let's face it. I haven't been a good judge of women in the past."

"Looks like you've hit the jackpot this time, son," his father commented with a wink.

Dana blushed, and Philip laughed.

"Enough of all this gloomy talk," he said, jumping up. "Come on, Dana. We're going out to the lake. I want you to see the place now that it's fixed up. Susan might have done me a favour there. It looks better than ever!"

Dana laughed at his enthusiasm, which was wonderful to see. "And grab your bathing suit!" he added. "It's warm enough for the first swim of the season, and we won't have to worry about crocodiles or deadly snakes like I did in Africa!"

At that moment, a few raindrops hit the patio umbrella over their heads. Dana looked at the sky. Dark clouds were gathering on the horizon.

"Oh, darn!" she said. "Looks like we're going to get rained out."

"Oh, I don't think so!" Philip gave her a sly smile and

grabbed her hand. "After all, aren't you the one who insisted there's nothing more fun than swimming in the rain? You're not going to chicken out, are you?"

Dana's heart raced. She truly believed she'd even brave those crocodiles and deadly snakes to be with this man, but she was too shy to say it out loud. Instead, she teased, "Me? Chicken? I'm the girl who saved your life, remember?"

"You tell him, Dana!" Mr. Marshall laughed. "She's got you there, Philip!"

Dana's eyes shone with mischief. Before Philip could get a word in, she added, "You're not going to make me regret that now, are you?"

"We'll see if you regret it," Philip replied softly, and before she knew it, she was in his arms, being deeply and thoroughly kissed to a round of delighted applause.

When she caught her breath, she opened her eyes, only to become lost in the deep longing in his. "Oh, my goodness!" she confessed. "Absolutely no regrets at all! Not one!"

THE END

Wendy B. Truscott, a native of Toronto, Ontario, has taught Kindergarten and French, but her primary role was that of "Domestic Goddess"— or stay-at-home mom. After she and her husband moved to their home on a peaceful lake in beautiful Muskoka, Ontario, she joined a memoir-writing group, where she was encouraged to venture into fiction as well. She has since published two successful YA historical novels, *Haunted Journey* and *MacGregor's Curse*. A life-long volunteer, her other interests include painting, genealogy, swimming in that peaceful lake, and memoir-writing, where she often includes comical anecdotes of life experiences she hopes future generations will enjoy.

www.ingramcontent.com/pod-product-compliance
Lightning Source LLC
Chambersburg PA
CBHW072056190726

48294CB00005B/1547